I'll Make My Arrows From Your Bones

Brandon Faircloth

Other Works by Brandon Faircloth:

Mystery

Darkness

On the Hill and Other Tales of Horror

Whimsical Leprosy

The Outsiders: Book One

You saw something you shouldn't have

One Bite at a Time

My Uncle Makes Dolls to Replace Souls in Hell

Incarnata

The Outsiders: Book Two

Table of Contents

The Convenience Room

They call it "The Convenience Room", even though it isn't always in a particular room or spot. It travels from place to place, setting up in an area for sometimes a single night and other times an entire month before moving on. In some ways, it is like a traveling circus or fair, though it doesn't offer the multitude of sights and sounds those places tend to provide. In fact, it only offers one thing.

The convenience of another's death.

When the Room comes to a place, be it a city or a larger, more rural area, it shifts from spot to spot every night. That's one of the keys to how it has worked for so long, you see. There is so little connecting one place to the next, one murder to the next, that it becomes almost impossible for a pattern to be developed, much less relied upon. No one investigates the Room because there is so little to investigate. And if one was to begin…well, who's to say their death wouldn't become convenient sooner rather than later?

It works like this.

When the Room has come to town, a series of symbols will be marked in either paint or chalk at various points around the city. The logic behind the location of where the symbols are left is up for debate, but some loose rules seem to have developed over the years. First, there will be one symbol left within 1000 yards of one house of worship of every religion in the area. It may be on a telephone pole, on a street, or inside an electrical box, but it will be there somewhere. Second, there will always be a symbol near one of the last murders that occurred in the area prior to the Room's arrival.

That's the Room's calling card, you see. The way it announces it is on its way. A person is killed, often in a way that generally looks accidental, but amid whatever other injuries might have occurred, the last two fingers of their left hand will be broken. A small thing, and something that would never get reported widely. But for those awaiting the Room's arrival, it is an easy enough thing to watch out for and learn about if one knows the right people.

And then the hunt for the symbols begins. People begin casually searching near the crime scene, or if they worry about drawing undue attention there, close to various churches, mosques, and synagogues in the area. The symbols are found and decoded, giving specific GPS coordinates and a time frame. As I said, the location will change day to day, so new symbols must be found every day as well. The time of day changes also, but the duration of the window never does. It is always ninety minutes.

That is the window of time you have to mark someone for death.

Once you know the place and time frame, all that is left is to go there at that time with the person you want erased from the world. You would think this would be the hardest part, as you have to come up with a convincing but innocent-sounding reason for someone you want dead to travel with you or meet you at some obscure spot. The funny thing is, so often the people we want dead are the ones we are closest to, and it usually isn't hard to get them to show up at all.

Besides, the locations are never sinister. You aren't carrying them to an abandoned warehouse or a midnight graveyard. The places are all very normal.

A restaurant. A hallway in a college building. The changing area of a department store. Most of the places are well-lit, well-populated and wholly unremarkable. That's what makes it work so well.

Because for 99% of the people there, they are just living their lives: eating, going to a class, trying on clothes. For the other 1%...well, they are there as either victor or victim, or perhaps both. The third party present, unseen but ever watchful, are the servants of the Room. Their role is critical, as they must watch for the Signs.

The Signs are the other key information encoded in the symbols, telling the where and the when of the Room on a given day. The Sign of the Victor is the signal given by the person marking someone in the Room for death--it might be touching your throat three times within a minute or checking your phone twice within two minutes while yawning both times. Once the Sign of the Victor is completed, the "victor" will have thirty seconds in which to start the Sign of the Victim. The Sign of the Victim is what marks a specific person for death. It might be rubbing someone's back counterclockwise for three rotations or touching someone's arm while your other hand is in your pocket.

The Signs are always natural and common, and they are different for every symbol one might find--even different symbols for the same day. This means that on any given day there are several different Signs of the Victor and Victim that will work. But they only work if paired with the other Sign from the same symbol, and they are only taken as marking someone if done exactly right at exactly the right time and place. If done correctly, then you're finished. The person you marked will die.

Eventually. That's another trick of the whole thing. You aren't marking them to die right then or even that day or week. That would obviously call too much attention to the Room. Instead, some time within the following two or three months, the person will be in a terrible car accident. Or their house will have a gas leak. Or they will get shot in a robbery gone wrong. You'll never know how or when they will die until it has already happened.

And it always happens. I've heard stories of people who had second thoughts and tried to warn the intended victim. The victim still dies, and usually the other person does as well. The few times someone has tried to go to the authorities about it...same result, and nothing is ever investigated.

That is the thing you have to understand about the Convenience Room. No one knows who runs it or why. Not really. There are rumors, of course. Always rumors. You hear it was created by a rich madman that enjoys it as some kind of macabre game. There are stories about a supposed serial killer religion called "The Dark Path" that uses the Convenience Room as a kind of church. I don't know if any of that is true, and I don't know that any of it matters.

Because at the end of the day, the Convenience Room is a kind of machine. You turn certain levers and knobs, such as laughing while rubbing your nose followed by picking something off your husband's shirt, and the gears start turning. And when they have stopped, your husband is dead.

And there is no off switch. You aren't paying an assassin, you aren't having secret meetings with a hitman. You aren't paying any money and the killer or killers aren't doing it because you want it done, but because they want to do it. All you are doing is pointing them in a particular direction, and once you do, you couldn't stop them if you tried.

That thought eased my guilt when I plucked a hair from Ronald's jacket. It was one of his...he was going balder these days...but I still pretended it was a gossamer strand from that young whore he had been seeing. I wasn't killing him because he cheated...not really. But looking at myself as the jilted wife did make the whole thing a bit more palatable. Easier on the stomach than just admitting that over the last fifteen years I had grown to fucking hate him.

Still, I felt a sharp stab of regret as soon as I had completed the Sign of the Victim. Couldn't I just divorce him? I would get less money and more hassle, but I wouldn't have this stain on my soul. And was he really that bad?

I watched him for a moment. A short, dumpy man reading something on his phone rather than looking at any of the paintings in the gallery. Rather than sparing a glance for me. All the while scratching at his growing bald spot, no doubt sending disgusting flakes of his dry, crusty skin fluttering over the floor the same way he spreads them over my house. The same way he has spread his mediocrity over my entire life for nearly two decades, tainting everything I have.

No, fuck him, he deserves it. It's no different than in countries where the sentence for stealing is death. Ronald was nothing if not a thief of my…

That's when I realized he was looking at me. More than that, he was reaching out and rubbing my cheek in two short strokes. He never did that. What was he…

"Oh no."

I need you to kill me.

That's what the man said to me, his eyes suddenly clear and sharp as he regarded me over the table. I had met him two hours before when he offered to buy me a drink, and over that time I had grown to like him. He looked to be a few years older than me, but with the good preservation and polished sheen that you see on those that have the means to stay relaxed and well-groomed almost all of the time, probably with minimal personal effort. Normally I would have found that off-putting, but this man didn't seem soft or overly pampered. Instead he was worldly and wise, with an endless fount of interesting stories that somehow didn't seem like bragging coming from him, but rather just an expression of his intense desire for you to know him better.

In short, he was a really cool dude.

But that didn't change the fact that I was taken aback by his request. I would have chalked it up to the alcohol, but he hadn't seemed that drunk before and he certainly didn't now. And I've seen enough to know you can never tell what's going on with people. Not really. This guy looked like he was riding the world on a golden saddle, but that didn't mean much if he wasn't happy. And looking into his eyes now, he was clearly anything but.

"You are a good man. I can tell. And I believe you are smart enough to listen to what I have to tell you and believe what I will show you. I can only hope that after that you will be strong enough to do this for me."

I pushed back from the table. I was drunk, but not that drunk. "Dude. I don't know what this is, but let's dial it down a notch, okay? It is way too late to start some...bullshit philosophical conversation or whatever this is, okay?"

He reached forward and gripped my arm. "I'm not kidding. I'm just asking for a few minutes of your time. Listen to what I have to say, let me show you proof of it, and then you can make your decision. Fair?"

I pulled my arm back. "No, man. Sorry, I just don't..."

"Here's roughly five thousand dollars. Take it, it's yours. All I ask is that you hear me out." I looked down from his feverish expression to the wad of cash he had taken out of his pocket. We were far from America, but those were U.S. dollars, and I had never seen that much money at once in my life. Swallowing, I grabbed the money and gave a nod. "Okay, I'll listen, but I'm telling you it won't make a difference. I'm not killing you."

A look of relief spread across his face. "Thank you. Oh, thank you. I will be brief." He paused for a moment as though weighing how best to begin. Finally he looked up at me with a narrowed gaze. "How old do you think I am?"

I frowned. "Um, I don't know man. Maybe like forty-five? Fifty?"

He smiled. "I appreciate the compliment, but I am over four hundred years old."

I went to stand up again, but I remembered the bulge

of new money in my front pocket. "Ohhh kay. So you're four hundred. You must take a lot of vitamins."

He shook his head and began.

****

I know it sounds insane, but please bear with me. I first came to this island as a sailor back in 1698. I was on an exploratory ship that sank in a storm. Unbeknownst to any of us, we were only three miles from this island at the time. Myself and the first mate—his name was Sullivan—were the only survivors, at least as far as I ever knew. For certain, we were the only ones the currents carried to this shore.

The first few days we had hope of being rescued in time. We weren't that far off of an established trade route, and there were several expeditions to fully chart this area underway by different European powers. Our theory was that if we could just sustain ourselves, just survive a few weeks or months, we would be saved.

But this island was much different back then. There were no people or resorts obviously, but there was little to no animal life on the island either. The feral pigs and chickens you see on the tours? All imported in the 1800s. The snakes they warn you about in the jungles? Their ancestors were all accidently brought over in the landing gear compartments of the first planes that came to this place fifty years ago. When Sullivan and I searched this place, we quickly learned it was a lush wasteland. No insects under logs, no fish in the water. Even the handful of things that could be considered fruits or nuts were sparse and would make you sick to your stomach. We tried to subsist on bark and leaves, but that was a losing proposition from the start. By the end of the second week, we were wasting down to nothing.

This terrible wasting bred a kind of insanity in us. We became paranoid, and at some points, delusional. I began to suspect Sullivan was hiding food from me somehow, despite the fact he looked just as bad as I did. I took to following him everywhere, telling him I only wanted to help if he found us any food.

And then one day, he did. We were traveling under the jungle's wide canopy when he suddenly fell upon something. I was only a few steps behind, but by the time I made it to him, he was already sucking in the last of a wriggling, black tail as he chewed with a mixture of guilt and triumph on his face. I was insane with anger then, and I struck him across the face. He was shook by the blow, but not shaken. He said he was sorry, but it was just a small worm and in his hunger he had been greedy. He would, he promised, help me find another.

But there was no other to be found. We searched for as long as the sun allowed, but there was no sign of any other creature aside from the two of us and the thing that lay inside Sullivan's belly. It was that night, as I lay freezing on my bed of woven grass, trembling with hunger and rage, that I began to hate Sullivan and began plans to kill him.

Over the next few days, my plan was only estopped by my growing weakness and Sullivan's growing strength. By the second day, he looked as well as when we landed. By the third, he looked stronger and more vital than I had ever seen him in ten years of sailing together. He stayed with me most of the time, but every day he would journey back out into the jungle, promising he would find me a worm of my own. While it was never spoken, it was clear he understood the miraculous nature of the changes he was undergoing, and this only deepened his guilt that he had denied me the same boon.

I say that now, with a rational man's understanding. At the time, I was anything but rational. I was convinced that he had found a hidden trove of food and secreted it away for himself. That his "hunting trips" were nothing more than a thin lie to cover his daily visits to gorge himself while I lay there dying.

So I mustered my strength, a strength borne purely out of madness and ill will, and I followed him one day. He appeared to be hunting for food, but I decided it was just another sign of the lengths he was willing to go to in order to deceive me. He wanted to sit and laugh as I starved to death…me, the fool who believed his lies.

I caught him unawares with a rock and bashed his head in. He never had a chance to struggle or resist, and by the time I was done, his face was a bloody, broken ruin. I only stopped when I did because of the movement I saw from within that gory mess.

It was the worm. Fat and black and quite whole, it pushed its way out of the red meat at the top of Sullivan's neck and seemed to regard me. What it might have done, I could not say, because I immediately picked it up and consumed it whole.

It was nearly two years later when a trade ship went off-course and found me on the island. I had not eaten anything for all that time, and yet I was more fit and strong than the men that rescued me. It was another ten years before I began to suspect I truly wasn't aging. Ten more before I knew for certain that it must be true.

And in those twenty years, I had encountered two events that should have killed me. Instead, I was wholly unharmed. I didn't get sick, I rarely even cut myself shaving, and if I did, the cut was healed before I had time to wash away the blood. I had become immortal.

I have spent hundreds of years sampling all this life has to offer. At first it was such a miracle, such a gift. But over time…I have lost so many friends and loved ones. I have seen so much pain and suffering. And I am so very, very weary. I understand how this sounds to one who has lived so short a time, but I need to die. To rest. To move on to whatever comes next. People are not meant to live like this. Endless time is endlessly cruel, you see. It strips away all that is good and leaves you with the repetition of countless losses and miseries.

But I cannot kill myself. Believe me I have tried, but nothing I do works. Yet it is in my failures that I think the answer lies. The one thing I haven't tried, I cannot try, is to destroy the worm in my chest. I know that is where it lies, for it stops me if I try to do myself harm in the area of my heart. I have tried totally obliterating myself with explosives and heavy machinery, but the thing inside me can somehow cause such implements to fail if it senses its own impending doom.

But my hope is that another person, particularly back in this place, will be able to do what I cannot. End my miserable life and that of the thing inside me. Please. Help me find peace at last.

****

"Goddamn. That's some next level b-movie shit right there, man. I like the pirate thing. Or whatever you were.

You had me going at first. I was like…shit, this fucker is crazy." I laughed nervously as I drained my glass. "But good gag, dude." He just sat staring at me silently as I finished. "Look, it's getting late and…"

I stopped as I saw the man had pulled a knife from his pocket. Recoiling, I stumbled away from the table as he brought it across his own neck and slit his throat wide open. I started to scream, and looked up to get help, but there was no one else left in the bar. Looking back down, I saw he was still staring at me. His neck, while bloody, had already healed.

"This is what I'm talking about. I cannot die by my own hand. Perhaps not by yours either, but I am desperate to try."

"What the fuck..."

"I know this is all fantastic. But I assure you it is all very real and you are my best hope to finally be free. And as a reward, I will leave you fifty million dollars in my will, along with a certified affidavit that this was an assisted suicide done at my behest."

"There's no way…"

The man sighed as he wiped at his neck absently. "Mr. Ferry, I did not come upon you randomly. I have been planning this for years now. The paperwork, all the arrangements, have been in place for several months, just waiting for the right person. Just waiting for you, as it turned out. I already texted my attorney an hour ago. Your name has been added to my will and the aforementioned affidavit. It is all done except for the deed itself. And, of course, for you to live a long and wealthy life as a reward for freeing me from my own."

I took another step back. "This…is all insane. I can't do this."

Rolling his eyes, he fished his phone out of a jacket pocket. "91 Caskill Lane. Does that sound familiar to you? How about Apartment 16B at Smithfield Apartments? Ah, you're starting to understand." The man stood up as he put his phone away. "I own this island now, at least in the legal sense of the word. You were on our radar as soon as you booked a room at one of my hotels. Utilizing various projected models of behavior, online spending and social media profiles, you were selected as one of three potential candidates on the island this week. You weren't my people's first choice, but I…well, I just had a good feeling about you."

"What are you going to do to them?"

He raised an eyebrow. "To your mother and sister? Nothing if you do as I ask. If you don't, then tomorrow I will send their names and addresses to a very skilled professional killer. And by the time you arrive back home, you will have two funerals to attend."

"You son-of-a-bitch, you're crazy."

Shrugging, he walked over to the bar. "Perhaps, but how does that really change anything?" He gestured around the empty room. "Do you doubt I am who I say? Do you doubt that I'm in control?" Leaning over the bar, he pulled out a pump shotgun as a man in a dark suit entered the room. "This is Mr. Leipold, my attorney. He is happy to show you the will and affidavit before we begin."

The man strode toward me with a dispassionate look on his face. "First, the will. If you look at the marked and highlighted portion of page twenty-four, you have been

14

identified as the beneficiary of a lump sum payment of fifty million dollars U.S. currency, payable upon the death of my client." I glanced at it, my hands shaking. I didn't care about the money, not anymore. But I needed to play along so he didn't hurt my family.

"Next is the affidavit, signed and witnessed by two others. This specifies that you are killing my client at his behest and with his full permission, and that he is of sound mind and under no duress in making this request. As he may have mentioned, this island falls under the legal jurisdiction of a nation that has no criminal or civil penalty for suicide or assisted suicide. So there are no ramifications for you other than becoming a very wealthy man." I looked over the affidavit, and they were right. It said everything they claimed, and my name and date of birth were right there in it. When I handed the paper back to him, the attorney gave my host a small nod before leaving the bar without another word. I watched him go, and when I looked back at the supposed immortal, he was holding out the shotgun.

"Take it. Shoot me in the chest, right here." He tapped the left side of his chest as I took the shotgun. "One shot should do it, but you've got five shells if you need them." Pausing, he gave a laugh. "You do know how to use a gun don't you? I never thought to ask."

Gritting my teeth, I stuck it to his chest and pulled the trigger.

The sound was surprisingly muffled, but the effect was profound. The man flew back several feet before crumpling onto the floor, and when I rolled him over with my foot, I saw a large chunk of his chest was gone all the way through to his back. I sat there staring at the wound for what felt like several minutes, my mind skittering this way and that. Was what he said possible or was he just some rich nutjob? And if it was true, why didn't he just hire an assassin to kill him instead of an innocent bystander? And how was he able to kill Sullivan without killing the worm?

Because I didn't like Sullivan as much as I did him. Or you.

The voice thundered in my head as I saw something small and dark wriggling out of the ragged hole in the man's chest. It was a fat black worm, and it was looking at me. Talking to me in my head.

So I ran.

I ran for help, but I couldn't find anyone. It was as though everyone had vanished. I considered going to my room, but I hated the idea of being trapped there if that small and terrible thing came for me. So instead I went up to the main road. I was only a couple of miles from the airport, and I knew there was a police station there as well. Surely I could find someone to help me there.

I went up the road as fast as I could, the last of the alcohol burning away as I pounded my way up the midnight road. I rounded the last corner and saw lights burning at the police station. Almost crying with relief, I raced to the front door and beat on it until a sleepy and irritated officer opened it and asked me what was wrong. I told him that I needed help. That someone was after me.

Nodding, he asked me my name. When I told him, I saw a slight change in his expression before his gaze shifted to someone behind me. Then everything went black.

****

I woke up strapped to a gurney in the back room of the small island's clinic. They had woken me up so I could see when they fed the worm to me. The creature was silent for the moment, but I could still feel its gaze on me as they pried open my mouth and began to stuff it inside. I gagged as it began pulling its bulk across my tongue and down my throat, and when the nurses let go of me, I tried chewing on the last of it, trying to kill it. It didn't complain, and I felt sure it couldn't really be hurt.

Just like me now.

That was three years ago. I was released the next morning, and by that afternoon I was on a plane back home with the necessary information to access my new bank account. I was now a millionaire many times over. True to his word, my family was never hurt, and I've never heard from any of the dead man's people again. I suppose in many ways, he was honest with me.

But not in all of them.

Because what he omitted was the nature of the worm itself. How it talks to you. How it constantly, endlessly talks to you. Perhaps it knows it's torturing me, or maybe it is only bored and lonely. But the only thing keeping me from going insane is that it won't let me go insane. Instead I find myself trapped with another on the island of my mind, unable to leave or die or escape. And all the while, even now, it keeps telling me so many terrible, terrible things.

It tells me I'll be like the man I killed one day. That I'll do horrible things, and when I grow to hate myself enough, I'll sacrifice what's left of my soul just to be free of it. I used to argue with it. Then for awhile I would cry and beg. Now I just nod along with the incessant rhythm of its chatter. Not because I've grown accustomed to it, you understand.

No, it's because with this, as with everything else it says, I know it's telling me the truth.

The Chaos Engine

Ten years ago, I lived in a rundown part of Austin in an apartment that's only saving grace was the rent was cheap. Well, that, and the fact that my next-door neighbor was Tim Stapleton.

Tim could have afforded a much nicer place, even back then, but he looked at things differently than most people. He told me that he didn't care much about material things. He just needed an apartment so he had a place to sleep. A car so he could go where he needed. Clothes so he didn't get arrested.

He sounds like a weird guy maybe, and I guess he was in some ways, but he was a really good guy too. Over the two years I lived there, we got to where we would hang out on the weekends or after work, and I think he enjoyed it, though it was always hard to tell with him. What he told me once was that he liked having something to do other than just wait to go back to work, and I took it as Tim's version of a compliment.

And without question, his work was what drove him. He was working on what he called "an emergent AI project", and while he couldn't go into the details, it wouldn't have mattered if he had. Even his occasional vague and frenetic monologues on artificial intelligence tended to go far enough over my head that I was lost halfway through. Still, I could understand enough to know he was smart and passionate about whatever it was he was working on, and I was happy for him for that. I had moved from job to job for years, and a new potential career is what ultimately led to me moving from Austin a short time later. I envied him the passion and love he had for his strange work.

We had kept in touch over the years, but just barely, and I hadn't heard from him in over a year when he showed up on my doorstep last night, three hundred miles and nearly eight years distant from our last face-to-face encounter. He looked terrible. Not just older, but worn-through and paper-thin. He apologized for showing up unannounced, but I told him not to be silly and to come on in.

I asked if he was okay, and he just nodded as he made his way to the sofa. As he sat down, his stained t-shirt rode up enough for me to see a yellowed bandage across the small of his back. I almost asked again if he was sick or needed me to take him somewhere, but then he was talking, leaving little space for me to ask anything.

****

Paul...Paul, it's good to see you, yeah. I know I'm fucked-up looking. Again, I'm sorry for just showing up at your house after all this time. But I needed to talk to someone about all of this, and I thought about you. But this isn't something you say in a text or something, right? I wanted to talk to you in person. Needed to. Is that cool? Cool.

The project...the thing I've been working on for years...you know, the AI stuff? I'm running most of that lab now, and it's given me the latitude to try some more experimental...well, experiments. Different approaches to solving our AI problem.

The basic problem in most theories of AI is that they're a lie, or if that's too harsh, they're a half-truth. They rely on semantics and changing definitions to assert that we can create true intelligence, when in truth, AI is fundamentally a highly complex set of systems interacting to mimic true intelligence, true will.

Because that's the problem, isn't it? Intelligence isn't just about calculating power or memory speed. You wouldn't call a calculator "smart" in the traditional use of the word. Same thing for a supercomputer or an abacus. They are tools meant to be utilized to more efficiently and effectively navigate a set of systems, be that adding 2+2 or calculating the behavior patterns of a group of people based off of zettabytes of data. The calculator doesn't want anything. It doesn't love or hate or plan.

Even if...well, even if you made it look like a person. Talk and mimic the responses of a person, it would, at its core, be a fake. A sham. It hides its flaws with complexity and human affectations, but the flaws are still there. Even experiments with machine learning, while very useful for making better tools, cannot replicate true intelligence or will. It will always be a matter of improving imitation, not true replication.

Do you understand?

****

I shook my head slowly. He was clearly keyed up about something, but he didn't seem crazy or on something or dangerous. To the contrary, Tim was very focused and precise in everything he was saying. But still, I was growing more worried. "I'm sorry, buddy, but I'm confused. Are you sure you're okay? Did something happen?"

He looked at me for a moment before nodding. "I get it. I look a mess. I get it. Okay. Um, okay, so two years ago, we had a man nut up at the office. He was a stranger who no one knew. No connection to the lab, and I never knew why he did it, but he brought in a gun, held three people hostage, and then killed himself when police tried to get him to surrender. It was terrible...the whole thing was terrible...but it also gave me an idea."

"That day, all the systems of our office, of that part of the city even, were disrupted by that crazy man and his will. Because he wasn't worried about offending people or killing people or getting killed himself. Whatever his warped ideas were, whatever was driving him, he was operating beyond anything that was intended or dictated by the outside systems of our world—law, morality, basic survival instincts, things like that."

"So I thought...what if you could design an intelligence that did not rely on systems? Sure, you would have to have some foundational systems in place just like we have a brain, but what if instead of building those systems to follow constants and 'learn' from data and algorithms, you built those systems to learn from what would be an error or fail state in a traditional A.I.? It could be full of bugs, it could rely on faulty data, it could break any system rules it needed to break."

I raised my hand. "Are you telling me you tried to create an A.I. based off a crazy person?"

He laughed a little and shook his head. "Not an artificial intelligence, a true intelligence. One with its own thoughts and wants. But yes, by most definitions, completely insane. But sanity is a relative thing, right? And we're all a little crazy. I wondered if that randomness, that chaos, that drives people could also work for it. Would it just result in a broken piece of software, or could it create something that would truly grow and develop beyond the systems and information it was given?"

Tim leaned forward, his voice low. "And it worked. It fucking worked. Within six months I had a functional theoretical model. Another year and it was coded and ready to begin trials. The day we set it to running was the best and worst day of my life, Paul. I was so afraid it would fail. That I had wasted eighteen months and millions of dollars on a project that would either not function at all or would only be another mimic, another scam. But it didn't take long before I knew it was real. That it was alive."

"We called it The Chaos Engine. And at first, me and my colleagues were all convinced that it was the breakthrough that was going to win us all Nobel prizes and change the way technology functioned forever. It needed to be refined, of course, and taught to be useful, but we were its parents and we would help guide it."

Frowning, I stood back up. "Okay, so what the hell? If what you're saying is true, and not trying to be an asshole, but that's a big if, why would you think that's okay? Shit, did y'all never watch Terminator? How did you think it was safe to create an art...an intelligence that is batshit crazy? Don't you know how dangerous that could be?"

Tim looked wearily up at me. "We did. But scientific breakthroughs, the really big ones, come with risks. And we had every conceivable precaution in place. Believe me, we looked at every angle we could think of from both real world research and discussions on the dangers of A.I. to the speculative scenarios to be found in books and movies. It had no way to interact with other systems electronically or physically. It had no way to connect to other data or the internet either wirelessly or physically. It was housed in an underground bunker that only myself and three other people had access to, and none of us had seen any sign of any aberrant behavior outside of acceptable limits."

"What were the acceptable limits?"

Now he looked away. "It…it was very clever. Creative even, which is a term that is not casually thrown around when talking about something like this. But it was also…sadistic. Warped in ways we didn't understand. It was true to its name…it was very unpredictable and chaotic. But over time, we came to realize it wasn't random. There was a method to its madness."

Tim let out a sigh. "At the time, we had concerns, but they were eclipsed by our excitement at what we had achieved. And to be fair, if it was insane, even that insanity was a major sign of success. And this was only Mark I of the project. We could refine The Chaos Engine in future iterations until we arrived at something that would be safe in the outside world."

"But that's when we started seeing all the homeless people outside our office. At first it was a few, then it was more. They would just stand around and stare at us, twitching and mumbling as we passed. They were never aggressive, but it was disturbing. It became more so when we realized many of them weren't even the same people from day to day. What we had thought were fifteen people acting strangely was actually closer to a hundred."

His hands shaking, he buried his face in his hands. "Last week, they caught my assistant, Sandra, as she was being escorted to her car by a security guard. The homeless killed them both in the parking lot and ripped them apart in a very meticulous fashion. The police never caught anyone, but the security footage…it's the second worst thing I've ever seen."

"Three days ago, two more of my colleagues were killed in their homes. Again, torn apart, but this time with parts missing. The lab has been shut down officially, but of course, the Engine was still running down there. Always running."

He looked back up at me, tears streaming down his face. "I went down there. I tried to shut it off. Stop it. Some of those people…those servants of that thing…they attacked me. They were babbling in some strange language, and they barely looked human between their slack faces and the bits of metal and wire they had jammed into their flesh here and there. They drug me down, and I thought I was going to be torn apart. Instead, I woke up back in my bed, my legs and arms feeling like they were on fire and a strange numbness in my lower back."

Standing up, Tim turned around and lifted up his shirt with trembling hands before pulling off his bandage. "I…I can't see it well, but I know something is there. And I needed someone that I could trust. That might believe me enough to at least try and help. I know that fucking thing has done something to me, but I don't know what. Please, Paul. Tell me what it is."

I bent down and looked at the small white circle that

was embedded in Tim's flesh at the spine. It looked like a plastic disc, and reminded me of knickknacks I had seen before that were made on 3-D printers. Except this piece was buried in my friend's back and he was clearly terrified. Edging closer, I saw there was a faint etching on the disc, words that I said without thinking as I read them.

"Mark...Two."

That's when I realized Tim's shoulders were shaking. At first I thought it was from fear or sadness, but then he turned to me, his eyes blazing with a kind of fiery madness that made him look like something far less, or maybe far more, than human. He was laughing.

"You never asked me what the worst thing I ever saw was."

I was backing away now, grateful my keys were in my pocket and trying to guess the distance to the front door. "What? What are you talking about?"

"I told you seeing the videos of those people being ripped apart was the second worst thing I'd ever seen. But you never asked me what the worst was."

I was almost to the door now. He wasn't pursuing at all, just glaring at me and laughing as he talked. I'd ask this last thing and then immediately go for the door. Hopefully get to my car before he could react. "What was the worst?"

Tim suddenly stopped laughing as though a switch had been flipped. "What the Engine showed me, of course. It shows me so many terrible things."

I grabbed the knob and yanked the door open, turning as I went through so I could run to the car. I half expected to be grabbed any moment, but I made it to the car and got inside without any sign of Tim. It wasn't until I was pulling out of the driveway that he appeared at the door of my house and gave a small wave. Even driving away as fast as I could, I still heard the last words he called out across the growing gulf of night between us.

"It will show them to you too. It'll show them to all of you."

Watch out for the Takers

It was as I pushed the needle into his eye that I knew I had crossed a threshold. A life full of increasingly dark and self-destructive choices had led me to a doorway, and as I began to harvest this man, I walked through it. My hand trembled as I pulled up the plunger and his ocular fluid filled the vial as the eye beneath began to shrivel. I had thought he was still out, but as I finished, he began to stir. His good eye rolled in the silver frame of the eye speculum I had applied, and then it found me. Perhaps he recognized me. Maybe it would make it easier for him if he did, give him something to focus on other than the pain and the terror. He could spend his final moments wondering why his baby girl was treating him this way. Why she was taking choice bits of him, slowly killing him in the process.

As he began to cry and flail against his restraints, I found myself wondering the same thing. He wasn't a good man. By many definitions he would be called evil. But I had seen far worse things since running away at sixteen. Had become far worse myself.

But the time for regrets was past.

I had already walked through the door. And they were all waiting and watching.

****

There is the world as you know it, and then there are

worlds beneath that world. I stumbled into one of those worlds when I was a homeless and desperate young girl worried more about not starving or freezing to death than I was the mysteries and moralities of life. It was as I lay shivering in a shadowed corner of a rundown subway station that they found me and offered me a new life. A new path to walk.

They call themselves Takers. It's hard to say if it's more of a philosophy or a religion, as for the past five years I've only known the practical details I needed to perform my duties as an initiate. Like any good secret society or cult, they save the inner workings for after you are in too deep to get away or risk telling anyone. But to be fair, I never cared that much about my ignorance.

When they found me in that subway, I had been homeless for almost a year. A year of living on the street had hardened me, made me ruthlessly pragmatic. Social taboos and moral restraints start falling away the second or third time someone tries to cave your head in or rape you. I had more scars inside and outside than I had when I'd run away, but I had also grown up a lot. My priorities were surviving and improving my life when I could. Everything else was trivia.

They took me to a small, clean apartment. Told me it was mine now. Gave me a debit card to a small expense account and told me to use it to buy some new clothes and food. Gave me a burner phone and told me to always answer it without fail. They said someone would be by the next day to evaluate me further.

It's almost funny now, looking back at that seventeen year-old me. Dirty and tired, I sat there crying with a mixture of gratitude and disbelief at how quickly things had changed. There was stuff for sandwiches in the fridge, and I ate one and a half before my shrunken stomach rebelled. I took a long shower, the first in two months, and then I went to sleep in a bed softer than just about anything I had ever felt. I slept deep and well, never troubled by why I was being given this or what the price would be.

It wasn't that I was stupid. I knew there was a catch. There's always a catch. But I just didn't care. If it was sex, I would try to get away if it was more than I could handle or endure it if I could. If it was violence, I would do my best to hurt them worse than they hurt me. If it was anything else…well, I could tolerate a lot to not go back to that cold subway.

The next day a short woman in horn-rimmed glasses came in and asked me a series of questions. Weird, random stuff like you'd probably see on a psych eval or personality test. Whatever she was looking for, she seemed satisfied with my answers and moved on to explaining that I was being given an opportunity to begin a new job. A new life.

A new path.

****

One begins in the Takers as an Initiate. That's a fancy word for assistant. Several times a week I would get a phone call to go somewhere and do something. Both the where and the what would vary greatly. Sometimes I was told to just go and watch a location for awhile with no specific instructions of what I was watching for. Other times I was told to carve or paint a symbol in a specific location. Over time I figured out that there were two separate sets of symbols I was being given. One related to something they call "The Convenience Room". Those symbols wouldn't be requested except every few months. The others related to the main business of the Takers.

Taking people and harvesting them.

The marks were a way of letting a Taker know who a potential target might be and some details about them. Takers in an area would be told the general location of potential marks and then they could pick and choose which ones to seek out. The marks will always be near a place that the victim frequents, be it their home or work or a movie theater they always visit on Tuesday nights. This victim has been independently vetted as a good candidate that meets several criteria.

First, relative health needs to be good to excellent. Smoking, excessive drinking or drug use all decrease the likelihood of being taken. Second, they need to live a life where they won't be overly missed. This is important, but not as important as you might think. Most people, even if they have families or important jobs, aren't going to be truly missed by more than a handful of people. And there are many that won't really be missed by anyone at all.

If you think this just applies to the homeless or the aged, you're wrong. The first time I marked someone's house, it was a man in his late forties who worked at a local delicatessen. He lived within his means, he had friends at work, he even had a sister who lived in New Mexico. Within a month of him being taken, his house was rented and his missing person's report had gotten lost in a stack of others.

And to be clear, I'm not apologizing for what I've done. I'm not claiming I was tricked or ignorant of what was going to happen when I put the right combination of symbols underneath his mailbox. I was using a specific code, the code I had been taught, to convey who this person was and when they would be at home. And while there was no guarantee anyone would ever use that information, I knew if they did, it was going to be a bad time for the deli guy.

Because the Takers never lie to you. They're very matter-of-fact, and while they have a lot they just won't tell you, they aren't shy about letting you know what happens to the people that you watch, the people that you report on, the people that you mark for taking.

They become cattle. Vetted, safe to take and consume, cattle.

I've heard it ties into old Egyptian ideas of mummification and immortality. I've heard it ties into something called The Kingdom of Ash. Whatever truth can be gleaned from all the rumors and hearsay over the years, I can tell you at least part of what they do.

They take these people, these cattle, and they extract things from them. Bits of their brain and heart. Spinal or ocular fluid. Blood and marrow and bile. I don't know how they choose what they choose, but whatever they take, the person must be alive for it all and conscious for at least a portion of the time. And whenever they're done taking, they consume their prizes and dispose of what remains.

Before the night when I drained the fluid from my father's eyes, I only knew the mechanics, not the point of it. I looked at my graduation from initiate to a Taker as more of a job promotion than the key to unlocking some greater mystery. I had spent the last few months preparing for this, learning all the techniques and making sure I wouldn't make a mistake. The permissible amount of drugs for incapacitation, the surgical techniques for extraction, the various rules that must be followed so that the Harvest was not tainted. The day I took my father, I spent most of the day nervously reviewing my notes as though I was cramming for an important exam.

****

Hobbling: Hobbling describes the restriction of free movement through either binding the legs or feet together or through damaging or removing the same from the person's body. This is always permitted so long as it does not interfere with the Harvest.

Quieting: Quieting describes the severing of the tongue or vocal cords. This is only permitted when there is no alternative. It is always preferred that the person be allowed to vocalize their pain and grief.

Cleansing: Cleansing describes the use of antiseptic to cleanse an area before extraction. It can also describe sanitizing an unknown infected area if it potentially compromises the quality of a Harvest to leave it unclean. While cleansing has been frowned upon traditionally, with the increase of Methicillin-resistant (MRSA) bacteria and other hard to kill infectious agents, the practice is becoming more commonplace and widely accepted.

Harvesting: Harvesting describes taking specific items from the body for the purpose of induction.

Rendering: Rendering describes when an item to be harvested from the body requires changing the body's state for collection. This most commonly describes melting down a body to collect fat via an apparatus called a "sluice gate" or to more easily separate muscle from bone.

Stilling: Stilling describes utilizing either drugs or physical damage (blunt force trauma, a full-frontal lobotomy, etc) to render the person unconscious or unaware of what is happening after they initially awaken. This is forbidden, as it irrevocably taints the Harvest.

Induction: Induction describes consuming the Harvest and descending further down the Path through the consumption.

I kept those rules and dozens of others close to my heart as I began to cut my father apart. The first time they always make you take someone you know. That you can be connected to. It's their way of insuring you can never turn against them later. And that was fine by me. My hands kept shaking, but I knew I could make it through. That is, at least, until he spoke to me.

"Lori...I'm sorry...I'm...I'm so sorry."

I froze. What was I doing? What had I become? I knew they were watching me from the shadows, but gone was the mad desire to please them and the thrill of fear at what might happen if I failed. Instead I was filled with disgust and rage at myself.

I looked down at the man lying on the table in front of me. He was moments from dying and far past saving. He was still trying to look at me with his shriveled, useless eyes, but his strength was failing. It was too late for him. It was too late for all of us.

I slit his throat and ran from the room. No one tried to stop me, and I ditched my phone just outside the office building where my father's murder was conducted. I ran and ran until I got to a bus stop, and then I rode as far as it would take me before getting off and heading to an ATM. I would try for one big cash withdrawal to give myself some traveling money, and then I would disappear. I half expected the card to already be turned off, but it worked. I got out $300 and walked the five miles to the train terminal.

Four weeks later and I hadn't seen the first sign of them. I'm halfway across the country and living above the laundromat I work at now. I don't use anything but cash, and no one knows who I am. I should be safe.

But I know them too well. I know how good they are at what they do. So I keep looking for people that don't quite belong. For symbols and codes in spots that a Taker on the hunt would be told about. Places no one notices unless they've been told where to look—and waiting there, a private menu meant just for them.

I found the menu last night. It was scratched into the paint behind the trashcans in the alley. To most people it would look like nonsense, but I could read it just fine.

Female, early 20s, very good health. Works below. Lives above. Use caution. Take heart.

I eased the trash can back into place as calmly as I could. For all I knew, they were watching me, and I didn't want to give any more indication that I knew than could be helped. I went in, finished my shift, and then went back upstairs to write this down.

I've thought of running again, but what's the point? They'll just find me again. They've been doing this for too long. They're too good at it.

So instead, I'm providing this account and then I'm going to go back to living my life, however short or long that might be. Who knows? Maybe no one will ever come. Or if they do, maybe I can survive it.

And if not? Well, I'll do my best to take them with me.

This is not my house.

I woke one morning in my bed.
The sheets were green instead of red.
They were red the night before,
So next I run to my front door.

The door is closed, the lock is thrown,
But it is not a door I own—
The color's off, the knob is grey,
And wasn't it brass just yesterday?

Footfalls behind me and I turn to look,
What I see next leaves me utterly shook,
My husband alive after three weeks buried,
His face confused as to why I'm so harried.

I run into his arms, confused but not caring,
Want to ask how, but I'm not so daring,
Instead I just cry and laugh for awhile,
And when I pull back, I drink in his smile.

The next day is wonder, the next week--bliss,
I find there are dozens of things I don't miss,
The different models of cars and who has bright fame,
All the things I see now were just facts and names.

The things that mattered, they were still there.
Altered slightly, but not enough that I'd care.

Johnny was left-handed here and spoke with a slur
Left over from an accident some years before,
My parents seemed distant, emotionally bereft,
But it was due to my other's history of theft.

I was an explorer in this new version of my life,
Digging up my past as a daughter and wife,
Figuring out the differences both big and small,
Because I planned to stay here after all.

Except today we went to a park.

This was apparently a tradition,
It was a gathering of sorts, and by my own admission,
I began to get nervous as soon as we arrived,

Passing by groups of people laughing in the grass as they writhed and writhed.

The park was filled with a manic mob,
And as we plunged in, the crowd began to throb
With a frantic ecstasy that seemed insane,
Sending aching tendrils into my brain.

Ahead I saw a giant shape—an X made out of steel and fire.
A man hung chained on its burning frame,
the crowd pulling him this way and that across the pyre.

The man was screaming, he was laughing,
The crowd was singing, dancing, chanting,
I smelled him burning to their song,
I retched a little at so much wrong.

My Johnny looked at me with eyes gleaming,
I think he wept, for tears were
Coming down his face and I almost thought
He knew how bad this all was, even
Though he wasn't really my Johnny,
Oh God, surely he knew this wasn't right,

This world wasn't right…

I looked back and saw a pair at the park's edge,

A couple hiding near a hedge,

They weren't laughing or coming near,

Perhaps like me, they weren't from here.

Oh take me with you, take me back,

I can't stay here you see because it's changing me already and

Oh no, why is this place like this?

How could it be like this?

What is this song they're singing?

And why do I know the words?

I start to sing and the pain goes away.

I start to dance and the fear goes away.

I eat from the dead man's cooked heart,

And I go away.

And then I go home with my Johnny.

It's been a good day.

I'll make my arrows from your bones.

Part One

I remember the first time I caused two men to kill each other.

I was seven and was waiting outside a dressing room while my mother tried on summer vacation clothes. She had told me not to move a muscle, so that's what I did. The department store was quiet and I soon felt myself getting drowsy from boredom and the breathing in and out of the same warm, recycled air. That's when I noticed two men talking nearby.

At first I thought they were friends or worked together, but then I saw they were angry. They were standing on opposite sides of the check-out counter, and that seemed like the only thing keeping them from pushing or hitting each other. And then they *were* pushing and hitting each other. I heard someone yell from somewhere nearby, and when I looked back, I saw that one of the men had pulled a knife and was stabbing the other. As they fell down and out of view, I heard both of the men begin to scream.

My mother had come out at the commotion, and without another word she grabbed my hand and pulled me from the store. I was shaking as we walked across the parking lot to the car, but I didn't cry. I never cried in front of her. Instead I just waited, tense and tight as a spring, for whatever my mother had to tell me. Five minutes down the road, she began.

"Did you see those men?"

I nodded from the backseat and then spoke up. "Yes, ma'am. I did."

She was gripping the steering wheel tightly, her gold and silver rings standing out from her white fingers like strange, glittering mountains on some distant, hostile world. I saw her dark eyes flick up to mine in the rearview mirror.

"Did you see the dark cloud around them?"

I frowned, shaking my head. I knew my mother saw a great many things. Knew a great many things. And while she could be harsh, she was never dishonest or cruel. Even when I was afraid of her, I loved her. Wanted to be like her and never disappoint her.

In my heart, I considered lying. Saying I had seen the cloud around them, just so I could be like her. But she would know I was lying and it would make her angry. Worse, she would think less of me. So I kept shaking my head as I answered.

"No, ma'am."

She nodded, her eyes unreadable. "Well, that may be for the best. It was a terrible thing to see. It was a dark cloud that made those men fight and have the lust for killing. Just a little thing swimming around the two of them. But that's not the worst part." She let out a deep breath. "No, the worst part was I saw a black string of it trailing back towards us like the string on a balloon. Trailing all the way back to my sweet little girl."

I remember feeling so scared then, so ashamed. It wasn't the first time my mother had told me secret, hidden things that she saw, or the first time she had hinted there was something wrong with me. But even at that young age, I understood how her mind worked. The meanings and implications of what was said and left unsaid. Normally I kept that all to myself, but this time I just couldn't. I had to know.

"Mama, was the cloud coming from me?"

She closed her eyes for a second, and when she reopened them, I saw her mascara smudged from the tears welling in the corners of her eyes. "I'm afraid so, honey. You made those nice men fight. Maybe kill each other." We rode on in silence for several minutes then, the only sounds the road beneath us and my mother's sniffling. I still wasn't crying or even really afraid. There was a terrible inevitability to it all that made sense, as though my inherent badness had finally grown so strong it had spilled out into the outer world.

I looked back at Mama's face in the mirror. "Am I going to hurt more people?" And then at the panicked thought, I added, "Am I going to hurt you with this cloud?"

Mama favored me with a watery smile. "I hope not, honey. I'll do what I can to stop it." She was suddenly slowing down the car until we were stopped dead in the road a few miles from home. Turning around, she looked at me intently, her face no longer smiling, but not unkind. "But don't you worry, baby. I won't leave you. And I'll do my best to keep everyone safe from you."

****

43

Six months later, Mama woke me up to tell me that the world was ending.

I hadn't been back to school since the day in the department store, and aside from Mama, the only person I had seen was the mailman when he stuck his arm out to put mail in the mailbox. She told people I was being home schooled, but for the most part I was left to my own devices so long as I stayed inside. The house was huge, and even growing up there, I felt like there was always something new to explore in a forgotten room or a dusty corner of the library.

I loved books already, and once the outside world was foreclosed to me, they became my only real friends aside from Mama. I would carry them through the shadowy halls of the old family house, whispering secrets to them and holding them up to my ear like a seashell to see if they would answer. They never did, of course, but I didn't hold that against them. I knew sometimes it was best to stay quiet.

The night the world ended, Mama carried me down to the lower basement. It had been fashioned into a storm cellar decades earlier, with a heavy metal door and rooms set aside for storing food and water. I had always been intrigued by my earlier glimpses of it, but now I was afraid. When she pulled me inside and twisted the door handle shut, I felt my stomach clenching.

"What's happening, Mama?"

She was dressed up like always—wrapped in a green cocktail dress and glittering with jewels, from behind she looked like she had just gotten home from attending some fancy party or hosting an elaborate dinner. She was even holding her little metal box like a tiny purse a model or actress might carry. But when she turned to look at me, her face was pale and drawn, with make-up caked and running into a thick, melting mud of sweat and tears. In the unforgiving sodium lights of our little underground bunker, she looked like a monster when she told me of the death of our world.

"It was your cloud, honey. It was such a terrible thing. I thought if I kept you hidden away, you wouldn't be able to hurt anybody." She shuffled over to one of the two small metal beds stuffed against the walls of the front room of the storm cellar. Her eyes were distant and her lips trembled as she sat down unsteadily on the edge of the mattress. "I…I started hearing news stories and gossip about people fighting. Killing each other. At first I hoped it was just normal evil that people do to one another. That my safeguards were keeping everyone safe from you and your little cloud."

Leaning forward, she bit the knuckles of her clenched hands. "But I was stupid. And I supposed I always knew in my heart of hearts. Then, just today, I saw it when I went into town. It was almost as big as the sky, and I saw people fighting in the streets. Going crazy."

Turning to stare at me with her wide, raccoon eyes, her voice cracked with emotion. "It's only a matter of time before they figure out it's coming from you. And then they'll come for you, those that are left. That's why we have to stay down here where it's safe. In a few months, everything will be settled one way or the other, and we can go back outside. Try to make a life in whatever world is left." Mama smiled weakly. "I know it won't be fun, but if we're careful we have enough food and water to last a year down here. I've been getting ready just in case."

I went over to her, hugging her both to comfort and to be comforted. I was so ashamed and guilty for all the bad I had done without even realizing it, but what I hated the most was what I was putting Mama through. She already had so much on her with her special sight. She had foreseen Daddy dying weeks before it happened, and she had known since I was a baby that something wasn't right with me. But she always stuck by me, forgiving me, protecting me. I squeezed her tightly, my heart thudding with fear and sadness, but most of all, love.

It was hours later, when I was still softly crying in some twilight realm of not-sleep, that I felt her crouched in the darkness next to my new bed. I felt her hand light on my head, gently stroking my hair as she murmured to me.

"Nothing to worry about, baby girl. I've seen what needs to be done. We're going to stop this bad ol' cloud."

Looking up from my tear-stained pillow, I stared at her voice in the dark. "How?"

"Well, I'm going to wait a few days and then I'll head up into the house. Into the attic. Your father's old bow is up there somewhere. With it, I can try to kill the cloud, or at least drive it off."

What she was saying made no sense, but she seemed so certain. "How do you know that, Mama?"

I heard the rasp of metal on concrete as she reached down to find the small box in the inky black surrounding us and give it an affectionate pat. Of course, the box. She had seen something in it. That was part of how she got her visions, and while I had never been allowed to touch or look into the box myself, I knew how powerful it was. It was what had first showed her I had something wrong with me when I was just a little baby.

"The box of shadows, dear. It showed me the way."

I could have left it there. I knew the rhythms of conversation with my mother well enough to know when she was satisfied, and I could have just let the silence stretch out until she tired enough to go back to bed. But I wanted to show her how much I cared. That I was a smart little girl that wanted to help, even if I had wickedness in me.

So I sent one more question out into the dark.

"Where are you going to get arrows for the bow, Mama?"

Her breath was hot on my neck as she leaned close, crooning the words into my ear as she began stroking my hair again.

"Why from your bones, my heart. I'll make my arrows from your bones."

Part Two

I didn't sleep that night. At first, I was too frozen with fear to even think about closing my eyes or moving at all. My brain felt like jelly, and my thoughts were dull and ponderous, sliding past each other in the congealing dark of my mind. I remember thinking that I was turning to stone, and that was all right. I would just turn to stone and then it wouldn't hurt when Mama came to rip me apart.

But the thought didn't last. Didn't satisfy. Soon it was replaced with a new, stranger idea that I liked better. The idea that if I was still enough, not moving a muscle or making a sound, I would just fade into the background until I disappeared like a ghost. Once I was invisible, I could move around without Mama noticing. I could try to help her, and if I couldn't, I could try to escape. I was still fearful of what the world had become outside our little shelter, but I was also starting to doubt what she had told me. If she was sick or confused, maybe things weren't like she thought after all.

Hours passed with me staying still, barely breathing enough to stir my chest. It felt as though I could feel myself fading away from the world, growing thin and insubstantial before slipping away entirely into some ghost version of the storm shelter. Breathing a little more deeply, the only sound I heard was the placid snoring of Mama across the room.

I eased off the bed an inch at the time. Twice the unfamiliar springs beneath me creaked and my heart shuddered in my chest. Both times, Mama stopped snoring for a moment before the familiar drone of her sleeping began again. My bare feet were silent on the cold concrete floor as I crept in what I thought was the direction of the door leading out.

My initial thoughts had evolved into a rudimentary plan. I would sneak outside, see how things looked, and if there was help to be gotten, I would get it for myself and for Mama. If everything was as bad as she said, I could always turn around before she even missed me.

But when I twisted the doorknob, I found it was locked, with no way of unlocking it except for the small keyhole I felt under the knob. Biting my lip, I turned back to stare unseeing in the direction of Mama. She would have the key somewhere, probably on her body in a pocket or on a chain. I might wake her up trying to find it...but I might not. She was sleeping hard, and besides, what other choice did I have?

So I made my way back in the direction I had come, following the sound of her snores to guide me to the side of her bed. Every step I was scared I would bump something or fall—make some noise that would wake her and arouse her suspicion. But I reached her easily, and crouching down beside her, I sent out a trembling, questing hand.

She had changed into pajamas of some sort, and at first I wondered if there were any pockets at all. I was drifting my hands over her, light as a spring breeze, trying to sense the geography of her clothing without waking her. It wasn't working very well. I had no points of reference in the dark, and I hadn't paid attention to what she was wearing before she put me to bed. Just as I was losing hope, I felt a hard lump on what I guessed was her hip.

It was Mama's box of shadows.

She'd had the box for as long as I remembered. She told me once it had been in the family for some time, and that it was always passed down to the oldest child, which she was, when they were grown. Mama said that one day it would be mine, but that until then, I was never to touch it or look in it. Such things, she said, weren't meant for me yet. They could ruin someone so young.

As with everything, I had taken Mama at her word. Worked to do as she wanted. And while I still had curiosity about it, for the most part I had learned to act as though it didn't exist.

But I was not an idiot either. I knew the box had shown her terrible things. Had affected her, making her strange—especially in the hours and days after she used it. When I was smaller, she had looked into it very infrequently, but within the past few months, I had seen her with it more and more. And every time she used it, she came back to herself a little less. It was as if she was leaving some part of her sanity or her soul in that thing every time she looked into it, trying to see…what?

I didn't know. Possible futures and how to avoid them? Hidden knowledge from some distant, forgotten place? She rarely talked about what she saw, but it was clearly important given how it had captivated her. The thought didn't occur to me at the time that she was an addict—an addict hungry for whatever poison that box offered. At the time, I just thought about how I needed to see what was in the box for myself so I could try and understand. So I could help Mama.

I carefully reached into her pocket for the box. It was icy to the touch, but not unpleasantly so, and after one gentle tug, it slid easily out into my hand. I froze again for a moment. Still snoring? Yes, at least for now, but I needed to be quick. Standing up slowly, I crept away from the bed, my free hand stuck out in front of me. I needed the door to the storage rooms. I could look at the box in there.

I went too far at first, but when I came back in the other direction, I found it. I sat down after I was through the doorway—if Mama decided to turn on the lights, I'd be around the corner out of sight. Feeling the box with my hands, I found the small metal door on the top of it. I knew from watching Mama that all you needed to do was trigger the door with a tiny button on the side and two small glass windows would be revealed. Then you simply held the box up to your eyes and looked through those windows into…whatever it was it showed.

It hadn't occurred to me growing up how insane the idea of the box was, perhaps because I had never known life without it. Questions like how was it powered, how did it work, how could it possibly work…those things never crossed my mind. In part because I'd seen how it affected Mama whenever she used it. She wasn't faking it, and I hadn't thought she was stupid or insane. So whatever the box was, whatever it could do, it had to be real, right?

I triggered the button to release the lid covering the glass viewing circles. It sounded impossibly loud in the dark, and I strained to listen for the rhythmic sounds of Mama sleeping before relaxing my death grip on the box. I felt an untapped well of fear rising in me. I didn't want to see what the box would show me. I didn't want to be like Mama.

Shaking badly, I opened my eyes wide and brought the box up. My eyelashes brushed against the glass lenses and I blinked as I stared into…nothing. There was nothing in there. It was just a dark, empty box, and my mother…

****

"…was just crazy."

I looked up from my notes at Addison. She seemed slightly emotional now, leaning forward in her seat as she spoke. I would normally take that as a welcome change from her typical flat affect and guarded body language, but something was off. Staring at the floor, Addison was wiping tears from her cheeks as she waited silently for my reaction.

I took a moment to pick up her file off the table and flip back through my earlier notes from when she first started having sessions with me a year earlier. Not notes from the sessions themselves--a troubled and angry fourteen year-old girl at the time, she had barely spoken to me in those first meetings. No, the notes were from things her grandparents had told me before I started counseling Addison. Ah, here we go.

Addison is a sweet girl who has been through a lot. Her mother had mental health issues, which lead to her isolating herself and Addison from the family. This culminated when, after two months of attempts at contact with no response, her grandmother went to check on them and found Addison trapped in a sub-basement with her mother's dead body.

She had been there for several days.

There was some investigation into the cause of death, which was ultimately ruled a suicide. Grandmother showed signs of dishonesty during the discussions of this death and Addison's ongoing behavior. This may be partially unintentional, as she seems very protective of the girl, and seems unwilling to assign blame to Addison even after the incident at school...

Looking back up from my notes, I saw that Addison was looking at me. Even at fifteen, her gaze was unnerving at times. She was highly intelligent, and while she often showed little emotion, I never got the sense it was due to any lack of feeling. Instead, I had recently began developing the theory that everything this girl did was extensively planned and tightly controlled. This could simply be the product of an unfortunate but charismatic young lady who was working hard to be liked and fit in, to find love and acceptance after a traumatic early childhood.

Or it could be signs of a budding sociopath.

"When you had this realization about your mother, how did that make you feel?"

There was a buzz from the office phone, and then Janice's voice telling me that my 3 o'clock, Mr. Evans, was here. I told her it would be a few minutes. I looked back to Addison and apologized for the interruption.

I saw that her tears were gone now. She sat back in her chair, and crossing her arms, she gave a shrug.

"Well, not good. I had trusted her. Knowing she was crazy, had been delusional or lying or whatever…it sucked. Knowing she might hurt me…that was worse."

Nodding, I weighed my options. I could let her continue to guide the session and retreat back to her normal posture. That would lose any real progress we might make today, especially if I was wrong and she was being genuine. Or I could try and provoke a reaction. See if I could breakthrough to…something.

"Did you kill your mother?"

Addison's expression didn't change at first. Then she smiled slightly. "Why? Do you think I did?"

I mirrored her earlier shrug. "I don't know, Addison. There are details about what I've heard about your time with your mother," I flipped through the remaining pages of notes I had from her family and a childhood counselor, "that don't seem to match up with what you're telling me."

Her smile widened. "Like what?"

I flipped to the third page and scanned it. "Like, according to your grandfather, there were never any reports of a fight or murder at a department store near where you lived. Not during the relevant time frame."

She nodded. "And what else?"

"There's the pre-interview notes of the counselor you saw briefly when you first went to live with your grandparents. According to those, she reviewed an incident report from when you were found in the sub-basement with your mother's body. That when police found you, you were in good condition and sitting on the front lawn. Your grandmother had gotten you out easily, because the door wasn't locked."

Addison crinkled her nose slightly. "Couldn't it be I just remember things differently? Trauma and all that?"

I tried to keep my expression neutral. "It could. But in my experience, you are very intelligent and self-controlled. You don't make many mistakes. And while a traumatized seven year-old unlocking the door and then still choosing to stay with her dead mother is feasible, it seems less likely in this case."

"Because I see here that I asked your grandmother about when she found you. She said she searched the upper floors and then went down to the basements. That she found you easily enough then by the smell. That the door opened right up, because there was no way to lock it. Never had been."

Addison smirked at me. "What else did she say?"

I closed the file back. "Addison, if you want to make

progress, if you want me to reach the point where I can sign off on you having completed the mandated mental health component of your pre-trial diversion satisfactorily, I need you to be honest with me. Tell me what really happened to your mother."

I felt my breath catch as her smile fell away. For the first time, I was actually afraid of her. "She died and I lived. That's the only part that matters." Suddenly her smile was back as her eyes began dancing with mischief. "But if you want to know how, it's going to cost you."

Part Three

I swallowed. She was trying to bait me, but how or why I wasn't sure. I held her gaze for another moment before nodding. "Sure. I want to know. How did your mother die?"

A small chill ran up my back as she looked at me. She was still smiling, but her eyes were no longer full of life and merriment. Instead they looked flat and dark, empty pools of night ringed by a thin rime of dark green. Pools that were deep and filled with terrible things ready to pull me down...

I blinked. "What did you say?"

She chuckled as she stood up. "I told you I needed to go. We're over our time and your next patient is waiting."

I rubbed my eyes as I rose from my chair. "He won't mind waiting a few minutes. I wanted you to tell me what happened to your mother before we ended our session."

Letting out a light laugh, Addison looked back at me

on her journey toward the door. "Oh, I never said I'd tell you." She waved as she went through the door and then she was gone. Harold Evans, with all his social anxieties and inability to make eye contact or speak above a whisper, stared at Addison as she passed through the outer office. It was only when I called his name that he looked back at me and came in for his session.

****

"That's the last of the notes I have from Dr. Chester Bailey, dated ten years ago. Because that's the last time you saw him, wasn't it?"

Addison nodded. "Yep. I heard about what happened to him later." She looked up at me, her lips twitching upward. "Very sad."

I held her gaze. "You know, Addison, this whole act you've got going on here? It doesn't work with me."

She raised an eyebrow. "It doesn't, huh?"

Smiling thinly at her, I shook my head. "Not a bit." Standing, I started walking around the therapy room. The sounds of the footfalls were muffled—every surface was padded with dense foam cushioning, even the floor and the furniture, and Addison's wrists were strapped into padded cuffs secured to the table at which she sat. I didn't think these precautions were necessary though. Not because she wasn't dangerous, but because I didn't think attacking me fit her profile or her plan. I made a point of turning my back to her as I went on.

"No, because I know who you are. Or at least I'm starting to. You're in here for attacking a neighbor, right? Bit her thumb off, I understand. Now why would you do that? You're very wealthy, or at least your grandfather is, and my understanding is you have a trust fund large enough that you could never spend it all. That's the main reason you're here instead of a jail somewhere, right? Your family supposedly pays to get you help instead of you getting locked up. Just like in high school. Just like Dr. Bailey."

Nothing but silence behind me. Gripping my hands, I continued.

"But I have a great deal more resources than poor Dr. Bailey. And I have a greater appreciation than he did for just how dangerous you are. So I've researched you. Dug deep. Read all the reports, evaluations, everything from your elementary school records to your mother's autopsy." I turned around now so I could gauge her reaction. Addison was just watching me placidly, paying attention but seemingly unaffected. "I've seen enough that I don't need to ask you those questions, Addison. I don't need to play your games. I'll tell you what happened to your mother and to Dr. Bailey. And after the cards are on the table, maybe we can start from a place of honesty, or at the very least, respect."

Addison smirked slightly. "Sounds peachy. Go for it."

Sitting back down, I ticked off points on my right hand. "Your mother's autopsy showed ligature marks and bruising on her neck and ankles, and her body was found on one of the beds in the storm cellar. The incident report doesn't mention these details, of course, because things were kept intentionally vague to protect you. But it doesn't matter. The first week you were committed here, I went and reviewed the original physical file. Looked at the handful of pictures that were taken after her body was removed. One of those pictures showed the stained mattress where she voided herself as she died. The same bed you describe in your little fairy tale as the one she was laying on when you took the box from her."

Folding my hands together, I caught her eye again. "So what happened is this. You were down there with her for whatever reason. Perhaps she had gone insane, or perhaps you tricked her down there and got her laid out on the bed somehow. The autopsy didn't show any drugs in her system or any signs of head trauma, so that part is unclear to me. But it's also largely unimportant. What is important is how she died."

"You were too small to move her or easily kill her when she was awake. But just like now, you were very smart as a little girl. So you waited until she was asleep on that bed. Then you gently tied a sheet around her ankles and to the metal footboard of the bed. Not too tight, or she'd wake up. Just tight enough that when she tried to pull free in a panic, it would tighten down more. And then you prepared a second sheet. A noose, really. Because this one you slipped around her neck."

Addison was smiling wider now, her dark gaze unblinking as she studied me, watching me like I was a stupid animal doing something funny at the zoo. "You were only seven at the time. Weighed what? Fifty pounds, maybe? But you weren't just using your weight to pull the sheet tight around her neck were you? No, you were braced against the back of the headboard, pulling as hard as you could while your mother suffocated to death. You must have been a strong little girl."

She nodded her head. "I've always been gifted with some degree of natural athleticism. Thank you for noticing."

Frowning, I went on. "Even if everything I've said so far is true, it could arguably be justifiable. If she was dangerous, if she really was threatening your life, you could have just been trying to protect yourself." Sighing, I went on. "But then we come to Dr. Bailey. Dr. Bailey, who by all accounts, was a good man, and based on everything I've looked at, was earnestly trying to help you."

Addison lowered her head. "Yes, such a shame about him. Such a nice guy."

I stood up again, standing over her. "No. You don't get to play your games here. You don't get to…"

She looked up at me. "Sit down."

I backed up. I had to fight a strong compulsion to do as she asked. "You don't tell me what…"

"Sit down and quit attacking me please. This is all very distressful and unprofessional, Dr. Bridges."

I shuddered and went to the far corner of the room. I was losing control of this, and I just wanted to be out of the room now. I felt like I couldn't breathe. Turning away for a moment, I forced myself to calm down. She was just a twenty-five year-old girl with signs of narcissistic sociopathy, not Hannibal Lecter. I had to take the reins back.

I just couldn't look at her yet. As long as I didn't have to look at her, it would be okay.

"Harold Evans killed Dr. Bailey during their session one week after your last time meeting with Bailey. You were scheduled to meet Bailey the hour before the murder for your weekly appointment, but the logs say you called and rescheduled it the day before."

"Why don't you turn around, doctor?"

I jumped at her voice. I couldn't turn around. Couldn't meet her eyes. I had to just keep going.

"But Harold showed up for his appointment. Harold, who had no history of being violent. He was seeing Dr. Bailey for severe anxiety disorder and mild agoraphobia. That man…he tied Dr. Bailey's feet to one end of his desk and then nearly pulled his head off with a noose."

"It's hard to hear you, doctor. Why don't you show me your face?"

Shuddering, I began sidestepping for the door. "I'm going to help you, Addison, but it's going to take time. You have to be willing to work with me." I held up my card and the door unlocked. "That's all for today." I felt my stomach roiling as I opened the door and went out into the hall, narrowly closing it behind me before I was bent over retching. What was wrong with me? I had to…

****

"…get ahold of yourself, Monica."

I glared at Dr. Talpin. "Richard, don't patronize me. I understand I crossed a line in my initial interview last week, but that's no reason to take me off her case."

He raised his eyebrows. "Monica, it's not my call anymore. Addison filed a complaint, the interview tape was reviewed, and yes, you were too combative for a first session. Or a tenth, if I'm being honest. But I understand what you were going for, and hell, I might even allow it if things were different. But her grandfather is friends with two people on our board and he's already talked about donating money to the hospital. They are not willing to risk pissing him off, and right now, the best thing I can do is keep you from getting fired."

I stood up, clenching my fists as I began pacing. "Fired? What are we even talking about? This girl is dangerous. It is documented that she broke a girl's jaw in high school. It is documented that she bit the thumb off of a woman who lived in her apartment building just last month." I stopped walking and pinned Richard with my gaze. "And all the things I was telling her in our interview? All true. I'm pretty certain that she killed her mother and somehow convinced Harold Evans to kill her last therapist."

Talpin rolled his eyes. "Look, Monica. This isn't a movie. You aren't a detective. Even if you're right, and that's a really big if, that's not our job. Our job is to assess and treat, that's all. And don't get me wrong. You're a great clinician. One of our best. But taking you off this case is the right move. You've lost sight of the priorities here." He looked down at random papers on his desk, as though signaling the end of the conversation through a subtle reminder of his bureaucratic authority.

I wasn't done yet. "Have you seen how the other patients act around her? She's gathered quite the following while she's been in here."

Looking irritated, Talpin glanced back up. "She's a very charismatic, very pretty young woman who is new to the environment. It's not unexpected that the other clients would flock to her. I imagine that will calm down as the new wears off. Either way, there's nothing sinister about it."

I stared at him incredulously. "Really? We've had three violent attacks between patients since she's been here. Three. In a month. Before that, we hadn't had one in years."

Looking back down at his paperwork, Talpin began, "Monica, you're looking for connections that simply aren't..."

I cut him off. "And by the way, they're patients not clients. I know all you and the fucking board care about is money, but we're actually responsible for people's lives and well-being here. And I'm telling you that woman is fucking dangerous."

Talpin struck the desk as he glared up at me. "Enough, Dr. Bridges. Enough. You're off Addison Hawthorne's treatment team, and that's final. If I hear another word from you, or if I hear you're contacting that girl again, you will quickly realize what it's like when I'm not on your side. Do I make myself..."

****

"...clear? Any questions?"

I was trembling, not from fear or worry, but excitement. The time was almost here. I would finally be able to do my part and show her how worthy I was.

"No, I've got it, Addison. I throw the package over the fence at four in the morning. And then I come back at ten that night and park down the road at the gas station."

"Not at the gas station, they could have cameras. You park at the ride-share lot down from the station."

Oh no, I'm so fucking stupid. Now she'll think I can't help. The poor thing has been locked up in that stupid place for two months, and now that she's ready to leave, I can't even get the simplest thing right.

"Terri, it's all right. You've got this. I trust you. Just breathe."

I felt tears spring into my eyes. She was so good to me. Still believed in me. And I wouldn't let her down. Not now, not ever.

"Th-thank you. I...I'll go to the park and share. I'll have clothes, money, and two burner phones. Is my car going to be big enough? Are we taking anybody else with us?"

"No, the others will have to find their own way. The risk is too great otherwise." There was a pause and then, "I have to go. I'm using someone else's phone account, and they apparently don't have many minutes. See you tomorrow night."

I held the phone to my ear for several seconds after it clicked and fell silent. Everything was prepared and now I just had to wait, which of course was the hardest part. Sighing discontentedly, I shifted the phone to my other hand, planning on sitting it down on one of my moving boxes. Instead, it slipped from my grasp and clattered to the floor.

Stupid, Terri, stupid. I still wasn't used to the thumb being gone. I had already broken a plate and two glasses that way while packing. The last thing I needed to do was mess up my phone, especially with everything going on. Bending down to pick it up, I let out a relieved breath when I saw it was okay.

I laughed shakily as I sat the phone down with my

good hand. I just needed to calm down. Everything would be fine. This was Addison's plan, after all. It would work just so long as I did my part.

I looked over at the cardboard box sitting apart from all my belongings. Addison said there was more things to go in it, but the first one was already sitting on top. The small metal box drew me to it whenever I thought about it, and with a twinge of guilt, I walked over and touched it again. I had the familiar impulse to trigger the button on the side and lift it to my eyes, but I wouldn't. I couldn't. Addison said it wasn't for me, at least not yet.

I checked the time. Eight hours until I needed to throw the package over the fence. Twenty-six until I needed to be ready and waiting for Addison. I wanted to go right now and be waiting, just so I'd be ready, but I knew that was stupid. I might draw attention that way. Instead I would just keep packing and then go get some sleep.

I looked down at the mottled stub where my thumb used to be. I needed to remember to take my antibiotics too. Hopefully this round would finish off the infection, because I did not want to have another surgery.

But no, I needed to stop being so negative. It would all be okay. And besides, nothing great ever came without sacrifice.

Even all the people that are going to die? Is that okay?

It had been some time since I'd heard that small, meek voice in the back of my head. Some vestige of who I had been before meeting Addison, before coming to understand things. It was a weak, scared voice that wanted me to doubt myself. To fail Addison. I spoke aloud when I responded to the thought, my voice echoing strangely in my increasingly empty apartment.

"Yes, even that. The Path is a razor that bleeds you. Until you finish it or it finishes you."

Part Four

I could see the hazy glow of orange in the night sky as I waited in the rideshare parking lot for Addison. The hospital, or at least part of it, was burning. The fire would eat eight patients, including one I would soon find out was named Janet Oberman. Out of the patients in the woman's ward of the hospital, Janet was the one that most closely met Addison's criteria.

First, she was similar in build and age to Addison herself. Second, she had no one that came to visit her. Third, her "intake bag" contained not only her purse, cellphone and car keys, but credit cards that were not set to expire for another few months. I knew all of this because Addison knew all of this. Because among the people she had befriended during her two-month stay at the asylum were a custodian and an orderly. They had been shown a new path for their life. And as I could attest to from personal experience, once Addison showed you that path, there was very little you wouldn't do to walk it by her side.

The package I had chucked over the fence earlier had looked from the outside like little more than a duct-taped beach towel wadded up into something approaching the size and shape of a basketball. But it was what was inside the ball that mattered. A burner phone, a book of matches and a plastic glue bottle partially filled with lighter fluid, as well as a small bag of Addison's blood. I had not even made it back to the car before I saw the shadowy figure of the custodian coming out to collect the package.

The plan was simple. All patients had to be in their rooms by 9 p.m. Doors were locked at 9:30, and the lights went out at 10 p.m. That was the routine of the hospital, and routine is very important in such a place as that.

Except tonight, the routine would be disrupted. Janet Oberman would be taken to Addison's room instead of her own. Once there, she would be struck in the head with a bookend that had been taken from Janet's own room. Then she would be set on fire. The bookend itself would be cleaned before being smeared with Addison's blood (which had been in my refrigerator next to the tofu for the last two months) and discarded back in Janet's room which, as luck would have it, was on a different hall that would likely be untouched by the fire.

The rooms near Addison's wouldn't be so lucky. The plan was to burn all eight of the rooms on that hall so Addison's didn't call special attention. There would be a knife from the kitchen used to wound or kill the other patients, and that, like the bookend, the matches, and the glue bottle filled with lighter fluid, would be left in Janet's room when it was all done. Eight people would die that night, and another five would escape. I worried what might happen if one of them was caught—they wouldn't know all the details, but they would know that Addison was still alive; that it was Janet Oberman's body that lay twisted and smoldering in her room.

But I forced my doubts aside. They wouldn't betray Addison any more than I would, and even if they did, what did it matter? The ravings of lunatics in the face of the physical evidence, Addison's family demanding the remains immediately, and the ongoing proof that Janet Oberman was alive and out in the world.

Because Addison was bringing Janet's purse with her. The orderly would have gotten it from the patient intake storage room and given it to her before opening the back gate. After I dropped Addison off, I would take the purse and drive south for three days, making sure to use the cards in out of the way places once every few hours. So long as I kept my face and damaged hand off of any cameras, it shouldn't be hard to give the impression that Janet, after killing Addison and several of her fellow patients, had escaped and was slowly traveling south toward the border.

When Addison had told me about the plan two months earlier, I was worried. What if I got caught? What if they checked Janet's body for DNA or dental records? What if someone made a mistake?

She had listened to my questions patiently before replying. If I got caught, I was to say that I had been paid by a woman matching Janet's description to use the cards for a few days while she traveled in a different direction. They might charge me with theft, but it wouldn't go anywhere. As for the rest, Addison said that everything that could be taken care of had been—there would be no autopsy or detailed examination of the body before it was turned over to her grandfather. No security footage and no investigation into why the accelerants seemed to match gasoline much more closely than the small amount of lighter fluid found in Janet's room. As for the rest? Addison had just laughed.

"Danger and uncertainty are always going to be there,

Terri. I know you're not there yet, but once you reach the point on the Path that you can fully embrace it as the gift that it is, the fear and worry fall away. All that is left is your Will."

We had been sitting on my sofa at the time, moments away from some of the worst pain I've ever had in my life. I had smiled and nodded. "I know, it's just hard sometimes. I worry that I'll mess something up."

Addison watched me silently for a moment before standing up. "Did I ever tell you my father was an archer?"

I shook my head.

"Yeah, he was. Not professional, of course. I think the only thing he did professionally was spend my mother's money. But he would practice a lot and do the occasional tournament. I don't remember a lot about him, but I remember one time, just a few months before he died, he tried to show me how to shoot a bow."

Addison had stepped back from the sofa and gone into an archer's stance, left arm out straight as she drew back an invisible bowstring. She looked at some unknown, distant target as she went on. "He told me that the trick to making the hard shots was to not think about it. Not worry about it. The bow was just a platform for your desire. The arrow was the important part, because it carried your Will. Not your thoughts or your doubts, but something purer, something higher. You didn't release the arrow wondering if it would hit. You had already decided it would hit. You released it simply to force reality to conform itself to what you already knew to be true."

Addison had broken her stance to look back down at me, wiping her left eye with the back of her hand. "He was a bit drunk at the time, and I don't know that he expected me to get it at such a young age, but I understood it very well." Crouching down next to me, she grabbed my hand tightly. "This Path that we are traveling is something purer and higher, too. And we survive it by living without fear, without doubt, without hesitation."

She yanked my hand forward as she opened her mouth. Pain exploded up my arm as she began biting through my thumb, yanking her head back and forth so violently that as she backed up, I fell off the sofa. I could distantly hear myself screaming, but my mind was focused on getting it over with. I turned my body so I could brace against Addison as she grinded down between the bones and yanked again. I saw my vision go red and then white. One last forceful tug and the pain changed. The feeling of pressure was gone, replaced with the hot shock of damaged nerves screaming in the open air as blood pulsed out onto the rug.

Then Addison was beside me. I think she must have swallowed my thumb, as I didn't see it anywhere and she was talking to me clearly, telling me it would be all right as she put one of the towels we had prepared against the wound. She said I needed to stay with her, at least long enough to call 911. I had numbly agreed, though I don't remember what I told the operator or the police when they arrived.

The next memory I had was two days later in the hospital. I had woken up in a panic, worried that something had gone wrong, that they had hurt Addison somehow instead of just taking her to the institution like she had wanted. It was a foolish worry, and not at all bec...

I let out a small scream as Addison opened the back door and climbed into the seat behind me. I met her eyes in the rearview mirror. "You scared me."

She let out a laugh. "I could tell. Give me a second to change clothes before we get going." She opened up the duffel bag I had brought and changed out of the smoky-smelling green scrubs she had been wearing. Those went into a large sealable garment bag that we'd dispose of after we left the area. As she was pulling on her shirt, she glanced back up at me. "Did you get the burner phone?"

I nodded. "Yes, it's in the glove compartment."

Addison squeezed my shoulder. "Good job. Now let's head to the drop off point. After that, start out on Janet's last wild ride."

I laughed. "I'll feel like a spy in a movie."

She grinned as she laid down in the back seat. "Super Agent Terri. Just make sure you're back in five days, okay? Remember, you're my movie director too."

My smile fell away. I remembered. I was dreading this part, though I knew it was just me being weak. Trying to hide my dismay, I raised my fist as we pulled out of the parking lot.

"That's right! Lights! Camera!..."

****

"Action!"

"Oh God, why are you doing this?"

The old gymnasium smelled of stagnant water and disuse, and at the edge of our light I saw several small, furtive shifts in the shadows I suspected were rats.

Shuddering, I looked down at the bound naked man sitting on the floor before me. He had been crying and whining for the last half hour, ever since Mr. Paul and Mr. Soto, his former patient and employee respectively, had roughly stripped him down and bound him. Every time he complained, one of them struck him, but it only cured the noise for a short while. It was like he had a geyser of fear in him that had to erupt every few minutes, no matter the price. I felt around in my heart for any pity for him, but thankfully, I found none.

"Dr. Talpin, you're only making this harder on yourself. You should be savoring these last few moments of peace before filming begins."

The woman, Dr. Bridges, looked up at me with dejected anger before glancing at the man. "You might as well save your breath, Richard. They are under her control. We have no chance of persuading them. We either fight or…"

Her head rocked back as I slapped her across the face. "You need to be quiet too. There is no fighting this. And I've seen your notes. You should be grateful to be part of something like this at all, particularly after how you treated Addison."

Eyes watering, Bridges looked back up at me. "Why don't you get Addison out here so I can talk to her directly. Try to make amends."

Talpin looked at Bridges incredulously. "Addison? Addison is dead, you stupid bitch! If anyone is behind this, it's Janet."

I almost left it alone, but all of this was going to have to be removed from the final movie anyway. I didn't want talk of Addison or my voice on the disc we left behind. And if it was only going on the director's cut, I might as well have my fun too. "I'm afraid you're the stupid bitch, Dr. Talpin. Janet's all burned up." I enjoyed watching his eyes go wide as he started to understand. He began sniveling again, which earned him another hard slap from the orderly's beefy hand.

Turning back to Bridges, "And as for you, you don't get to talk to her again. She's not even here. You're not worth her time." She lowered her gaze as the last of the hope left her eyes. Suddenly, she started stammering to Talpin.

"Richard, she's the only one that can call this off. If we don't escape, we…"

Her words cut off as I kicked her in the ribs. "Enough of that. Get up. It's show time."

Paul and Soto yanked them to their feet and began shoving the pair from our small circle of light under one of the rusting basketball hoops out to our main stage. I stopped the camera and then started back under a new file. It would make editing it easier, and I wanted to capture the scene before the pair changed it with their screams and blood. It wasn't anything fancy—a thin mattress covered by clear tarps, all of it highlighted by a pair of powerful spotlights. But it was simple. Simple and beautiful. Full of potential.

I felt my breath quickening as Soto pulled the pair into the light. I had been afraid of being too squeamish for this job, but instead I was excited, anxious to get started. Talpin looked toward me and let out a low moan as Bridges began to cry softly. I stepped closer, making sure my phone's camera stayed in focus. I didn't want to miss capturing a single moment. Addison said it had to be clear enough that whoever watched it wouldn't think it was just a low-budget horror…

****

"…movie? What if no one ever watches it? Especially sticking it in another movie's Blu-Ray case?"

Addison smiled at me, her eyes dancing. It was now three weeks since she had been out of the hospital, and she had never looked more radiant. At least part of that was because she was so happy with the job I had done on the movie, and I felt so excited and proud I thought I might burst. She'd taken it a few days earlier to encode it with what she called "special magic" so she'd be alerted as soon as it was played on pretty much anything connected to the internet.

When she brought it back today, it was in the disc case of a sci-fi movie—Independence Day. I was already worried that the movie might go to waste, that the whole box might go to waste, if no one ever found it. But like always, Addison wasn't worried. She had already decided what was going to happen. Now it was just a matter of making it so.

"It'll be watched, Terri. Don't worry about that." Addison pulled out a sealed plastic bag. Inside I could see several small Halloween toys that looked like they had been smeared with blood. She handed me the bag. "These go in the box near the bottom. On top of this."

My breath caught as she took the old skin-bound book from her bag. I felt an electric charge go through me as I touched it, and I found myself wanting to ask her if it was okay if I read more of it before putting it in the box. But I already knew the answer. The book wasn't for me any

73

longer, at least not for now. Still, I couldn't help but voice one last worry.

"What if the book gets lost or destroyed?"

My blood froze as Addison's gaze changed. "Your questions and doubts are starting to get tiresome, Terri. Do you doubt the plan? Do you doubt me?" I wanted to answer, but I felt as though my throat was constricting to a pinhole. Why wouldn't she stop looking at me? I was so sorry I had made her angry, if she would just stop...

She looked away and I sucked in a breath. I used it the next second to say how sorry I was. That of course I didn't doubt her or the plan. I just knew how valuable the book was. I was being foolish. Smiling, she turned back to me and stroked my cheek.

"It's okay, Terri. Just let it be the last time." Shifting her gaze to the back seat, she regarded the cardboard box. "Everything else already in there?"

I nodded. "I put everything else in before and..." Swallowing, I went on, "I put the box of shadows inside this morning."

Addison frowned for a moment. "It's almost right...but it's still missing something." She glanced at me. "Do you have a pen or something?"

Digging in my purse, I came up with a black marker I had been using to mark moving boxes. I glanced at the dash clock as I handed it to her. 4:30. I had to hurry. This was the last day of my lease's early-termination period, and the rest of my stuff had already been moved. I needed to get the box into Addison's old storage unit tonight or I'd call attention trying to get back into the building after I was supposed to be fully moved out.

But Addison didn't have much left to do. Leaning over the seat, she scrawled two words on the side of the box.

Private Valuables

Handing me the pen back, she leaned over and planted a kiss on my forehead, making me giggle as she got out of the car. Leaning back in, she looked at me seriously.

"Be careful and then go to the gathering as we planned. Remember, this is just the beginning." Tipping me a wink, she added, "We still have much work to do, yes?"

Loss Parameters

"What's that?" I pointed to a blue line that trailed across the chart up and down.

Ben looked serious as he followed my finger's path. "That's a measure of happiness in the sample population."

I raised a hand to cover my smile. For a nine-year old boy, he was incredibly articulate, and in the two days he had been in our home, I'd already started to love him. Part of it was because he was a smart and quirky little boy that talked like a little adult and tended to dress like he was late for a business meeting—polished shoes and jackets, clip-on ties and slicked back hair. Part of it was because it was so clear he needed that love. He had sad, haunted-looking eyes that had clearly seen too much, likely even before the accident at the orphanage.

"What about that one?" I pointed to a purple line that intersected with the blue happiness line in several spots.

He rubbed his chin thoughtfully. "That's a measure of sadness in the sample population."

Patting his shoulder gingerly, I imagined I could still smell the gas wafting up from his jacket's little shoulder pad. When I'd asked where he had gotten all the grown-up looking clothes, the lady at foster care had just shrugged. Said it was her understanding he'd had them when he was abandoned at a fire station the year before.

They told me that he wouldn't talk about where he had come from, who his family had been. One of my goals was to get him to trust me enough that he felt comfortable sharing that in time.

"What about the red line?"

He glanced up at me. "That's the measure of fear in the sample population."

The poor kid. The red line had several spikes, shooting up at the end before the line stopped abruptly. My guess was this was his way of trying to process his time at the orphanage. At having to watch ten of his little friends burn to death, and several more suffocate, as gas filled that place just two weeks ago.

"What about that one?" This green line shot up at the end too.

"That's a measure of death in the sample population."

I felt tears springing up in my eyes and I tried to fight them back. "I...I see. What's the black line going across right above the green one?"

He looked up at me again. "That's the acceptable loss parameters in the sample population. As you can see from the green line, that parameter was not met in this instance."

I lifted my hand from his shoulder. I should have asked more, but I was suddenly afraid to. I needed time to process and regroup first.

"Okay...Well, dinner will be in an hour."

He nodded to me as he pulled out a new piece of poster board. "Good. I have to start working on my new chart. I'll be hungry again soon."

There is only one of us.

I sat watching Brent sleep, knowing what a waste of time it was. I was coddling him, feeding into his delusions, instead of doing the hard thing, the right thing. Telling him that yes, he needed help, but from a therapist or a hospital, not an old girlfriend. That whatever he thought, I wasn't going to see some kind of strange event or monster that night.

He lay snoring peacefully in the same bed he'd had back when I dated him three years ago. Most of his furniture and decorations were the same actually, and it awoke a disorienting mix of nostalgia and discomfort from seeing familiar things in an unfamiliar apartment across the country from where they had been when I'd seen them last. Reflecting again on the last couple of days of hurried travel preparations, the flight out, the expense of it all, I found myself questioning again what I was doing there.

When Brent had moved out to the west coast for grad school, I was the one that had chosen to end things. I didn't want to move and I didn't see us working well long-distance. It was hard, but I had made my peace with the decision a long time ago. And the truth was, while neither of us was dating anyone at the moment, I didn't feel any desire to get back together with Brent. We had both grown up and moved on, and while we didn't talk often, we had developed a comfortable long-distance friendship that had made his phone call two days earlier a bit of a surprise, but a welcome one.

****

"Hey Cassidy. How're you doing?"

My initial automatic response of something like "Hey, I'm doing good. How're you?" died in my throat as I realized how he sounded. I'd known from his voice it was Brent, but I'd never heard him sound like that. He sounded defeated and exhausted, but more than that, he sounded scared. My first thought was that he had been in an accident or gotten arrested for something terrible, though I couldn't imagine what that would be.

"Umm, I'm okay. Brent, are you okay?"

After a pause, "Not really, Cass. I…I've got some kind of problem. It's going to sound crazy…maybe it is crazy, but I don't know who else to ask about it. My folks would just freak out and accuse me of being on drugs, which I'm not. And I can't talk to the people I know out here about it. I…I know I don't have any right to ask, but you're the only one I trust with this. Can you come out for a couple of days?"

My mind was racing. My gut instinct was to tell him no—I had work, it was too short-notice, it might be weird, and it would be super-expensive. But…I knew Brent. He was a good guy. An honest guy. And he didn't like asking for help unless he really needed it.

"Okay, yeah. But first tell me what's going on."

"I think someone is invading…is coming into my

apartment uninvited at night. I've got camera footage of it, but I want you to see it before I try to explain. See what you think. I know this all sounds very mysterious, but I swear, I'm not on anything and I don't think I'm crazy." He sighed. "But I also know the old saying about crazy people never thinking they're crazy, so that's why I want to talk to you. To show you. If you tell me I'm wrong, that I need help, then I'll trust that and get treatment. If I'm right, maybe you can help me figure out what to do about it."

I felt my stomach twist uncertainly. "Brent, do you think your apartment is haunted or something? Because I can already tell you that…"

"No! No. I don't think it's haunted. It's…well, the video shows a person. I really need to show you the video, okay? I won't be able to explain everything well over the phone or internet—it'll just make me sound crazy if I try. So will you come?"

"Yeah. Yeah, I'll come."

****

Brent had picked me up from the airport the next morning. He looked pale and tired, and he had a yellowing bruise on one cheek, but other than that he looked like his old self. We hugged and then drove to a restaurant closer to his apartment. He'd said he wanted me to be comfortable, so he was sticking to public places until I had a chance to make sure he wasn't some kind of lunatic.

"I don't think that." I patted his arm. "Look, I know after what happened with your sister, you're afraid your parents will think you're some kind of junkie or…well, suicidal or something. But I know you're not, and they probably would too. You're not Deidre. She had a lot of

81

problems for a long time. A lot of pain, and a lot of substance abuse trying to stop it. You? You're like the most normal, stable person I know." I grinned at him and he smiled back uncertainly.

"Yeah, I know. I think I know. But then this all started happening." He looked distant for a moment and then pulled himself back to me. "The first thing was when the man punched me." He gestured to the bruise on his face as he began.

****

I was coming out of Cutter's Grocery—it's a little weird place not far from my apartment—when this dude comes up to me. At first I thought he was going to try to give me a flyer or maybe ask me for directions, but then I saw he looked angry. Not just angry, like, really mad. Before I could really process what was happening, he had gotten into my face and was yelling.

"It's you, isn't it? I recognize you."

I started backing away, but he was right on me, and I wound up just backing into a car's bumper. "What? I don't know what you're talking about. Got the wrong guy."

This only seemed to make him angrier. "No, you son-of-a-bitch. I know you. You're him."

I was starting to get scared and mad myself, but I was trying to avoid a fight. I'll admit part of that was because the dude was like twice my size, but I still really thought he was just confused or maybe crazy, and I just wanted to get to my car and go.

"I don't know you, man. Where do you think you know me from?"

He grabbed the front of my t-shirt. "From outside my fucking house. You were standing outside, staring in at my wife, my family, last week. Scared the shit out of them. She called me from work, but by the time I got home, you were gone." The man pulled me forward and then pushed me back against the car. "But she took a picture of you. It was dark, but not where you were standing. I could see you well enough."

I pushed him off me, my bag spilling in the process, but I didn't care. My heart was hammering and I moved to the side so I wouldn't be pinned again. "That wasn't me. I don't know you or your family, and I wouldn't do that. It must have been someone that looked like me, man. Honest." He looked uncertain for a moment, so I added. "I'm sorry that happened though. If that guy comes back, you should call the cops."

His fist flashed up out of nowhere and my vision went white. Clutching my face, I fell back against the next car over, but kept my feet. I put my arm up to protect myself from another punch, but he didn't try for one. Instead, he started crying.

"They're gone, you fuck. My wife, my kids, they're fucking gone. Police said there were no signs of a struggle, no signs they were taken against their will, but she wouldn't have left me. We had a good life...a good fucking life..." His eyes burned with hatred through his tears. "It was you, wasn't it?" I could see he was preparing himself for another attack, and I held up my hand as I pulled out my phone.

"Wait. Fucking wait, okay? I'm calling 911. If I'm the guy, then the police can catch me, right? But I'm telling you, I'm fucking not the guy. I don't know you or your fucking…" I forced myself to take a breath and calm down as I wiped at my watering eye. "I don't know your family. But I can tell you're upset. So let's get this settled okay?" Blinking, I punched 911 and showed him my phone. "See? Legit calling."

Fifteen minutes later a police cruiser showed up, though it felt more like an hour. The man was tense the whole time, as though he was ready to tackle me if I tried to run. I guess he was. When the cops arrived, they talked to both of us. I told them I wasn't wanting to press charges on the guy, but I did want this cleared up, and if I ever saw the guy again after that I'd be calling them back to arrest him. They asked if I'd be willing on going back to the station and answer a few questions, and I agreed.

The interview was a lot more casual and laid back than what you see on t.v. The detective that talked to me said that the guy had been calling them constantly even when they had already told him there was no sign that a crime had occurred. The poor guy just didn't want to hear that his wife had left him and taken the kids.

"But what about the picture?"

The detective had raised an eyebrow. "Picture?"

I nodded. "Yeah…the guy, the guy that punched me, he said his wife had taken a picture of someone that looked like me standing outside their house, looking in all creepy-like. Just last week."

The man chuckled and shook his head. "Oh yeah. We heard about that too. Except wouldn't you know it, the wife took her phone with her when she skedaddled, and the alleged picture was on it." He smiled at me. "Look, you seem like a nice, normal guy, and I'm sorry this happened to you. And honestly, if anyone had messed with that guy's family, I'd put my money on him." He puffed out a breath. "But, the reality is that people "disappear" every day. They have affairs, they steal money, or they just get sick of putting up with some kind of shit. It happens. So unless you've got something to confess, I don't know this interview is going to amount to much."

I shook my head. "I...no. But I can try and tell you where I was if I know when they left. Or when the guy was supposed to be outside the window."

The detective nodded. "That was my next question. He last saw them last Thursday morning. And the man was supposedly standing in the yard looking at them late Tuesday night...I think he said around eleven o'clock."

I thought a moment and then shrugged. "I mean, Tuesday night I think I was at home. I would have went to bed early because I've been getting to work early the last two weeks. I'm in grad school, and I work part-time too, but lately I've been having to work early shifts because of some of my meetings with professors."

"Where do you work?"

"Um, the archives section of the university library. I'm working toward becoming one of those people that studies and restores old books and stuff." I laughed nervously. "Super-nerdy, I know."

He shook his head. "No, that's good. My daughter is going for a degree in...I think they call it information technology? I'll tell you the same thing I tell her. Nerdy is where the money is." He smiled. "What about Thursday?"

"I spent the morning at the library, then meetings and

classes in the afternoon. I played softball that night with some buddies, then went home. Went to bed early again."

The detective asked me the names of people he could contact if he needed to verify my whereabouts at any of those times, assuring me he wasn't going to actually call unless something else came up that made it necessary. I gave him the names, he showed me out, and then I went home. For a few days, nothing else strange happened.

But then I noticed I was missing clothes.

I still have a lot of the same clothes and stuff from when we were together. Poor student and all. But even the newer stuff, I know what it is. Where it should be. And I started noticing that I couldn't find a particular shirt or pair of pants. I'm used to misplacing a sock here or there, but nothing like this. And not with this pattern.

Because it was never underwear or socks or shoes. Just shirts and pants. And, I started to realize, I seemed to be missing an equal number of each. It may sound dumb, but it kind of freaked me out a bit.

Maybe it was just because of the deal with the guy attacking me, or maybe because I've been tired and stressed lately, but I started to think someone was coming in and stealing my stuff. Maybe even trying to impersonate me or something, if what that guy said was true. So I borrowed a little security webcam from a friend at school and set it up in my bedroom. I don't think I really expected to find anything, but I figured it would help ease my mind at least. Get me out of…well, whatever mindset I was slipping into.

****

"The first three nights there was nothing. Just me

coming in and out, sleeping, watching t.v. It kind of freaked me out at first to see the camera watching me, but it was on a new account that I had set up and only I could access, and after the first couple of days, I got used to it. I didn't even remember to check the fourth night's footage until I was about to go to sleep the next night." Brent looked visibly paler as he fiddled with his phone. "I…well, I saved a clip of what I'm talking about on my phone. You look at it. Tell me what you see."

He handed me the phone and I saw it already had a video pulled up. Hitting play, I watched a five-minute night-vision clip of Brent sleeping. He did jerk and twist some early on in the video, and that caused the sheets to pull down and his t-shirt to ride up some. Maybe it looked a bit weird, but I figured it was just him having a nightmare. And aside from that, everything looked normal. I tried to hide my worry as I looked up at him.

"I…I mean, I saw you twisting around some like you were dreaming, but that was it. Was there something else I missed?"

His eyes went wide. "No…wait…" He grabbed the phone back and played the video again, watching it while angling it where I could see it. At various points he would say things like, "Do you see anything there?" or "There! What about that?" Every time, I would just sadly shake my head.

I could tell he was getting more agitated, but his voice was even when he put the phone down. "Okay. Well…that's not good." He was lost in thought, pulling at his lip the way he always had when he was nervous or upset. After a moment, he looked back to me. "Look, I'm starting to think maybe I really am just crazy. What I see when I watch that video…it's a lot different. And that's just one example."

I frowned. "What do you mean?"

He grimaced as he put the phone back in his pocket. "I mean I've been recording myself sleeping for three weeks, and every fourth night…something happens. Or at least I think something happens. When I've watched the videos, I see things that, well..." I could see the fear on his face at the memory, imagined or not. "The video I showed you was from the first time, and it's still the longest and clearest one I've got. So if it's not really there…" He shook his head slightly. "But there's also the clothes."

"The clothes you've been missing?"

He nodded, his eyes lighting up again, if only a little. "Yeah! I…I started keeping closer track of them. And every fourth day, I seem to be missing a new pair of pants or shorts and a shirt. That matches…well, it matches what I'm seeing on the video."

I put my hand on his. "Why don't you just tell me what you think the videos show?"

His eyes narrowed as he pulled his hand away. "Because I don't want to be humored or patronized. Not that I think you'd do that to me, but still. I need you to see it on your own or not. I have to know if it's real or I'm crazy."

"But how? Other than the video, how?"

He gave a slight laugh. "I need you to watch me sleep. Because tonight is the fourth night."

****

Brent had armed me with a baseball bat before going

to bed. He apologized again for me going to all this trouble, told me again how much it meant to him. That he realized it was likely he was just having some sort of breakdown—and that was the only reason he was okay with me being in the apartment during the fourth night. Because, he said sadly, it was probably all just in his head.

He had taken something to make himself sleep, but it still took a while before he finally drifted off. And while I had taken a nap earlier in the evening, I was feeling myself beginning to fade by midnight. It had been a hard, stressful couple of days and...

Brent was moving around again.

Watching from closer up and in person with the bedside lamp on, I could see much more clearly than on the video. Like before, his shirt starting riding up as the sheets drifted down, exposing his bare stomach. But it looked strange and artificial somehow. Like a ghost movie where unseen hands are moving things instead of them just sliding around because of Brent's own movements. I felt my heart beating faster and chided myself. I was tired and spooked, that was all. There was nothing...

A pair of hands suddenly erupted silently and bloodlessly from Brent's stomach. His body jerked again, and the hands were followed by arms and the top of a head. I stood up and started backing away, my mouth open to scream. But no scream would come out. In fact, I couldn't hear any sound at all, not even the scraping of my shoes as I backpedaled into a corner. The head that freed itself from Brent's stomach was...it was identical to Brent himself. This second head's eyes glanced around, raking over me without seeming to notice or care.

As the shoulders and elbows cleared the surface of Brent's rippling skin, the hands braced on the bed for leverage as a man continued to pull himself free from Brent's shuddering torso. The entire process probably took less than a minute, and in the end, a naked shape that looked just like Brent climbed off the bed and went to the nearby chest of drawers. Staring in horror at the man's back, I noted dimly that he was perfectly clean and dry. There was no sign of blood or other fluid. Similarly, Brent himself seemed unharmed, with no trace of what had just occurred showing on him or the bed he still slept on.

Looking back to the intruder, I saw he was pulling on a pair of shorts and a t-shirt. I recognized the shirt as something I'd given Brent the last birthday we'd had together. I wanted to say something, but I was too terrified, and silence still pressed down on the room like the strange gravity of a black hole. I just needed to stay still and hopefully he would just leave without looking at me.

As though hearing my thought, the man turned toward me as he finished pulling on the shirt. He really was indistinguishable from Brent except for his eyes. Where Brent's eyes were kind and intelligent, this thing's gaze was hard and terrible, with a yellow glimmer that came and went as it smiled at me. I felt myself shudder.

Raising a finger to its lips briefly, its voice penetrated the unnatural stillness when it spoke. The sound was harsh and guttural, like the first words of someone who survived a hanging, but I could still hear each syllable clearly.

"There is only one of us."

It stared at me a moment longer and then turned toward the door. I began shaking uncontrollably, and it was several minutes after I heard it leave the apartment before I was able to stand and wake up Brent. He was groggy at first, but he snapped awake when he saw how upset I was. I told him what had happened, and at first he looked oddly relieved. But as I told him about the other thing looking at me, speaking to me, his eyes darkened with concern.

"And that's all he said? All he did?"

I nodded. "Yes, that's all it did. Then it left." I was still shaking, but talking about it had helped. "Do you know what it meant by 'There is only one of us'? Have you heard it say anything before?"

Shaking his head, he got out of bed and picked up his phone. "No, the camera doesn't do audio. But we should have the footage of tonight I can pull up. It uploads to the cloud every few seconds." He sat back down as he pulled up the video feed and began scrubbing through it. He glanced at me. "This was just a few minutes ago, right?"

"Yeah. Should be within the last ten minutes."

He stopped the video ten minutes back and let it play. On the screen, Brent began to jerk and twist, and I felt my nails digging into my palms as I forced myself to keep watching. I didn't want to see it again, but I needed to. I had to…

I started trembling. "Wait, this isn't the right night. Nothing's happening."

Brent looked at me, bewildered. "What're you talking about? I see him coming out of me. Just like I see them coming out of me every fourth night now. You don't see it?"

I shook my head, a tear rolling down my cheek. "No. I-I know it happened. I remember it. But that's not what I see on the video. It doesn't look like anything but you moving around some." I snatched the phone from him. "This has to be the wrong…" I stopped as I saw myself stand up at the edge of the camera's frame. Standing up several seconds after I had in my memory, and instead of retreating to the corner, I was turning and looking at the camera.

Looking at the camera as I smiled, holding a single finger to my lips.

****

I left Brent's apartment just a few minutes later. He begged me to stay, to try and help him figure it out, but I couldn't. I was too terrified and I had no idea what was going on. I told him I'd call and check on him in a few days, and that he should go to his family about it. His family or a psychologist, or maybe a priest. I didn't know. All I knew was I wasn't able to help him and I had to get away from there.

That was five nights ago.

Since then, I've had trouble sleeping, trouble concentrating, trouble doing much of anything other than feel guilty and scared. A part of my mind keeps suggesting I imagined things, or maybe he was into drugs and had slipped me some, but I know that part of me is a liar. I know what I saw, even if I don't know what it means.

Tonight I finally took a sleeping pill. My thought was I could sort through things, cope with everything better, if I wasn't teetering on the edge of exhaustion all the time. I just need ten to twelve hours of sleep, and things would be better. I had been out for about four when I suddenly jerked awake.

I had heard something. Or felt something. I looked around in the dark of my bedroom, blood pounding in my ears as I looked into the shadows for any sign of danger or disturbance. I didn't see anything, but that meant very little. Breath coming in quick gasps, I leaned over and turned on the light on my nightstand. As I did so, I looked around again.

No.

My eyes had fallen on my closet. I always kept the door shut, but it was open now. The light from the lamp didn't penetrate far into it, but it was enough for me to see a pair of my jeans lying on the floor just inside the closet door.

Nononono.

I started easing up in bed, trying to get into a position where I could try to make it out if something came at me from the closet. It would be a near thing, as I had to go past the open door to make it out of the bedroom. That's when I heard something. A stealthy, scraping sound. But not from the closet.

It was coming from underneath my bed.

I almost ran then, but that same small voice came back to me. Told me I was driving myself crazy. Running from shadows. Letting whatever delusions Brent had infect me somehow. I needed to be better than that. Stronger and braver than that. Confront what I was afraid of and see that, just like the video, nothing was actually there.

Biting my lip, I grabbed up my phone and turned on the flashlight app. I gripped the bed tightly as I slowly leaned over, my body tense as more of the floor underneath my bed came into view. There were a pair of my shoes, and an old book I was reading, and…

Farther back, I saw twin yellow sparks glittering softly in the dark. Turning my phone, I saw myself, or something that looked like me, staring unblinkingly into the light before shifting its gaze to my own. Naked and grinning, it began slowly inching toward me as I realized that I couldn't move. Couldn't scream. Couldn't hear anything as it scrabble-crawled to within a few inches of my downturned face.

Until it spoke.

Its breath was spicy and strange, but aside from that and the occasional flicker of light from its eyes, it had been like looking into a strange upside down mirror until I heard its voice. It sounded different than the thing at Brent's, more feminine, though still very hoarse.

Like a hanging victim. Or someone speaking for the first time.

"There is only one of us."

Leaning forward, it planted a searing kiss on my forehead before bringing a finger to its lips. I dreaded it touching me again, but it didn't. Instead, it slid soundlessly past, and I watched under the bed as it headed to the closet to get dressed. Once that was done, it padded silently out of the house and into the moonless night.

The Audition

Come in, come in. We're glad you could audition with us today.

Thank you for having me.

Your mark is there where the circle is.

Oh, okay.

Tell us about yourself.

Well, I grew up outside of Dallas, and I went to University of Texas as a drama major. I acted in a few plays there before moving to New York and working on several off-Broadway plays. Now I'm out here wanting to expand into movies and television.

Great. So you know the scene we're reading, right?

Yep. Ready to do it. I don't have much context, so if you have any notes beforehand or after, just let me know. Happy to make any adjustments.

No, I'm sure you'll do fine, dear. You know the hand gestures and body movements described? The pages described them adequately for you?

Yeah, I think so. I've practiced them, but if I need to adjust any of it, just let me know. I took two years of dance in high school, and I'm a quick learner.

I'm sure you are. So…when you're ready, begin.

We beckon to you, Wacalu, we beseech you, Wacalu. King of pestilence, Scion of the Rot, we writhe in supplication and beg for your audience.

Very good. Two notes, if I may. One, bend forward enough that you touch your head to the edge of the circle when you are saying the word "supplication". And at the end, your fingers should be against the outside corners of your eyes with your palms facing out, not in.

Oh, I'm so sorry. I guess I pictured it wrong in my head. Can I try again? I'll nail it this time, I promise.

Of course, dear. Go ahead.

We beckon to you, Wacalu, we beseech you, Wacalu. King of pestilence, Scion of the Rot, we writhe in supplication and beg for your audience.

Very good. Again, faster this time.

We beckon to you, Wacalu, we beseech you, Wacalu. King of pestilence, Scion of the Rot, we writhe in supplication and beg for your audience.

That will do, yes. We'll be in touch.

Thank you for the opportunity. Have a good day.

****

Come in, come in. We're glad you could audition with us today.

Sin Eating

To many, sin is just an idea. A religious or spiritual concept meant to describe an act or the condition of one's soul. To others, it is something more real and tangible—it has a weight and substance to it like the gravitational pull of some distant black star.

For me, it was just a word. I had been raised in a strictly religious family in the middle of nowhere Oklahoma, so it was a word I was intimately familiar with, but one which held little meaning for me other than stirring up fuzzy memories of fiery sermons and harsh admonitions when I'd done something my parents found to be "sinful". I wasn't religious or spiritual myself, and if I had a soul, I imagined it must be a dim and shabby thing that I was getting little use out of.

When I went to visit my best friend Melanie the summer before our senior year of college, I'd had no idea I would be attending a funeral. My first indication was the line of cars filling her family's driveway as I pulled up. When I got out and found Melanie, she tearfully explained that her grandmother had passed away the afternoon before. She apologized for not calling and warning me, but things had been chaotic and she was glad I was here anyway.

I had some misgivings about intruding, but in the end I stayed. I kept out of the way most of the time, occasionally giving Melanie or her mother a break from the steady line of family members and well-wishers who were coming and going for the next two days leading up to the funeral. I was amazed at how many there were—I knew her grandmother was old, but I could live to be two hundred and I wouldn't know that many people. Melanie's family had some money, but this was like the old woman had been *famous* or something.

Still, while the constant stream of people got tiring, it was nice to feel like I was of some use. I helped clean a bit and got groceries while they finished making the funeral arrangements. I was dreading going to the funeral itself, but I figured after that I should be good to leave. I wasn't trying to be selfish, but I'd had my fill of family time, even if the family wasn't my own.

It was the night before the funeral when Melanie came and knocked on my door before opening it a crack. "You still awake?"

"Yeah, I am. There's so many weird noises here. Hard to get used to."

Melanie gave a little laugh as she stepped in and closed the door behind her. "That's called crickets, and they aren't weird. You've just never lived anywhere that didn't have a sidewalk."

I shrugged as she sat down on the bed. "I guess not, but damn, do they not get tired?" She didn't respond, and I saw the troubled expression on her face. "Everything okay, Mel?"

She frowned as she looked down at the floor. "I...No, not really. There's this weird family thing, and there's a problem with it, and Mom wanted me to ask you and I'm not really comfortable with doing that, but now that I'm telling you about it, it's kind of like I'm already asking you, which makes me a hypocrite or something." Melanie looked up at me sadly. "Ugh. Sorry. I should go. I suck."

I grabbed her arm as she went to stand up. "No, don't be dumb. What is it?"

Sitting back down, she rolled her eyes. "Look, my grandma was super-old, right?"

I nodded. "Sure."

"Well, apparently she was also super-crazy. She had some old custom from like old-timey England that she wanted a sin eater to perform a ceremony before her funeral."

I stared blankly at her. "Am I supposed to know what the fuck a sin eater is?"

She gave me an exasperated sigh. "I know, right? According to Mom, there used to be these people called sin eaters that would perform a little ritual when someone died. They'd eat some food that was supposed to have the dead person's sins in it, and that would transfer the sins onto the sin eater. What sense any of that makes, I couldn't tell you. But I know my Mom is taking it serious, which means my grandmother took it serious. Where she got the idea in the first place, I couldn't tell you, but it's apparently a big deal."

I raised an eyebrow. "Okay, yeah, that's sounds super weird, but what does that have to do with me?" I already had a suspicion, but I didn't want to jump to any conclusions. "Are there people that still actually do that kind of thing?"

Melanie smiled weakly. "Apparently a few. And you can find just about anything these days, I guess. My mom found someone—a guy from Pennsylvania that is supposedly a "reputable soul eater", whatever the hell that means. Problem is, he just called and canceled, and there's not time to find someone else the night before the funeral." She paused and swallowed. "So…well, Mom wanted me to ask if you'd be willing to do it."

I felt goosebumps coming up on my arms. "Why me?"

She shrugged. "Well, you're the only one here that's not part of her family but close enough we'd be comfortable with asking. And I know you don't believe in all that soul stuff anyway, so I guess Mom thought it was worth a shot."

I shook my head slightly. "I…I don't know. I never said I definitely don't believe in a soul, I'm just not into religion and stuff. But even if I don't, it seems like a kind of big, weird deal that I wouldn't want to mess up. I don't know that I want to be responsible for some ritual I haven't ever heard of."

Melanie nodded. "If you don't want to, that's cool. But the ritual is very easy. You just take bread we've got, place it on her chest, then pick it up and eat it. Then you take a glass of…I think it's ale or something, sit it on her chest, then pick it up and drink it. There will be a coin on her throat, you take it off her throat and keep it. That's literally it."

She kept telling me details and trying to reassure me, so I knew she wanted me to say yes. I still felt uncertain, but why? It was a bunch of hocus pocus, and if it made Melanie and her family feel better, what was the harm in it?

Trying to not look uncomfortable, I gave her a smile. "Sure, why not?"

****

The funeral was being held in a large, non-descript building outside of town. I hadn't seen any signs on the way in saying whether it was a church or a funeral home or what, and when I asked Melanie, she had shrugged. Said she thought it was just a building someone rented out for various functions. It seemed strange, but I'd never been to a funeral that wasn't a little weird, and I already knew this one was going to get weirder once we got inside.

The main floor reminded me of some modern churches I had seen at past weddings and funerals, but we kept on going toward the back and down a flight of stairs to a large, cold basement. The space was empty except for a heavy metal table holding a cream-colored open casket. I felt the breath catch in my throat as I stepped forward and saw the woman inside.

She didn't look especially old, or even that dead. In other circumstances, I'd have said she was in her early fifties and taking a nap. In these circumstances, I suddenly realized I wanted to be anywhere but there. Why had I agreed to this?

Melanie's mother gave me a quick hug with one arm as she placed a hunk of bread on the woman's chest. I swallowed and looked at Melanie, who responded with a smiling nod. I had a moment where I almost rebelled, told them no, I was sorry, but this was too freaky, felt too weird.

But instead I forced myself to reach forward and take the bread. I ate it down in three fast bites, barely chewing before swallowing the tasteless, oddly greasy wads of dough.

Next was the "ale", which Melanie's mother poured

into a metal tumbler she held steady on the woman's chest. The clay jug she poured from looked old, with carvings that were hard to make out in the subdued lighting of the basement. I wondered if the grandmother had picked that out to be her ale jug too? Old people were so weird.

The thought distracted me for a moment, and I'd picked up the tumbler and started to drink before I had time to have more misgivings. I almost gagged as the liquid hit my tongue. It was overpoweringly sweet, and the taste and smell of it seemed to fill my head as I drained it down in a rush. Fuck that was nasty.

But almost done. What was the last part? Oh yeah, the coin.

I hadn't noticed it before, but looking back down I saw there was an oblong coin of dark metal resting on the grandmother's pale throat. I glanced at Melanie again, but she just stared back at me blankly. Ugh. No help from that corner. I just had to finish it, get through the funeral, and then I could get out of here.

The coin was surprisingly heavy in my hand as I picked it up, and I wasn't sure what to do with it after I had it. Looking back at Melanie, I asked her where I should put it.

She shrugged. "It's yours now. You can do with it as you like."

I frowned slightly at that. What was going on? Why was she acting all weird and aloof now? Trying to lighten the mood, I held up the coin. "What kind of coin is this anyway?"

Melanie did smile slightly at this. "It's called a

tumerin. It's very old, and it used to be very valuable. Some say it still is." Her smile fell away as quickly as it had come. "Sorry, but we have some other ceremonial stuff we need to deal with. Private family kind of a deal. If you'll wait upstairs, I can give you a ride back in a few minutes."

I felt my eyes go wide in surprise. "Um, what about the funeral?" I looked from her to the mother, who was already arranging sticks in some strange pattern on the floor. "What about all the people who are coming?"

Melanie shook her head distractedly. "No, no. No funeral. We're taking care of everything down here." She glanced at me and then the way out. "If you can wait upstairs."

Feeling confused and hurt, I dropped the coin into my purse and went upstairs. Twenty minutes later, Melanie came back up and took me back to their house. It wasn't long before I was packed up and about to hit the road. I wasn't sure if Melanie even wanted me to give her a hug goodbye, but when I started to make the gesture, she grabbed me up and squeezed tightly. For a second I felt better about things. She had just been grieving and stressed, that was all.

Then I heard what she was saying.

"I'm sorry. I'm so sorry."

She pulled back from me at the threshold of the house, and before I could respond, the front door was closed. I thought about knocking, but what would I say? Whatever was going on, it was probably better just to leave it alone for the time being. So instead I got in my car and started driving home.

I had been driving for over an hour before I noticed I wasn't alone in the car.

I saw it in the rearview mirror. Something that was more than a shadow but not fully formed either, hovering at the edge of my view when I started to look away. At first I thought it was a trick of the light, but I realized I could see the sun streaming into my backseat. Could see it stop dead when it touched that shifting, midnight skin.

Gripping the steering wheel tightly, I began to feel the weight of the coin in my pocket and the burden of that old woman's wrongs on my heart, but that wasn't the worst part. No, the worst was how that thing sat watching me. Silently studying the new soul it had been bound to.

I could tell you about stopping the car and trying to run from it. About the weeks that followed when I tried to convince myself it wasn't there. But by then it had started talking to me. Doing things. And it didn't take long before I knew that any ideas of insanity were just wishful thinking on my part.

Melanie never came back to school. Never answered my calls. Three months later I went back to that family house of theirs…it was up for sale and there was no sign of any of them. When I saw that, I just sat on their lawn and wept for awhile.

Out of the corner of my vision I could see its shadow stretched long across the afternoon lawn. It told me everything would be all right. I just had to listen to it. Do what it asked. If I would do that, I'd never want for anything. Money? Sure. Power? You got it. But most of all, it added with its terrible, buzzing laugh, I never had to worry about one thing.

I'd never, ever be alone.

Dewclaw

We call it a dewclaw. It's how you know you're one of us.

I...ah, I see. And when you say 'we' call it a dewclaw...

I mean me and Mama and Daddy. And Uncle Freddy and Aunt Sandra. And, well, our whole family.

So...they all talk about that as being a dewclaw?

Yep. It's like what my dog Roscoe has, only bigger. That's how Mama first told it to me.

Okay. So now, who else comes around your ranch? Other than your Mama and Daddy and Uncle Freddy and Aunt Sandra.

Hmm. That's mainly it except for Jonathan. That's Uncle Freddy and Aunt Sandra's son. He used to play with me when we were little, but he's all grown up now. And he don't come around no more anyway.

That's Jonathan...Peterson?

Yep. That's him.

Why doesn't he come around anymore?

I dunno...Maybe because he got mad last time. He saw me after the docking and he started crying and cursing and stuff. He said it wasn't right. Wasn't right what they'd done to me. He tried to talk to me, but my parents, they protected me. Daddy told me later that it wasn't anything to worry about. Said Jonathan was just upset because his adult dewclaws hadn't come in yet. Because he hasn't done the Necessary.

Okay. So because I want to make sure I understand everything, let's kind of break down some of what you're talking about, okay?

Yes, ma'am.

So what is 'docking'?

You don't know that? You're playing with me. No? Okay, if you say so. Well, docking is when you get to a certain age—with girls it's usually when you first get your color—they have to clip off your baby dewclaws. It hurts something awful, but they have to do it so your adult dewclaws can grow in right.

Um...sorry, give me just a second.

Yes, ma'am. No need to cry about it. It hurts, but we're made tough. We can take it.

Yes, well, that's good. Um, you said...you said something about Jonathan's...his adult dewclaws hadn't come in because he hadn't done the Necessary. What's that?

Gosh, I thought you'd know that part for sure. Okay. Well, when one of us reaches sixteen, we have to do the Necessary. We have to kill a person and eat their heart. And it can't be one of us. It has to be one of you. After that, our adult dewclaws grow in and we get real strong, real tough.

Okay. When you say 'us' and 'one of you', what do you mean?

Well, I mean, we're werewolves. And you're just a normal person, right? I don't mean no harm, ma'am. You can't help it. And you're in no danger from me. I made a promise to myself a long time ago I'd only take one life, and that was for the Necessary. I just don't feel right about it.

So the social worker, the woman who was out at your ranch yesterday. Do you know what happened to her?

I do. That lady was my Necessary. I promise, I killed her quick as I could. She didn't scream for long, and she was dead when I took her heart…(*whispering*) Don't tell, but Daddy helped me with getting it out. I had trouble holding the knife good.

So are you saying you killed that lady yourself?

Yes, ma'am.

Because she was your Necessary?

Yes, ma'am.

And your parents are the ones that…that 'docked' you?

Yes, ma'am.

How old were you when they did that?

Um, I was eleven going on twelve.

And they told you that you and your family are werewolves. That your…your dewclaws would grow back when you did your Necessary?

That's right.

Okay. Have you ever been away from the ranch before today?

Sure, plenty of times. Out in the woods learning to hunt and fish and camp. I love going out there.

Well, yeah. Alright. I meant more like, have you ever been to towns or cities. Places like where you are now. Not this building, I don't mean that. But you saw all the cars and people on the way in, right?

Yes, ma'am.

Have you ever been around anything like that? Been to school or talked to people other than your family?

No, ma'am. Mama told me it wasn't safe for our kind to mix too much until we're grown. They taught me themselves, and they did a real good job. But I am excited about getting to meet more people. I think I'm more excited about that than I am getting so strong and tough when my dewclaws come back in.

So, what di-

When do you think that'll happen, ma'am?

When do I think what will happen, honey?

When do you think my dewclaws will grow back? I woke up last night because the spots were itching, and I was so excited I could hardly go back to sleep. But when I got up today, they were just the same. Do you know when they'll come back?

I...I don't know, baby. I guess I don't know a lot about werewolves and dewclaws and stuff. I'm sorry.

Oh, it's okay. I bet it'll be soon. Hey, what do you call them?

What do I call what?

Your dewclaws. I mean, I know they're not for-real dewclaws like mine if you're just a regular person, but you didn't know to call them that, so you must call them something else. So what do you call them?

Thumbs, baby. We call them thumbs.

There is a needle hunting me.

Last year I finished a four-year residency as part of becoming an emergency medical specialist (aka an ER doctor). Working in a metropolitan hospital, I had seen a lot of crazy things over time—shootings, stabbings, freak accidents and mysterious illnesses, to name a few—but the patient I remember the most was Martha Jennings.

Martha had come in originally after police had been called to her home due to noise complaints from neighbors. When the officers arrived, they had found her frantically moving to and fro between a cellar door and a backed-up truck filled with sheets of metal and wood. According to one cop I spoke to later, she had been wringing with sweat as she yanked an eight-foot sheet of plywood off the truck bed and began dragging it toward the doorway that led underneath the house. She'd barely looked up at the officers' arrival, but when they offered to help her carry it down, she accepted gratefully.

The cellar was in chaos, with power tools and cords strewn across the floor from one end to the other. It didn't take long to figure out that Martha was in the process of adding layers to all the walls down there, and not just one layer either. Instead she was attaching sheets of wood and metal in alternating panels, and in places the layers were

111

already five or six sheets deep. When the cop casually asked her what kind of project she was working on down there, she had blinked several times before answering, her voice quiet and wavering in between pants of exertion as she propped the latest board against a wall.

"I'm making the walls thicker. So it's safe down here when it comes for me."

They naturally followed up with more questions, which led to her being brought in for examination. She was brought to the ER first due to concerns that her "confusion" might be caused by either dehydration, heatstroke, or some kind of bad reaction to medicine. We pulled blood and I did an initial exam right after she arrived, but I wasn't noting anything other than her being slightly underweight and looking exhausted. That and her being really pissed off.

"You can't keep me here. You have no right. I haven't committed any crime, have I?"

I had smiled at her then, both because I wanted to reassure her and because I thought it was a fair question. I knew they had brought her in because she was being "disorderly", but I honestly figured they did it more because they were worried about her and the things she was saying. At the time, all I knew was that she had supposedly been "acting crazy" and "talking out of her head", but looking at her now, fuming but clear-eyed, it was hard to imagine it.

"No, I don't think you did anything wrong. But...well, I think they were scared something was wrong. That maybe you were sick or weren't feeling yourself. Do you remember talking to the officers that brought you here?"

She rolled her eyes. "Yes. I'm not crazy. Or if I am,

I'm not senile at least."

I laughed. "No one said you were. But do you mind telling me what you talked to them about? It may just be some kind of misunderstanding."

She sighed. "Look, I was having a bad day, I ran my mouth, and they took me for being serious. It…It was all just a bad joke that got out of hand." She looked down at the wristcuffs that secured her to the bed. "Can you take these off? They are itchy, and I promise, you don't need them."

Nodding, I unbuckled them as we talked. "So, it was a bad joke? Tell me about it. What did you tell them?"

Rubbing her freed wrists, she scowled. "I was…I am…renovating the basement of my house. My husband died a few months ago, and I've been trying to keep busy ever since. I guess I was making too much noise, and one of my stupid neighbors complained. I was mad because they called the cops, so I made up this silly story just to mess with them. That's all there is to it." She glanced around. "So can I get my clothes back? I'm ready to go now."

I shook my head slightly. "Miss Jennings…"

"Call me Martha please. I'm not *that* old."

"Martha, I…I can't make the call to release you. When someone is brought in by the police, they have to either sign off on the release or they take you back when we're done treating you. I understand this might have all been just a bad joke like you said, but I'm going to have to talk to them first."

She started to argue and I raised my hand. "If you will, please tell me what you told them, if you remember. It will put me in a better position to help get you released if I know what we're talking about. Okay?"

Martha closed her eyes and pushed her head back into the pillow, her lips a thin line of resigned defeat as she began.

"I told them that there is some kind of alien or magic needle that is hunting me. That I needed to make the walls of my basement thick enough that it couldn't get through, even though I didn't know if it would matter."

I raised an eyebrow. "So that was your joke? That you thought a magic needle was after you?"

Glaring at me, she nodded. "Yes, it was a bad and stupid joke. Will you please get me released now? I need to be going."

"As I said, it will be a little while. They're going to want to see the bloodwork before we release you, and I don't control what the cops do after that. But I don't mind talking to them and trying to help, like I said."

Leaning forward, she stabbed a finger toward me. "I'll sue. You understand me? I'm being held against my will, and I. Will. Sue."

I shrugged. "Ma'am, you do what you need to, but I'm telling you, if they arrested you, it's going to be at least another couple of hours before you get out of here, one way or the other."

Her eyes widened. "No. I can't stay here that long. You Goddamn idiots, you don't..." She started to get up and I raised a hand to stop her.

"Please don't. They'll just put the restraints back on you, and it'll make it harder for me to convince them that you're okay to go home. Can you try to be patient?"

I was surprised when she laid back, tears in her eyes. "You're killing me, that's what you're doing. You're all killing me."

"Miss…Martha, what do you mean? What are you afraid of? The tests? I can assure you they're all harmless, and no one will do anything…"

"No, you fool. Not the tests." Her voice was lower but more strident now, the angry hiss of a snake. "The needle. *The fucking needle.*" Her eyes darted around as she spoke. "I lied before. The needle is real and it's coming for me. I need to keep moving or be somewhere protected, not stuck here talking to you."

I felt new unease stirring in my belly. She wasn't joking now, and I didn't think she was lying either. Which meant she was crazy after all. I almost went and got help right then, but I wanted to know more. Maybe she could tell me something that could help before they took her away for the 72 hour psych observation, as I could see now that's the direction this was all heading.

"Martha, will you tell me what you're talking about? The truth? That's the only way I can help."

The woman looked at me for several moments before seeming to make a decision. Scowling, she gave a shrug. "Why not? It won't make you think I'm any more crazy than you already do. And apparently I have at least a little bit of time to kill. But for the record, this is all a joke, I do not consent to my restraints, and if I'm not released in the next few minutes, you can expect a lawsuit." These words lacked the same energy and conviction that had crackled off of her just moments before. In fact, as I watched, she seemed to be deflating, her fear and panic being replaced with a dull gray sheen of resignation that was somehow worse. I was going to ask if she was okay, but she had already begun.

****

My husband wasn't a bad man. A bit boring and clueless yes, and too in love with his work to be sure, but not a mean bone in his body. He...well, he was passionate about his work. It was all molecular chemistry and metallurgy and...well, it was interesting to him and the paint on the wall. But it paid well enough, especially when he got hired by a hush-hush outfit to work on some secret project.

When he first went to work there, I tried getting some details out of him, but he wouldn't budge. Too much work integrity, you see. They said don't tell anything, so he didn't. That's how I knew how bad things were when he came home six months ago, pale and shaking.

It wasn't his constant, nervous glances. He'd been acting more jittery for a few weeks, and I'd assumed it was either work stress or because he knew our marriage was heading toward the edge of something that might interrupt the orderly existence he'd crafted for himself over the last ten years. It wasn't even the fact that he poured himself a drink as soon as he walked in, despite the fact that he never drank more than once or twice a year.

It was the fact that he was talking to me. Telling me things. Things I knew he wasn't supposed to be telling. Him breaking one of their precious rules scared the shit out of me.

He said for the last three years he had been part of Project Arcadia, a long-term, multi-disciplinary study of

116

several objects provided to the group he worked for. When I asked if it was the government, he just laughed and shook his head. Said I watched too many movies and was thinking too small. But that it didn't matter. What mattered was what had happened two weeks earlier. What had happened two hours before he came home to me terrified and shaking.

And it all came down to the thing that his team had been working with for the past year.

They called it the Needle. Two inches long and the width of five human hairs, it was a straight line of metal that defied any kind of explanation. For one thing, the metal seemed indestructible—they couldn't even scrape it for a sample, and the tests they could run came back with results that made little sense and gave fewer answers. Second, it appeared to be solid and made of one piece, but all attempts at internal imaging had failed, so they couldn't say for sure. Third, and this is where I started thinking he was crazy, the needle floated. Just floated on its own like a balloon, though it never raised or lowered itself more than about four feet off the ground unless pushed. If you did push it, it would drift away like a floating bar of soap before slowly creeping back to its original spot.

I asked him then, kind of making fun if I'm honest, if it was from an alien ship or something. He hadn't laughed, but only shook his head slowly. Said he didn't know. They were only told to learn what they could about how it worked. But, he'd added wearily, one of his partners had said it had come from some kind of "benefactor". That the guy had worked on other objects before, and they were all different and all strange. One had been some kind of mask, another was a tissue sample from a tree or something.

For a long time he enjoyed working with the Needle. They made very little progress, but the chance to work with something so unique was exciting. He started staying longer and longer hours in the hopes of making some kind of breakthrough. He didn't say it, but I think he was afraid he'd be kicked off the project if they didn't get results. Joke was on him, wasn't it?

Fuck. That's petty. He didn't know. I don't guess any of them did. But...where was I?

Two weeks before my husband told me all this, they were doing a round of what he called "behavioral tests" on the damn thing, because they had figured out it had to have some kind of computer in it or something because of how it acted. It was fine with being moved around to wherever, but it wanted to stay at the same height above the ground. They constructed big vertical mazes and it would navigate them. According to Reese...that was my husband...it was just like watching a smart rat after it had memorized a path. They had this...this fucking thing, and they were just playing with it like it was a shiny toy.

Except one day, when one of his lab buddies, Becker, was pushing the Needle into the maze opening, his hand slipped and the Needle pricked his finger. Reese said it never should have happened. They had protocols for handling the thing, but they had gotten used to it, which made them careless and sloppy. For a few seconds they were just laughing nervously as Becker sucked his bloody finger. Then they heard a terrible screeching sound as the Needle pushed its way out of the maze, shot through a nearby wall and disappeared.

They were locked down for the next twelve hours—

questioned again and again while security watched the surveillance videos and tracked the trajectory of the Needle out of the facility. It had shot through dozens of walls before flying off to places unknown. Well, unknown for the time being. As far as Reese and the rest of them went, there was no signs of them doing anything to cause it other than Becker pricking his finger. The rest of them were reassigned while Becker was "asked" to remain at the facility for further testing until the investigation was complete.

Reese heard about the first of the killings a couple of days later.

Becker had a grandmother in Arizona. She suddenly dropped dead in the produce department of her local grocery store, the only visible injury a tiny well of blood on the front and back of her head as though she had been pricked by something. The next day, Becker's high school girlfriend, who he apparently hadn't seen for years, died in a single car accident with no apparent cause for the wreck. By that weekend, his brother and the brother's entire family were found dead in their camper of "indeterminate causes". Then it was Becker's college roommate, his parents, his fucking pharmacist.

Because of the way the grandmother died, they suspected from the start it was the Needle. And while they didn't know why it was doing what it was doing, they began to understand the pattern and the practical effect. It was killing off anyone connected to the man who had pricked his finger on it.

Two hours before he came home, Reese had been talking to one of his old lab partners. They were on different teams now, and this was the first time they'd talked in a few *days. Reese said the first thing he'd noticed was that Theresa was spilling her coffee. He went to mention it when he realized she wasn't spilling it at all. There was a small hole in the side of her mug, and as the cup fell away, he saw blood blooming on her shirt as she fell to the ground. I remember him saying she shouldn't have died so fast...not unless it had darted around inside her before flitting away again.*

Reese was killed two days after telling me about the Needle. His death was a bit more mundane, however, as he was shot to death in a "robbery" while coming back from the ice machine at the motel we had checked into that night. Apparently his employers weren't very happy with him spilling the beans and trying to run away from the killer needle.

I'd expected to follow him soon after, but no one ever came. No assassins or black cars following me or whatever it is they might normally do. I moved around for a few days, but I realized there was no point. They could find me if they wanted, and I'd started to figure out that they didn't want to kill me after all. No, they were content to let the Needle do that for them while they gathered the data. Another fucking "behavioral test".

So I went back home. That's when I got the call that Rory, the man I'd been sleeping with for the past three years, had died mysteriously in the shower. Rory, a man that Reese had never met, let alone Becker. That's when I knew that Reese had been telling the truth, and that some time, somewhere, the Needle would be coming for me.

That's why I have to get out of here.

****

I tried to keep my expression neutral as Martha finished her story. It was insane, of course, but letting my disbelief and pity show would have only upset her more. So instead, I thanked her and told her I needed to finish my rounds, but I would be back in shortly. She said something else as I walked away, but I pretended I didn't hear and kept going.

I was on the other side of the ER a few minutes later when I heard Martha begin to scream.

Running over, I pushed through a throng of nurses and PAs to see what was bad enough to cause her to scream so loudly for a few seconds before falling silent. My breath caught as I saw her dead eyes staring up at the ceiling, the right one red from hemorrhage. I staggered back a step, and that's when I noticed her bare foot hanging halfway off the bed.

On the bottom of her heel was a tiny drop of blood. When I wiped at it, I saw a small puncture wound there. I was moving back toward her upper body to more closely examine the injured eye when something on the wall behind the bed caught my attention.

It was a small hole, about the width of five human hairs. It looked to be lined up perfectly with the top of Martha's head, and when I checked, I found a matching hole in her scalp.

I went home early that night. I couldn't get her story out of my head, but worse was the sound of her scream—full of fear and pain as the thing she feared the most found her and pushed its way relentlessly through her body.

I checked later, and there was no autopsy. No record of who claimed the body or where it went. It didn't matter.

I suspected I knew exactly who had taken it.

The next few months were hard for me. I kept waiting for guys in black suits to pay me a visit or to wake up in a dungeon somewhere. I kept my head down, finished my residency, and moved to the other side of the country. When I started my new job, I didn't take more than a day off for the first six months, and it was only this weekend that I actually got away with a girl I've been seeing. It's the first time in a really long time that I've relaxed, and when I got home, I realized I had gone more than twenty-four hours without feeling scared for the first time in…well, a long time.

Laying down on my bed, I felt myself getting drowsy as I stared up at my ceiling. Things were going good with Sidney, and work was fine now that…

There was a hole in my ceiling.

I sat up and looked closer. That hadn't been there before. There hadn't been a hole right over my bed, right over where I laid my head.

I looked around in a panic. There were no signs of anything else being disturbed, but still…I stood up and examined my bed. That's when I noticed that there was a similar hole in my pillow, though when I picked it up, it didn't go through the other side. As though it realized I wasn't there…or was letting me know that it had been.

Shaking, I grabbed my suitcase again. Headed for the bus station and got on the first one that was going far with infrequent stops. Planned infrequent stops, at least.

Because as I'm writing this on my phone, the bus has pulled over in the middle of nowhere. A flat tire and engine trouble, if you can believe that coincidence. I know I can't. There's no service out here, so the driver is walking back to a spot in the road with a gas station that we passed a couple of miles back. I'm not waiting on that though. I'm going to start walking in the opposite direction as soon as this is finished.

Not because I think I'll outrun it, you understand. But because people get nervous in a crisis, or even just the inconvenience of being stranded for a couple of hours. They want to talk, get to know each other, make connections so they feel more normal and less alone. I'm already terrified about what may happen to Sidney and my Uncle Mike, the people I work with or I've treated. I don't want more lives on my conscience.

So I'll walk and hope it doesn't find me. That if it does, it will end with me. And if it's coming for me, I hope it's soon. Because I still remember the last thing Martha said to me as I walked away, pretending I didn't hear.

"The worst part isn't that it's coming, you see. It's not knowing when or why. That it's out there, taking its time, maybe enjoying itself. Enjoying thinking about when it catches you. When it catches you and pushes a hole right on through."

The Midnight Hind

When you approach the pub known as the Midnight Hind, you would be forgiven for thinking it is abandoned, or at the least, closed. It only operates between dusk and dawn, and the ancient leaded glass of its cross-hatched windows are so pregnant with swirling colors that, in the moonlight, they take on the dead-eyed opalescence of an oil slick.

Opening the door, most blink at the contrast between the still darkness without and the riot of light and sound within. People talking and arguing, playing cards at corner tables, and gathering around the small stage where an odd little band plays. But none of that was why I'd entered that place. I had come to play the Bar Game.

You sit at the far end of the bar facing the other player, the span of polished wood in front of you deeply etched with white lines and runes. Among these carvings, several rows of silver nails have been hammered halfway deep, and when you are bade to slide your hand in, you find that the spaces between the nails fit your fingers just perfectly. Further, regardless of the players, when both have their fingers planted between the silvery rows, their fingertips always lightly touch.

Then the game begins.

The bartender has a card he or she produces from

beneath the bar. On it are three questions.

What is the best thing you have ever done?

You immediately get flooded by not only the best answer of your own heart, but that of your opponent. And it goes beyond mere telepathy. You see all the good and bad consequences of what you both did—things you could never know. This question breaks many people right away.

What is the worst thing you have ever done?

This is, almost without fail, a different answer than one expects. A buried, secret shame. It is what undid my opponent only a moment before I was going to yank my own hand free. The third question was never asked of us, but I saw it on the card.

Who are you truly?

I shuddered at the words, in part because I saw the look on my opponent's face. I had won, so I kept the memories of my best self while my worst crimes were wiped away. Not just from my memory, but removed wholly from the world. Her penalty for losing was the truth. Not only did she keep a perfect recollection of her worst act and its effects, but she had the last question answered for her. She was irrevocably shown who she truly was, without all the self-delusions and comforting lies.

I avoided her eyes as I got up to find a cheerier corner of the pub. The bartender was gentle as he ushered her out of the bar, and while it made me uncomfortable, I understood why she couldn't stay. After all, this was a place of light and laughter.

And the damned deserved to walk alone in the dark.

My friend Benji

I've never believed in imaginary friends, but I still had one growing up. His name was Benji, and much like his existence, his name wasn't my choice. You see, when I got to be about six years old, my mother disappeared and my father went through a real rough time. He slept a lot, cried when he thought I couldn't hear, and lost thirty pounds from sadness and worry. Then one day, when I came inside for dinner, I saw a third plate at the table.

For one bright moment, I thought that Mama had found her way back to us after nearly a year. I asked and saw my father's face crumple slightly. No, he replied thickly. That plate was for my friend Benji. When I asked who Benji was, my father acted surprised. He explained that Benji was my invisible best friend who would always be there for me. Who would never leave my side.

I was seven by then, and while still a little kid, I was well past believing in invisible playmates. But I was also old enough to see how much my father was hurting, and that, for some strange reason, having Benji around seemed to make things a little better. Over the years, I came to understand it was probably just his warped way of reassuring himself that I'd never be alone the way that he was.

Outside of the two of us, no one knew about Benji. I

didn't bring friends home—instead I always went to their house to sleep over or hang out. When I got to college, my father would always ask how Benji was doing when I called, and I would always tell him he was doing fine. You know Benji, up to his old tricks. And I could hear the relief in my father's reply. The peace I was giving him with this odd family ritual.

The last ritual I shared with my father was his funeral two weeks ago. I kept a seat empty next to me, the black "reserved" placard marking Benji's place. I was filled with sad anxiety as I walked out of the graveyard an hour later. Silly as it might seem, I felt like I was losing not only my father, but Benji as well.

A middle-aged woman approached me as I neared my car. She said she was my distant cousin, and she had come all the way from Maryland for the funeral, though she'd only made it to the graveside. She said she was sorry for my loss. That my family had been so burdened with loss over the years. My father, my mother, all the way back to my brother. My brother Benji that died when I was a baby.

I tell you this because I want you to know that I know who you are even if I don't know what you are. You're my brother. My friend.

And you wouldn't hurt your friend.

Right?

Every night I fight the demon.

There are various definitions and traditions when it comes to the length of a lunar month. An anomalistic lunar month is around 27 days. A synodic lunar month is 29. I know this because I've always been interested in astronomy. I mention it because it is one of the few useful reference points I was able to carry over from the life I had before I went to visit my father two years ago.

I use the synodic lunar month as a basis for marking my calendar every month, not because I need it to keep track, but because it allows me the illusion of order and sanity. In reality, I keep track of the moon by the building pressure at the base of my skull, by the growing volume and frequency of the demands being whispered in the darkest chambers of my mind. Because this isn't a struggle I have once a month, or just in the last days leading up to the moon rising fat and full in the sky. No.

Every night I fight the demon.

****

"You look just like I remember."

I tried to hide my contempt at the empty platitude. My father hadn't seen me in nearly thirty years, and I'd only been eight at the time. I stood before him now a grown man older than he'd been when he left, and he wanted to act as though he would recognize me on sight. As though some dishonest reference to some long-forsaken memory would bridge the gap of all those years in a moment. Make me forget the fact that he abandoned his family not just the day he left, but every day since that he hadn't come back.

It was too strong a word to say I hated him though. If anything, my opinion of him was mainly one of disinterest and mild pity. He was in his early sixties, but he looked decades older than that. Whether it was drugs, hard living, or guilt, something had been burning away at him for some time. Maybe, I considered, it was just the cancer. The malignant tumor that lay sleeping and growing fat in his lung, and according to his letter, would see him dead within a month.

It wasn't pity that had brought me all the way from my life in Indiana, however. It was the inheritance that he promised if I would come see him just one time before he passed. Fifteen years earlier, pride might have made me crumple up the letter or write him back, telling him to fuck off and keep his money. But that younger version of me didn't have a mortgage or crushing student debt. The me that stood before this twisted ember of a man had seen enough of the world to know that it was a hostile, dirty place that was made more tolerable by money.

And money was something that my father had plenty of.

The day before this arranged meeting, I had met my father's attorney at an office upstate. The man gave me a booklet detailing all of my father's finances, holdings, and properties. He was a millionaire several times over.

I'd glanced up at the attorney as I read through the

booklet. Asked him how my father had made all this money when he had been poor last I knew. The man had shrugged with a smile. Said my father had been lucky over the years and made a few good investments that paid off big. Said he'd known him for twenty years, and my father was a great man.

He didn't look great when I met him. His eyes were wet and weak as he looked at my face, judging my reaction to his opening gambit at reconnecting with his long-lost son. I faked a smile and nodded.

"You look older. How're you doing? Pain bad?"

My father shook his head. "Nothing the meds can't handle. Main thing that bothers me is not being able to get out of this thing." He patted the arms of the electric wheelchair he sat in, his lower half covered in a thick woolen blanket. "Two months ago I was jogging five miles a day. And now I need help wiping my ass."

I shifted uncomfortably. I wanted this over with as soon as possible, but I knew there would be some expectation that I stay for awhile if he was going to give me anything in the will. Possibly even try to rope me into sticking around until he died. Even with all the staff and nurses, he might want someone here that gave a shit. I just wasn't sure I could fake it that long.

Waving his hand, he went on. "But you didn't come to hear me complain. And I have no right to bitch, especially to you. Not after I left you kids and your mother high and dry like I did. Never tried to reach out and help, even after I got all this..." He lowered his gaze. "I know it's cliché, but all this cancer shit has made me wake up. I know I did wrong by you, and I'm sorry."

I tried to fight down the anger, but it slipped through my fingers. "Yeah, you fucking are. Luke nearly died two years after you left. Mama didn't have the money for the medical bills and...What am I doing? Like you fucking care. Why am I here at all?"

He raised his hands. "Please wait. Just wait. We both know you're here because of the inheritance. I contacted you because you're the oldest child and you were always good and fair. I want you, want all of you, to share in all that I've acquired." My father gestured around at the massive study we were in. "And I want you to decide who gets what. Your mother, Luke, your sister Lynn, you dole out the remnants of my life as you see fit. I feel like it's the least I can do after all these years."

Gritting my teeth, I nodded. "Fine. What do you want me to do? Hang out for awhile? What will it take for us to get it?"

He smiled. "A straight, no-nonsense question. I like that." When I just stared at him, he cleared his throat and went on. "I may be a foolish man in many ways, but I am not a fool. I know you don't want to be here, and I have no illusions that the guilt and regret of a dying man is going to magically recreate a bond that I gave up long ago. All I ask is that you shake my hand, tell me that you forgive me, and that you accept taking on all my possessions upon my death."

I raised an eyebrow. "Is this some kind of trick? Are you in deep debt or something?"

My father laughed. "No, far from it. You saw from your meeting yesterday with Anthony that I've done very well these past few years."

Nodding warily, I shrugged. "Okay. So that's it? I shake your hand, say I forgive you, and that I want to inherit everything when you die. That's all? Then I can go?"

"That's all. You'll be provided a copy of the new will as you leave and it'll be filed in probate court in the morning. You don't even have to come to my funeral. All the arrangements have already been made." He leaned forward slightly in his chair and stuck out his hand. "Do we have a deal?"

I hesitated for a moment. This was all so strange, and while I could understand guilt and his impending death as reasonable motivations, I still wondered if I was somehow being tricked.

But to what end? I didn't think he was faking having cancer, and I didn't have anything to offer him other than a comfortable lie to ease his conscience before he passed. I glanced around the study, thought about the massive house it was a part of, the other estates he had around the world. It would change all of our lives forever. How could I give all that up, keep that kind of money and security from my family, just because I was uncomfortable?

The answer was that I couldn't. So I stepped forward and shook his hand. Told him I forgave him, and that I would accept taking everything when he died.

It was as his grip on my hand tightened that I first knew something was terribly wrong.

He pulled me closer even as he pushed himself toward me, the sudden shifts of weight sending me off balance and stumbling. I would have recovered, but his bottom half was free of the blanket now—a coiled tangle of black-green meat that lashed out and wrapped around me tightly, driving me back onto the ground as I began to scream.

My father pulled himself up my legs and torso, his strong hands and the whipcord legs that made up his lower body painful and heavy on me as I struggled to get free. My first thought was that he was going to kill me or start biting out chunks of my chest. I kept screaming and struggling, but I was barely moving at all now. As his face drifted down, I felt my body growing distant, as though pushed away by the tides of his dead eyes boring into mine. He was going to do it. Whatever he was, it was, he was going to eat me, starting with my face.

Instead, he planted a light kiss on my lips. I felt my face go numb as I tried to move my head, but then it was over. Not just the kiss, but all of it. When I sat up and looked around, my father was gone.

****

I sold off that house and all of the other properties. From the start I knew that I didn't want anything that had ever belonged to that man, that thing, near my family. It was a few weeks after the last house had been sold that I started to feel something growing inside of me. When it was strong enough, it started directing my actions when I slept. Speaking to me when I was awake.

Even when it was just a low hum of words scratching at the back of my head, I could recognize the voice of my father.

He said this was a necessary thing for him to live on. He needed a host and he needed to kill. He hoped that I didn't mind helping with both.

I refused, of course. It only took a couple of months to realize that he grew stronger with the moon, and when it was full, he could kill no matter how hard I fought him. I begged him to stop, but he only laughed. He told me that I needed to develop a stronger stomach, or if I was too weak, there was always the other option.

I could share my true inheritance with my family.

I wouldn't mind seeing your mother again. Could be fun. And Lynn is in college now, right? I could join a sorority. It chuckled. The choice is yours. I know what I'd pick. Time to see if you're really my son.

I didn't answer him. There was no point, because there was no real choice. He won't let me kill myself, and isolating or confining myself doesn't work. At the end of each month, I drive to a new random place. At least…I think it's my choice to do that…it gets blurry when the last day is close. I tell myself that the randomness makes the horrible things we do more fair. Like an accident or an Act of God.

And I can keep him at bay 28 days out of the month. Even on the 29th day I try, but it's no use. His grip is too tight.

I don't see my family anymore. They try to contact me, but I ignore it. I stay on the move and won't respond to messages. They need to forget about me, let me go. I don't know what my father is or what he can do, and I won't risk them getting hurt by him again.

I know I'm getting to where I don't go around people much at all. I spend most days watching t.v. or sleeping. Marking time alone until the sun goes down. Dreading how quickly the darkness comes.

Because just past twilight I feel the familiar scratching at the back of my head, like a cat asking to come in for the evening. And then it's fully awake, pushing at me, trying to shove me down, to take me over, until the next sunrise.

Someone watching me would think it very odd—a tired-looking young man sitting alone in a fancy room somewhere, staring into the distance with fixed concentration for hours on end. A strange, but very placid, scene.

But inside, it's very different. It's shoving and clawing and biting. Pain and fear and dread as I feel my strength begin to go. Every night I fight the demon, and every night ends with me crying and screaming as I push the thing back down for a few more hours. Most nights it slips back into the dark nest it's made in my soul without threat or complaint—it knows the sun is coming up soon anyway.

But some nights, when I'm at my most broken and alone, I beg it to stop. To leave. To end this. Without fail, it repeats the offer to share my burden with the people I love. So far, I've managed to refuse every time.

Those nights are always the worst. Not because I've been lowered to begging or because I feel so utterly isolated in my father's trap. It's because of what he does as he slithers back down inside me for the day.

He laughs. It's a nasty, inhuman laugh that says I don't see the joke yet, but someday I will. That someday I'll be laughing beside him, readying myself for the next night.

For the next time someone has to fight me.

I don't think my brother committed suicide.

Two weeks ago I got the call that my brother had committed suicide. It came as a complete shock to me. I know it's a cliché, but Jerry really didn't seem like the suicidal kind, if there is such a thing. Sure, he had problems just like we all do. He was in a bad car wreck in college, and he battled depression for months after he realized that surgery and rehab were only going to give him most of his mobility back, not all.

But that was seven years ago. He hardly even limped anymore, had a good job, and had just started dating a great girl a few months earlier. He hadn't said anything concrete, but I could tell from talking to him that they were in love; that he thought Laci was the one. She was the one who called me first, and she sounded crushed.

I drove out that night, and amid funeral arrangements and spending time with my parents and Laci, I was so busy taking care of things that I didn't have time to stop and really let it sink in. My brother, one of my best friends since I was born, was really gone. It wasn't until I was sitting in his empty house, surrounded by belongings that I had to pack up or throw away, that I broke down and began to cry.

I was crying so hard, so focused on my newfound grief, that I didn't hear the doorbell at first. When I did, I debated not answering it, as I rarely answered my own door. Still, Jerry had always been more friendly and outgoing, and it somehow felt wrong not to honor that and be hospitable while I was still in his last home. Wiping my face, I went to the door and opened it on an older couple.

"Hi there! I hope we're not interrupting."

I looked at them confusedly for a moment. "Um, I…Jerry's not here."

The woman frowned. "Oh, we know honey. We heard what happened to him." The man leaned forward, as though to whisper, though when he spoke, his voice was loud and harsh in my ears. "Terrible thing. Good guy. Terrible thing." The woman's frown deepened as she glanced at the man and then thrust forward a covered dish.

"We live just next door, but we didn't know him well enough to come over during the funeral and what-not…and we've been out of town recently as well. But we did want to do something, and we saw that someone was over here…um, cleaning up, so I thought we'd bring over this casserole." She paused before adding. "It's a bean casserole. My recipe."

I took the offered dish numbly. This wasn't the first food offering I'd had to take in the last few days, and I admit to being relieved that this was the purpose of their visit. It meant they'd go away, satisfied they'd helped in some nebulous way by giving food no one asked for or wanted. Except they didn't go away, at least, not yet.

"Everything going okay? Got anyone helping you?" The woman's eyes were roving past me into the shadows of Jerry's foyer. I quickly found my faint gratitude souring into annoyance. So was that it then? Nosy neighbors wanting a peek at the horror show?

I shrugged. "It's fine. I've got it handled. My brother was a neat guy, so it's mainly just a matter of figuring out what to keep and what to throw away." I was about to launch into the wrap-up speech about how I better "get back to it" when the man interrupted.

"Have you run across anything strange so far?"

I stared at him blankly. "Um, no. What do you mean?"

He looked away. "Oh, I don't know. They say you don't really know someone until you go through their stuff, right?"

Gritting my teeth, I started pushing the door shut. "Look, I need to go. Thanks for the casserole and…" The man blocked the door with his foot.

"We mean no offense, friend. Want us to come in and keep you company for a bit?"

I pushed against the door harder and felt the wood flex slightly, but it didn't budge. "No, I wouldn't like that. Please move your foot and go on."

The woman gave me a thin smile as she nudged the man in the side. "Sorry to keep you. We'll let you get back to it."

The man reluctantly moved his foot back and I immediately shoved the door shut with a solid thump. Fuck me. What was their deal? Were they just that pushy?

I jumped as my phone rang. It was the number of the detective that had worked Jerry's case. "Miss Sanchez, this is Jim Truett. How are you doing today?"

Swallowing, I backed away from the door and returned to the living room where I'd been packing. "I'm fine. Packing stuff up. Anything I can help you with?"

"Well, I'm closing out your brother's file and we have a few personal effects that we need to either release to you or destroy."

I felt my legs growing weak, so I sat down between a table and a half-full packing box. "Um, you mean like his clothing and stuff?"

I could hear how uncomfortable Truett was over the phone. "No, not his clothes. They were...well, they're considered a biohazard due to their condition, so those are typically burned once we're done with them. But he had a wallet with various cards, a couple of photos, and fifty-seven dollars in cash. He also had his cell phone...and the keys I already gave you...and, well. The note he left." He paused and then rushed forward quickly. "Not that you have to take the note. Or any of it. People feel different ways about that kind of thing, and we're happy to do whatever you and your family want."

The air felt heavy around me, making it hard to move or think. I knew what the note said. I'd seen it the day after I'd arrived in town, and despite being in a plastic evidence bag, I'd been able to tell Detective Truett that it looked like Jerry's handwriting, even if the words made no sense.

I've had enough. Good bye. Love you all, Jerry.

I felt fresh tears springing up in the corner of my eyes and I fought them back. "I...well, the wallet and stuff, yeah. But the note...I don't want the note. None of us want that."

"Okay. Fair enough. I'll have the rest up front for you

to pick up whenever you like. Just tell them that…"

"Are you sure he did it?"

"Huh?" The man sounded younger when he was caught off-guard, and it took him a second to process what I was asking and respond. "Did what, commit suicide?"

"Yeah. It just didn't seem like something he'd do."

His voice was softer and tinged with sadness now. "Look, I know why you feel like that. I…well, I've never told anyone outside of my family about this, but when my grandmother died a few years back, it was a suicide too. She was eighty-seven and had bone cancer, so I could see her reasoning even if I didn't agree with it. But there was still a part of me…and my dad too…that had trouble accepting that she'd done that to herself on purpose. I guess my point is that you never really know what other people have going on inside and what they're capable of. And it's not your responsibility to save them from themselves." He cleared his throat. "Not trying to preach at you. Just want you to know that what you're feeling is natural and will pass with time."

I sighed and wiped at my face again. "I appreciate it. Thanks for your help." I hung up, and it was as I was leaning forward to set my phone on the floor that I caught a glimpse of white under the table next to me. My first thought was that it was warranty paperwork or something similar that the maker of the furniture had stapled to the underside of the table and that Jerry had never noticed and removed. But as I looked closer, I saw it was a small white envelope that had been taped there.

My mouth was dry as I reached for it and gave it a tug. It was well-secured, and it took three yanks to free the

140

envelope without tearing it. Once I was holding it, I studied it for a moment. There was no writing on the envelope, and it looked fairly new—new enough that most likely Jerry had put it there during the nearly three years he had lived in the house and had this furniture. Licking my lips, I gently opened the envelope.

Inside was an instant camera photo and a short note. I felt my stomach lurch as I recognized Jerry's handwriting immediately.

If someone finds this note, please know that if I have died or gone missing, it was not of my own free will. They keep finding ways in. I don't know why they keep coming, but I know they do things to me while I'm asleep. The door keeps popping up. I took a picture of it. They're growing angry and I don't know what to do. Please help me if you can, or if it's too late, please get away. Get far away.

I read the note five times before turning to the photo. It was a picture of what looked like one of the walls in the dining room, and in the middle of it was a tall door of dark wood and black metal. I'd have to check, but I didn't remember any door like that in the entire house.

First though, I needed to call the Detective back. Tell him what I'd found. Pushing redial, I clenched my phone hard enough to make it creak when his voicemail picked up. I left him a vague but urgent message, but after I hung up, I was unsure what to do. I could call 911 or go to the police station, but odds are they would just give me back over to Truett any way since he'd worked Jerry's death. And I was angry and scared, but there was no reason to think that waiting a few minutes or hours would make some huge difference to anything now.

So I went over and laid down on the sofa, planning to just rest and organize my thoughts for a little while before trying to call the detective again. Before I knew it I was asleep, and when I woke up, night had fallen and the house was dark except for dim patches of light streaming in from the streetlamps outside. I began to sit up when I heard a noise coming from the kitchen. It was a stealthy, furtive noise, and my first thought was a mouse or rat.

Shuddering at the thought, I got up and began easing my way through the house. I knew the layout of the furniture well enough to avoid the chairs and tables, but the scattered boxes were a different matter. I stumbled on three between the sofa and the dining room. It was as I looked back up from bumping into the third that I thought I saw a quick movement in the shadows across the dining room and heading into the hall. I froze for a moment and then fumbled for my phone to turn on the light.

I shined the light across the far end of the dining room and the hall beyond, but I didn't see anything. I thought and also checked the walls of the room. No door like in the picture either.

Hearing blood pounding in my ears, I found the switch and flipped on the light. The light made everything feel less menacing, but I still felt dull dread as I opened the door to the kitchen and shone my light around on the floor. I hated mice, and if it was a roach big enough to make that racket, I didn't want to…

It wasn't a mouse or a rat or a roach. It was a folded piece of paper.

Finding the kitchen lights, I flipped them on before bending down to pick it up. I found myself hoping it would just be an old receipt, an invoice from the tombstone company, or some other scrap of what remained of closing out Jerry's business. But it wasn't any of those things.

It was a note, in what looked like my handwriting, signed with my name.

I've had enough of everything. Good bye. Love you all, Connie.

Dying gives the body over.

When I was in college, I spent two summers working at a local funeral home. I learned a lot during that time—the embalming process, the stitching and wax used in reconstruction, and even odd tricks like running condensed milk through the circulatory system to reduce the yellow tint of jaundiced skin. I'd gone into the job with a fair amount of dread and squeamishness, but by the end of the first month, I was half-convinced I wanted to do it for a living.

It was the respect that had taken me by surprise. Respect for the body, but also respect for the grief of those left behind. There was such care taken to present this decaying collection of meat and bone in the best light possible—not because it was still a person, but because it was the last reminder that had been left behind. A reminder of who had been lost, and what waits for all of us at the end of the road.

The idea of comforting people through their grief was appealing to me, and once I realized how much the work relied on appearances, it made the work easier—even appealing. I just had to detach myself from the emotions and distasteful aspects of the job. Remind myself that this wasn't about me, or even the departed, it was about the people who had loved them—what would give them peace or lessen their despair, the things that they could see, hear or smell.

Which is why I found it so strange when I noticed my boss, Mr. Wallace, marking something in the roof of a man's mouth before sewing it shut. If I had seen it the first summer, I likely would have ignored it. But I was comfortable with Wallace by that second year, and there had already been some talk about me coming back after I finished school. So I asked why. Why was he putting a mark that no one would ever see?

Wallace glanced up at me with a startled expression, licking his lips several times before giving a small, embarrassed smile. "You noticed that, did you? I suppose I've gotten too used to you being around, my boy. I should have sent you upstairs before taking up that little task." He studied me for a moment, seeming to weigh something in his mind before going on. "But you are a good boy, and you've shown me you can be trusted. Be discreet." He stepped forward and put his hand on my shoulder as he met my eyes. "If I share this with you now, will you keep it only for yourself? No telling your friends or anyone. It is very serious and very important, and if I share it, it will be a violation for you to spread it any farther. Do you understand?"

Swallowing, I nodded.

He returned my nod. "Good, good. I think you do understand."

Wallace turned back to the body as he went on. "There is a secret truth that most undertakers and coroners know, though no one will admit it. In old times, it wasn't a problem most places—the bodies rotted quickly enough, you see. Only in certain climates and locations did you ever hear tell of it happening. But now, with air conditioning and refrigeration, embalming and powders, we can make the body last far longer." He looked at the body as he began trailing off. "Too long, some would say."

I raised my eyebrows. "I don't get what you're saying."

He glanced back and waived his hand. "I'm rambling, forgive me. The point I'm trying to make is this: When something dies, the body is meant to rot away. This is part of the natural order of things, and not just because it saves space or feeds worms or whatever. It's necessary because dying gives the body over."

I frowned at him, and giving me a humorless chuckle, he went on. "I know how this sounds. But if a body doesn't decay quickly enough or is not disposed of in a way that prevents it, the corpse can become a vessel, a receptacle of sorts, for something else." I kept waiting for him to crack a smile or let me in on the fact that he was fucking with me, but he looked solemn and more than a little afraid.

"What, like a zombie or something?"

He rolled his eyes in exasperation. "That's all you kids fucking know nowadays is a damn zombie. Zombie this, zombie that. No, not a zombie. The body comes back to a kind of life, but it's not some brainless monster. It's just not the person that died either." Puffing out a long breath, he shook his head. "I don't know what it is, honestly. A spirit of some kind? Some kind of animal we don't know about or understand? I don't know." He pulled a cigarette from his pants, glanced around, and then stuffed it awkwardly in his shirt pocket. "But they're slow, and they have to crawl. They can smell or sense a dead body from a long distance, like a shark or something smelling blood, but it takes them a long time to get there and get inside."

I felt my heart hammering, less from his story and more from what it must mean. I was working for someone who was either insane or had some kind of substance abuse problem. What other explanation could there be? But then again, maybe this was just a practical joke, even if Wallace wasn't known for them. Besides, it was too good of a job for me not to play along for at least a bit longer.

"Um, okay. So have you ever seen one of these things before?"

He lowered his eyes, but not before I saw the haunted look there. "I...not the thing itself, no. They're invisible, or at least I don't know how you see them. But I've seen the signs of them twice before, and the end result just once." He looked back up. "You think I'm crazy. That's why this isn't how you should learn about it."

"What do you mean?"

He sat down on a nearby stool, and I felt a wave of sympathy as I watched at him. He looked old and tired, and crazy or not, I could tell talking about this was hard for him. Still, his voice stayed steady as he began telling me about what had happened to him forty years earlier.

"It's like a weird kind of club, I guess. Once they know you're dedicated, that you're in it as a profession, someone, usually a mentor or friend, will invite you to help them with a special body preparation. For me, it was my boss, Oscar Lews. He asked me to stay late one night with a vagrant's body that had come in that afternoon. Those are the ones you have to watch the most—with no one to pay for cremation or a proper burial in consecrated ground, they wind up going to a potter's field with no real sense of urgency from a grieving family."

I raised my hand and he stopped for me to ask a question. "So this doesn't happen if they're cremated or buried at a church?"

Wallace shrugged. "It doesn't matter if it's a church, or what religion blessed it, at least as far as I can tell. It just needs to be consecrated or the body needs to be so far gone from rot or fire or what have you that it's past the point of use." He waved away another question. "The point is, I was like you. I wouldn't have believed any of this unless I saw it with my own eyes, and when I went down into the basement with Oscar and saw that hobo's body on a gurney, surrounded by a circle of flour on the floor, my first thought was that it was a joke. My second was that Oscar had slipped a gear and I needed to find the nearest door out."

"But he convinced me to stay. To wait with him and watch, said that he would explain everything after. So we sat in the corner for three hours. He said it shouldn't take too long, as the man had been dead probably two days when a railroad cop had found him frozen to death in the back of a supply shed. He was already starting to decay despite the cold conditions both before and after we got him."

"Still, I was bored and sleepy, and while I was getting paid to sit on my ass, I was about ready to call it a night. That's when Oscar grabbed my arm and pointed toward the wide white circle surrounding the body. It was moving, or at least a strip of it was. It was like an invisible hand was flicking the flour this way and that, scattering it as it reached the body at long last. I let out a yell and Oscar seemed satisfied I'd seen enough. He went to the body and pushed the gurney toward the oven, yelling for me to get it open and punch the button. I did as he said, and within twenty seconds we were sliding the body toward the flames."

Wallace shivered. "But that was still enough time for the body to grab my arm. This wasn't an involuntary muscle spasm or trapped gas moving around. It grabbed my arm, and when I looked up, it was staring at me. Staring at me and saying my name."

"I don't know what would have happened if Oscar hadn't broken its grip and pushed it the rest of the way into the oven. I heard it scream for a moment, but then we were alone again, and everything was silent except for our panicked breathing and the roar of the fire."

He pointed back at the body. "That's the night Oscar taught me the other way you prevent a body from being used. There is a symbol—I don't know where it comes from or what it means, so don't bother asking—but it looks kind of like three stars touching each other. If you put that into the roof of a body's mouth, it protects it the same as fire or holy ground. Most people don't know it, but there are thousands of bodies all around that have that mark in their mouth or somewhere else no one will ever see it." Rubbing his cheek distractedly, he turned back. "And that's for the best. People don't need to know that things like that can exist."

When he met my eyes again, I could see he knew I didn't believe him. I liked him, even respected and trusted him, but this? It was too much.

I called in sick the next day, and the following week I slid my resignation through the mail slot on his front door. I felt like a coward and a traitor, but I won't deny that I felt relief too. I told myself it was just because I was free from having to worry about working around a crazy old man with sharp instruments. But I think that was a lie. I think I was glad I didn't have to keep worrying that maybe he wasn't crazy after all.

****

I moved away after college, and three years later I was living in a cheap apartment in a bad part of Chicago. I was between jobs, had no money, and while I would have eventually called my family for help anyway, one night in November made me go ahead and ask to come home.

I'd been sick with the flu for nearly two weeks, and my last fevered trip out to get food and medicine had been days earlier. I was low on supplies, but I also felt so bad that I didn't care. I slept most of the time, and in between periods of unconsciousness, I shuffled back and forth to the bathroom, occasionally glancing out the window at the street below. A bleak early winter had been sending snow blowing past for the last few days, and though my grasp of time was warped by being sick, I could still see the progress of white, icy banks of snow accumulating around the steps, alleyways, and mounds of trash dotting the sidewalk on the far side of the street.

I don't know how long he'd been there when I first saw him, but over my next few trips past the window, I kept seeing the same figure—a man sitting up against a red dumpster in an alley right across from my apartment. He never moved, and as hours turned into days, I saw snow pile up around him until I couldn't see his legs anymore.

There was no question that he was dead, and I didn't know what I should do about it. If I had felt better, been more myself, I likely would have called 911 and asked them to go check on him—or more realistically, come pick up the body. But instead, I just watched him for a few more seconds before stumbling back to bed.

Another day passed, and I was feeling better. Sipping on some broth, I walked back to the window to check on the body. If it was still there, I was going to call and...

There was movement down there at the dumpster. Not from the man himself, not at first. But from the snow next to him. It looked as if it was rolling down or being pushed aside. My first disquieting thought was that a rat was under the snow getting at the body. But why would it go down into the cold when it could get at his stomach and chest just as easy?

And while it was hard to tell at a distance and in the limited glow of the streetlights, it didn't seem like something was under the snow. It looked more like something I couldn't see was crawling across it to get to the dead man.

The snow stilled, but a moment later the body gave a quick jerk followed by a smaller shudder. Then, as I watched, the corpse rose to its feet. I wanted to back away, to get away, from the awful thing I was witnessing. Just seeing it, I felt somehow unclean in a base, instinctual way that I can't fully explain or describe.

But I couldn't. I was transfixed, staring in horror as this thing clambered to its feet and brushed the remaining snow off its frozen pants and stiff, blue hands. I had the desperate hope that the cold and time had done too much damage, that it would be forced to leave the body or be trapped there as the rotten meat collapsed around it.

That hope died as it turned its head to look up at me.

It just stared for several moments, a smile slowly spreading across its face like a time-lapse of some hideous flower in bloom. Its eyes seemed to shine, even at a distance, and I could feel its gaze boring into me as it raised a hand and gave a long and limber wave. I had the frantic thought that I didn't know what that meant.

Goodbye? Or hello?

The smile fell from its lips as it lowered its arm, and after staring up at me a second longer, it sank back into the shadows. I imagined I could still see its eyes on me, shining up out of the dark, if only for a moment. And then, it was gone.

Something has always lived with us.

I remember the first time my mother told me about Chigaro. It had been the day before my sixth birthday, and I was excited about the decorations she had been stringing up around the house and the smell of a cake baking in the oven. That warm anticipation turned icy cold when I saw her standing at the door to my room, a solemn look on her face. She told me to come and take her hand, and when I did so, she began to walk us through the house, room by room.

I wanted to ask what we were doing, but something about her stern expression and the tight grip on my hand seemed to forbid it. So instead we walked into a room, paused for a moment in silence, and then moved onto the next without any comment. When we had entered every room, my mother brought me back to my bedroom and shut the door behind us. Only then did she crouch down next to me and speak, her voice a tightly-bound whisper in my ear.

"Did you see anything that didn't belong?"

I had pulled back slightly from my mother to look at her. Was this a game? Was I in trouble? I was very little, but I already knew to pick up my toys and keep things out of the floor. Had I forgotten something?

Meeting her eyes but still afraid to speak, I only shook my head slightly. Her eyebrows furrowed and she squeezed my hand harder—not enough to hurt, but almost.

"Stop and think. Did you see anything that didn't belong or looked out of place? Something you didn't remember seeing before."

I didn't dare pull my hand away, and I could tell by the intensity of her gaze that this was important, so I thought again, trying to go through each room in my mind. The hallway, no. The bathroom, no. Mama's bedroom, no. Her office...wait, wasn't there a different table in there? Yes, a low table of reddish wood I had never seen before. Pleased with myself, I smiled as I answered.

"Is it the table? The one in your office?"

My mother's eyes fluttered shut as a low moan escaped her. She gave a slow nod and pulled me toward her, cupping my head with one hand while rubbing my back with the other. Her voice was muffled against my forehead as she spoke, but I could still hear the sadness in it.

"Yes, sweet one. That's just the thing. That table." She held me for a minute or more, embracing me silently before gently grabbing my arms and pushing me back slightly. "Except it's not really a table. It's a living thing. A real living thing."

I frowned. "Like an animal?"

She nodded slightly. "Like an animal, yes. I don't think it's really an animal, and I think it's very smart, but yes..." My mother gave me a slight smile. "Yes, looking at it as an animal...a wild animal...isn't a bad way to talk about it." Sniffing, she went on. "Because you remember what we do with wild animals, right?"

I piped up immediately, happy to seize upon something more familiar. "We stay away from them!"

Nodding, my mother wiped at her eyes. "That's exactly right, sweet one."

But this led to other questions, and this time I did ask. "But why do we have a wild animal in the house? And what is it?"

She stood up and led me to the bed where we sat down. I didn't like that she was crying, but her voice grew steadier as she talked. She told me that the thing that looked like a table was called Chigaro, or at least that's what she had been taught to call it since she was a little girl my age.

My mother said the word meant *chair* in a language they spoke in a far-off place called Zimbabwe, and while that might sound silly when it looked like a table, Chigaro didn't always look like a table...or a chair for that matter. Every few weeks it changed to look like something different—a new lamp or dish, a new book or ottoman. There were only two ways to recognize where it was— either realizing that there was some object that didn't belong or by actually touching it. She said if you touched it, you would get real sick to your stomach until you stopped touching it again. I could tell from her expression that touching it was really bad.

I asked her where it came from and again, why was it in our house? She said it had been in our family for nearly eighty years. My great-grandfather had traveled a lot in his later years, and one time when he came back, everyone noticed a new painting hanging on the wall. The family assumed that he had brought it back as a surprise, but he swore he hadn't. A few days later, the painting was gone, but there was a new radio in the parlor.

This had been a source of excitement and mystery at

first, until my mother's father, himself just a little boy at the time, had tried to turn the radio on. Instead of hearing static or music, he heard a shrill screech through the speaker as he collapsed to the ground, vomiting. Chigaro's effect on those that touched it had grown much less severe over the years, but it still paid to avoid prolonged contact.

Over the next few years, they had tried different solutions to the Chigaro problem. They tried talking to it, but it did not respond. They tried attacking it, but it was always back the next day in a new form. They even called in a priest, but he left angrily after hearing their incredible story, convinced they were playing a prank on him. Eventually they moved, but that didn't work either.

Because it follows the family. It was always assumed that my great-grandfather accidently brought it back on his trip, as it stayed with him until he died. After that, it went to my mother's father, and then to her. One day, my mother told me, she would be gone and it would come to stay with me.

She could see I was growing scared, and she reached out to stroke my hair as she went on. "It's nothing to be afraid of, not really. Just don't touch it if you can help it, and move away quickly if you do. And don't stare at it. It…well, it doesn't like that very much." She offered me a smile. "Just follow those rules like the smart little girl that you are, and everything will be fine. Okay?"

And for the most part, it was fine. I grew up in that house and then later another across the country when my mother remarried briefly. My stepfather was rarely home and I doubted she ever told him about Chigaro at all.

She rarely talked to me about it either. She'd

occasionally ask if I had noticed what it had changed into or if I had seen it do anything "different". I never knew exactly what she meant by that, and she would never elaborate, but that question and its implications would always fill me with sharp new dread. It reminded me that we had an intruder in our lives—a monster that was frightening not because of what we knew about it, but because of all we didn't understand or suspect.

I would have periods where I wouldn't sleep more than an hour or two a night, and when I did, my slumber was plagued with night terrors. Between the ages of eight and twelve I had a terrible stutter, and I frequently wet the bed until I was fourteen. Therapists attributed these things to "underlying unspecified stressors", "a nervous temperament", and my favorite, "growing pains".

Not that any of these things were wrong, I guess, and I know there are people who grow up much harder than I did. I always had food and a fairly stable home life, I was kept clean and healthy, and even my fears of Chigaro would periodically fade with the passage of time and familiarity. It was only when I was newly confronted with the strangeness and unknown danger of it all…well, those were the really bad times.

I moved out as soon as I turned 18, and aside from holidays, I never stayed in my mother's house for more than an hour in the years that followed. In some ways, the infrequency of my stays made it harder—I was less sure of what items were supposed to be there and those that were Chigaro in disguise. It was disquieting in a way I can't fully explain, as though I had lost one of my senses. Or like I was walking across an unfamiliar field littered with mines, afraid of touching that cup or sitting on that chair, and terrified of staring at something long enough for me to finally learn what Chigaro did when it was displeased.

I felt guilty leaving my mother in that prison, but she honestly seemed content enough most of the time. She would try to get me to come back home more often, but I think she understood why I couldn't. And for all her flaws, I know she loved me.

She died six months ago in her sleep, and it was two weeks later before I received all the keys and documents I needed as executor of her estate. I had access to her bank accounts, her cars, the house, of course, and…a storage unit key. I had never known my mother to keep anything in storage—our homes were never mansions, but they were always large and well-furnished—full without excess. Yet when I went and talked to the manager of the storage unit lot, he said she'd had one of their largest units for nearly twenty years.

I felt a mix of nervousness and excitement as I unlocked the padlock and rolled up the front door to the unit. Perhaps it would be empty or full of junk, or maybe there would be prized items of monetary or sentimental value. Either way, it was a distraction from my constant worry about when Chigaro would finally show up in my home and start haunting my own family.

The door slid up with a solid thunk as my eyes adjusted to the shadowy interior of the unit. It was a huge space, and most of it was filled. Not with one kind of thing, but several of every kind of thing. Furniture, electronics, books, plates, statuettes…I had the passing thought that maybe my mother had been a burglar and this was her hidden stash from years of taking random objects from neighbors' homes.

But then I saw the red wood table.

It was sitting on top of a small floral loveseat that I remember almost bumping into when I was ten or eleven. I had come around the corner one morning and it was just sitting in the hallway. Sucking in a breath, I had recoiled and given it wide berth as I went on to the bathroom.

And there was the coatrack that had appeared the night of my junior prom. I had been coming downstairs to get picked up by Josh Breslin, and he was standing so close to it, and I was afraid he would bump it and get sick and...the night hadn't gone very well after that.

Or the teapot. The little flowered teapot sitting on a stack of cardboard boxes in the back corner of the unit. That was the first time that Chigaro had appeared in my room. I had woken up when I was seven to see it sitting on my dresser, and when I realized what it had to be, I peed myself a little.

That's when I knew that nowhere in the house was safe.

But how could this be? How could all this be here? Unless my mother had just...?

Biting my lip, I turned on the light against the wall and stepped inside. My harsh breathing and the irritated buzz of the fluorescent lights above me were the only sounds I could hear. It was as though everything else was frozen. When I looked back out, nothing seemed right or real, as though the angles were all wrong.

That's when I reached up and pulled the door back down, shutting out the world.

Tomorrow is my little girl Jessica's sixth birthday. My husband is baking her a cake while I hang up balloons inside and get an inflatable jumping castle blown up in the back yard for her and her friends. She's old enough now for birthdays to be really fun—for her to remember things more clearly and realize there's a point to the things we do.

For her to follow rules and understand why they can't be broken.

So I go into the sunroom where my daughter is watching a cartoon on her tablet with her stuffed bear, Jasper Scruffins. She's loved that bear since she was a baby, and while it's old, she's always treated it with a surprising amount of respect and care. Jessica has always been a smart and thoughtful child, which is why I think this will go so well.

I take her by the hand, forcing myself to hide my excitement as I lead her quietly from room to room. She giggles a bit at first, but a couple of glances from me and her face grows drawn and worried. When we are done, I take her back to the sunroom and Jasper. Maybe I'll use the little blue bear as a way of explaining Chigaro to her. It's just another companion that you have to treat with care.

Her big blue eyes are troubled as she looks up at me, searching my face for some sign of what is wrong. Letting out a sigh, I stroke her hair for a moment before I begin.

"Did you see anything that didn't belong?"

It won't stop growing.

I remember when I first saw the truck weaving in front of me. It was one of those old and battered white work trucks that you see government crews and old handimen driving. My first thought was that it was a drunk, and that I needed to slow down in case he slammed on the brakes suddenly. Then I was watching as the truck lurched violently to the right and tumbled down the embankment to the creek fifteen feet below.

I stopped and got out, and while my brain was still buzzing with adrenaline and surprise, I slid down the hill and yanked open the driver's side door. The man inside was in his fifties, and from the angle of his head, I thought his neck was probably broken. I couldn't tell if he was alive, and I knew better than to move him, but I was also starting to realize I needed to call 911. There was a colored piece of paper laying on the man's leg, and thinking it might have information I could give the hospital or the police, I plucked it out while dialing the number.

It was a work order. It said that Salivador Petty, I guessed this guy, had serviced the pool filter at some house out in the county. I told the 911 dispatcher where we were and what I thought the guy's name might be. He told me to go wait up by my car until emergency services arrived.

Ending the call, I glanced up to find the man staring

at me, his lips working soundlessly as he tried to say something or maybe cry out in pain. I told him to stay still and quiet, that help was on the way. This just made him more animated, his eyes rolling and his lips twitching as he tried to force something out. Finally I heard him speak, though it sounded more like a gasp of trapped air than a human voice.

"It…won't stop…growing…"

The man's eyes fluttered back closed, and I decided to take 911's advice and wait by my car for the authorities to arrive. When they did, the EMT thanked me for waiting but said they'd take it from there.

So I left.

By the next day, I rarely thought about the accident, and it wasn't until I was cleaning out my car the following weekend that I found the work order tucked between my seat and the console. Holding that pink slip of paper brought it all back to me, and I found myself wanting to find out what had happened to the poor guy. I called the local hospital, but they said they couldn't disclose any information about patients. I even talked to my brother-in-law at the sheriff's department, but he hadn't heard about the accident at all. Finally, feeling a bit foolish, I called the work number on the paper.

After the fourth ring, a voice mail message picked up and an older-sounding man said to leave a message at the beep with your name, number and address, as well as what work you needed done. I tried to picture that voice coming from the gasping man trapped in the truck, and I found it wasn't hard. So I left a message, asking for him or someone to call me back. That I was the guy who saw his accident a few days earlier, and I wanted to see how he was doing.

Two more weeks passed with no word. Not only had I not forgotten about it again, but it had become a preoccupation—it got to the point that I would check my phone a couple of times an hour to see if I had missed a call. I didn't understand my need to know what had happened to him, but that didn't change how compelling it had become. By the end of the second week, I was searching for a phone number connected to the address where the guy had worked on the pool filter. It was a long shot, but if the people there used him regularly, maybe they had heard something about what had happened.

There was no number, but I still had the address, and that Saturday I found myself driving across the county to a massive house tucked deep into the woods. I almost stopped and went back home several times, but it never quite happened. Every time I went to turn around, I kept telling myself that it was a fun random adventure on a boring Saturday, it was me being a good Samaritan, or at the very least, it would put the final nail in the coffin of my bizarre curiosity.

There were no signs of people outside the house, and when I knocked on the door, no one answered. I felt a flutter of nervousness as I went around looking for a side or back door to knock at. It was getting dark and I was a stranger, lurking around in the back yard like I wanted to get shot. But just one last try and...

There was the pool.

I hadn't thought about the pool when I first arrived, and even when I went around to the back of the property, it hadn't occurred to me right away. That was because it wasn't out in the back yard, but rather in a large building of brick and glass set away from the main house. The windows seemed to be partially grown over with some kind of vines or ivy, but I could still see the shimmer of the water reflected in the windows. Maybe I'd have better luck finding someone in there.

I knocked at the door to the pool house and then opened it. Looking inside, at first I saw a young woman floating naked and face down in the hazy water of a large, well-lit swimming pool. I had the panicked thought that she must be drowning and I stepped forward. That was when I realized my mistake. The pool wasn't well-lit at all, but instead thick with a murky sludge that had more of those black vines pouring out of it like a fountain. I looked around in horror as I realized those vines were all around me and growing closer all the time. I tried to run away, but I was already trapped.

But then again, maybe I had been trapped for a while.

****

I live in a white room now. Most of the time I can see it as a white room, and things are better then. I can see my bed and table, my television and bookshelves, my computer and desk. They are clean and tidy and not at all tainted. They are all just right.

I try to ignore the red line painted on the far line of the room. Anything that gets past that line gets burned up. When I first got here, I used to toss pencils across the line just to watch them pop like firecrackers. But then they stopped giving me pencils and I learned to behave. Life has been better since then.

Now the only time it's really bad is when I don't see

the clean white room. Sometimes I see the twisted snarl of those black vines, running in every direction, wrapping around me, digging through me, always trying to grow and grow and grow. That's when I feel how angry and hungry it is, how much it wants to tear me apart but doesn't quite dare until it manages to get past that damned red line.

I have visitors occasionally. They come in strange suits and talk to me as though nothing is wrong. They give me books and let me access the internet and watch movies and play games. They seem nice, but they won't let me leave, or tell me why they brought me here or what's wrong with me. When I ask them about the vines, they act like I'm making it up. Like there isn't any such thing.

For a minute, they had me thinking I was crazy. For a minute, they had me wondering if I was just seeing things. If maybe it was all just in my head.

But then, last…well, I don't know time like I did, but a little while ago…one of those doctors or whatever they are, they came in to talk to me. I was seeing the vines then, curling and uncurling against the walls like a thousand angry clenched fists. I was trying to ignore them and talk to the lady in the strange suit when one of the tendrils suddenly shot out toward her face. It stopped just short of the burn line, like it always does, because it knows. But I wasn't watching it. I was watching the woman.

And she flinched.

What lay in the well.

When I bought Killian Farms, it was as an investment property. It was a lot of land in an area whose property values had only gone up in the last five years, in part because of major urban development the next county over. The property had been foreclosed on years earlier by a local bank, and after years of it not selling, I was able to get it for dirt cheap. In retrospect, it was too cheap, but I was seeing dollar signs at the time, and my real estate development company had been doing well enough that I could spend some money on the property and be patient on making it back.

I intended on investing fifty thousand dollars to fix up the house, the barn and the stable, landscaping a five-acre yard around it, and then selling it off. As for the other two hundred acres, my plan was to divide it into lots for a suburban subdivision. If it all panned out, I stood to make better than a million dollars profit by the time I was done.

But it didn't pan out. At all. Several other investments fell through, my business partner developed a nasty pill habit and stole nearly a hundred grand before the accountant caught on, and by the end of last year, the company had been dissolved. All I had left was a couple of thousand dollars in my checking account and Killian Farms.

The renovations had been partially done by this point, so the house...my home now...was nice enough, if a bit quaint for my tastes. The barn still needed some work and the stable was run down, but this was all far down on my list of priorities now. I needed to figure out what I was going to do for money, especially when I knew there was little chance of selling the farm any time soon.

Because I had found out why I had gotten the farm so cheap. It was a murder house. No one had fucking bothered to tell me that when I talked to agents or had attorneys and inspectors checking out the property before I bought it, but I had learned it a few months before our company folded. I was meeting with Rex Tolliver, the head of a local development company, about going in with us on a new subdivision there. I still remember the sound of his laugh.

****

"Hell, boy." The man had chortled, his wide, tan face crinkling with mirth as he looked at me with hard, pebble blue eyes. "That why you bought that place? Didya really think anyone around here would want to live out there?"

I could feel a mixture of anger and unease rumbling in my stomach at his words, but I kept the smile on my face. "What do you mean, Rex? What's wrong with it?"

He laughed again, taking a swig of bourbon before leaning back in his office chair. "Boy, there was a whole family, the wholetire Killian family, that was killed up there maybe...eighteen, twenty years ago. Man went crazy, killed his wife, his sisters, and his parents. They only found him and the wife, and he had torn her ALL to pieces. When

167

they asked him why, he said it was because she wouldn't stop singing."

The man tipped me a wink. "I reckon she was a powerful bad singer, given what he did to her."

I could barely breathe. This was bad. Very bad. Sitting in Rex's office, I already knew our business had taken a nosedive and my partner was acting strange, but I didn't yet see how bad things were going to get. But a death house…worse, a murder house? It was toxic when trying to do a sale to locals. And if it was a mass murder house….

"But…but what about the rest? You said he killed more people? He must have killed them somewhere else?" Please let it be somewhere fucking else. If it was a mass-murder house, I might as well go set it on fire now.

He gave a casual shrug, but his eyes were sharp on my own. "No, I 'spect it was there, or that's what everyone assumes. There was a terrific amount of blood and gore, you see. More than coulda come from just that one little lady. And they were all gone, never seen or heard from again. Everyone knew he done it, but no one knew where he put the bodies. And he wasn't telling." I found myself starting to hate this man. He wasn't stupid, and he was enjoying doing this folksy, aw shucks act as he fed me bad news on a slow drip.

Still, I sat up straighter at his last words, a flame of hope still twitching in my chest. "So he never said he killed them? Just the wife?"

Rex chuckled again, licking his lips as he stood to pour another drink. "Hell, boy. He didn't have much chance. Deputies didn't check him good enough. He killed himself with a pocketknife on the way to the jail."

****

I moved onto Killian Farms on a Tuesday, and by Friday I was no closer to adjusting to living there or finding a way to go elsewhere. The house itself was nice enough, but despite my internal admonitions to not get creeped out by living where someone (or several someones) were killed, I had to admit it was unnerving to be living alone in a large, strange house with such a bad history. Nothing had actually happened during my first nights, but it didn't stop me from feeling like I was in the opening few minutes of a rural horror movie.

Still, by Friday morning, all my attempts at putting out feelers for a quick deal or job had dried up, and I resigned myself to the fact that, at least for the short-term, I was stuck there. After laying in bed, staring at the ceiling for half an hour, I decided I'd feel better if I got up and walked around the property. I had never been over the whole thing, and some exercise might do me some good.

Most of it was what you'd expect. Very pretty, but somewhat bland, farmland. Fields bordered by fences that still needed repairs if the place wasn't going to become a subdivision, and on the back of the property, the irregular border of woods that straddled the line between my property and the one behind.

It was at the edge of those woods that I noticed an irregular stand of trees. From a distance, they blended in with the woods behind them, but closer up, they were obviously different. Large, twisting trees with white bark speckled red, they had sharp looking leaves of a mottled green-grey that looked vaguely diseased. I wasn't a plant guy, but I was still surprised at how odd the trees looked. I took out my phone to take a picture, but as I was lining up the shot, I noticed the dark shadow crouched in the middle of the strange trees.

It was a well.

Four-feet high and made of rough stone, it almost looked like something from a children's storybook. However, unlike many childhood ideas of a well, there was no well house or pitched roof above it, no rope and bucket to send down into the depths. Instead the well was capped with what appeared to be a large stone lid, though it was hard to say for certain because of the wax.

A thick, uneven layer of reddish-brown wax coated the lid and upper third of the well's outer wall, sealing it like a bottle. I approached it slowly, feeling a dim buzz of apprehension at the strangeness of it all. Who would do this, and why?

I reached forward and ran my finger across the wax. It was hard, but somehow still greasy to the touch after who knew however many years it had been there. Who would...Oh, God. Is this where he put the other bodies?

The thought terrified me for several reasons, and I began walking back to the house immediately. I would periodically look behind me as though I expected some dark monster to be following me back from the woods, and it was only when I reached the front porch that I took out my cell phone again and called Willie Band.

"Hey, Cap. Been a minute since I heard from you. How've you been?"

Normally I would have gone into some banter with Willie before getting into business, but I was in no mood.

"Willie, I'm out at Killian Farms. Didn't you inspect this property for me last year?"

There was a brief pause and then: "Yeah, yeah I did. Nice little farm out there. Why? Something come up?"

"Well, I'm out walking the property today and I found a weird well near the woods out back. And I don't remember your report ever saying anything about a well."

A longer pause this time. "A well, you said? Like a well house, or a well pump or what kind of well are you talking about?"

I gripped the phone tighter. "No, like a big, old stone well. With a lid on it and something that looks like fucking wax sealing it. That kind of well."

"I'll be honest with you, Cap. I don't remember seeing any well out there. And something like you're talking about...well, I'd remember that or have noted it in my report. You say I didn't?"

"No, I went back through it just a couple of days ago. No well."

"Well, hell, I'm sorry. I don't see how I missed it, but I must have. Mistakes will happen, but I hate that. I pride myself on being thorough. I'll take some off my next fee to make up for it." When I didn't respond, he went on. "Speaking of which, any business you need doing at the moment?"

Letting out a sigh, I sat down on the porch steps. "No, not just now. I'll let you know when I do."

When Willie spoke next, his voice was softer and I could hear sympathy in it. "I understand. I heard some of

---

171

what happened, and that was a raw deal. The other guy, Neal…he was always a bit squinty-looking to me. But keep your chin up, Cap. It'll get better."

I nodded to no one in particular. "Sure. Thanks Willie. Talk to you later."

I went back inside and looked at the land plat and the aerial photos I had of the farm. Maybe I was missing it, but I saw no sign of that well or stand of trees either place. I then put in a call to the lawyer who had handled the title search and closing, but he was as surprised as Willie had been. Apparently, no one knew about the well.

Which left me with three options. Ignore it, call the sheriff and have them come out and investigate it, or look into it myself. I didn't like the idea of unearthing some watery tomb full of murder victims, but I liked the idea of the publicity a bunch of skeletons might generate, either now or later after I'd sold it off without disclosing it, even less.

If I looked on my own and it was nothing, then no harm, no foul. I wouldn't have stirred things up for no reason. If there was something sinister in there, better I knew first so I could make an informed decision on what to do. On who, if anybody, needed to be told.

Still, I was getting ahead of myself. First I needed to see what was in the well.

****

I rustled around in the barn and stable for any tools I might use, but there were none to be found. The place had been picked clean long ago, I supposed. Sighing, I got in my car and drove into town. There was a big chain hardware store out near the interstate, but instead I went to the local Mom and Pop store near what faded signs dubiously declared was the "historic downtown" of the town of Galen. My thought was if I shopped local I might accrue some goodwill that could eventually translate to a sale, but when I went up to the counter with my wire basket of tools and rope, the woman at the counter gave me a suspicious glance. Her mouth set in a thin, tight line, she began to ring up my stuff.

"Hi, my name is Scott. I'm staying up at the Killian place outside of town." Feeling like I was swallowing a piece of gristle, I added, "I just moved here."

The woman paused, glancing up at me briefly before going back to her tally. "I know who you are. I don't mean to be unkind, but that's a bad place you have there. It's always been a bad place." She hit the total button on the old register, and it rattled and whirred before giving her the final cost. "That'll be eighty-three dollars even."

I felt worry crawling up from my belly. This was a big expense for something I didn't know existed before that morning. Still, spend a little now or lose a lot later. Better to go ahead and deal with it. Handing her my credit card, I tried to smile. "Yeah, I heard about the place's...bad history. But I've been in the real estate business for awhile now. Most places have had something bad happen at some point, right? But they've had good stuff happen there too. I don't know about you, but I feel like with some time and the right people, any place can be good again." This was a paraphrase of a little speech I had given five years earlier when I was trying to convince a couple that the brownstone I was selling them wasn't cursed just because the former owner had hung himself in the spacious upstairs walk-in closet. Unlike that couple, this lady seemed unmoved. If anything, she seemed angrier.

"Well that's some ripe bullshit you're peddlin'. That might fly where you come from, but around here we know better. And I don't know what 'history' lesson you've been given about that place, but I 'spect you didn't get the full story."

My smile was gone now, but I was more curious than irritated. The woman was clearly upset, but why? What was it to her? And why did she think I didn't know the details of what happened? I actually asked her that last question, and she just stared at me a moment as though I'd asked the silliest thing in the world before responding.

"Because if you knew much about that place, you'd never set foot there again."

****

I tried my best to shake off my encounter in the hardware store as I drove back to the farm, and by the time I'd made it halfway I'd turned my focus back to what I had bought and what I had planned. A flat-head screwdriver and hammer to break through the wax seal. Work gloves and a painter's mask. A high-powered flashlight that was waterproof. A bucket to lower down to see if there was water or…whatever down at the bottom of the well, as well as lots of rope. And finally, a small hatchet and a pack of blue plastic tarps.

Even while I had been in the store, a part of me had been preparing for the eventuality of my wanting to get rid of bodies. The idea was gruesome, and odds were, wholly unnecessary, as it was probably a boring, normal well that contained nothing other than maybe some spiders and old, smelly water. And even if I did find something, I hadn't decided that I was going to be doing anything other than call the authorities. But in my feverish, panicked state, I wanted to keep all my options open. Be prepared for anything. Most of all, I wanted it over with. So as soon as I reached the house, I grabbed up the bucket full of stuff and began walking purposefully out to the odd stand of trees.

It was just as I remembered it, though it looked vaguely more sinister this time. Whether that was due to the fading afternoon sun or the crazy woman at the store with her foreboding looks and cryptic warnings, it was hard to say. Either way, the sooner I started, the sooner I'd be done.

The wax was surprisingly resistant to my makeshift screwdriver chisel, and I started growing frustrated as the screwdriver's head kept slipping and doing little damage with each jolting impact of the hammer. Feeling a flush of reckless anger, I reared back and swung the hammer as hard as I could. It hit the butt of the screwdriver solidly before sliding off to strike my hand with enough force that I let out a curse and dropped my hammer and chisel to the brown grass surrounding the well.

Cursing again, I massaged my hurt hand as I looked for any sign at all that the wax could be chipped away. This time I found it—a large chunk had been dug out by the tip of the screwdriver. Picking the tools back up gingerly, I set my chisel back in the groove and hit another hard, but more controlled, blow. More chunks scattered away. Now we were getting somewhere.

It took nearly an hour and a half to chip away the wax sealing the stone lid to the top of the well all the way around. My shoulders ached and my arms and hands were numb from fatigue and the constant shockwaves each hammer fall had sent through them as I worked. Now that it was done, I found myself hesitating. Did I really want to do this? Particularly when it was already getting dark and I was so tired? Maybe I should…

No. What I should do was stop being a baby and get it done. I already had enough to worry about without this bullshit taking up all my time and headspace. I'd go ahead and look, and if I found something, I could think about it overnight. Assuming I could even move the stupid lid…

To my surprise, the lid was heavy but not difficult to slide. One hard, steady push with my hands and it slid off and rolled a foot or two before falling over with a soft thud. I had the thought that it looked like a lost quarter from a giant's pocket. Normally, the idea would have made me laugh, but I wasn't in a laughing mood. To the contrary, my guts were crawling like angry snakes as I gripped the greasy lip of the well and looked over into the darkness.

Unsurprisingly, I couldn't see anything. I grabbed the flashlight and turned it on, but it made little difference. I felt like it barely penetrated the inky blackness at all, with the light going down the opposite interior well wall maybe ten feet before petering out. The inner wall was stone, though the stone was much darker than the outside and covered with what looked like grey and black moss. The moss made me think there might be water down there still, but I needed to be sure.

I tied a fifty foot length of rope to the bucket and loaded the bottom with just enough small rocks to make it sink into the water a bit if it found some at the bottom. The encroaching blue-black of twilight made the preparations harder, but I managed and began lowering the bucket down by the rope as I held the flashlight in my teeth. The light bobbed as I worked, the dancing pool of illumination seeming to grow brighter as night settled in around me. How long had I been lowering the rope? I had to be...

I reached the end of the rope. Fifty feet down and the rope was still taut, which meant the bucket hadn't found water or some other obstacle—at least not yet. I weighed my options and decided to go ahead and pull up the bucket. I could tie more rope and keep going, but it was almost completely dark now. Better to start fresh in the morning.

I grabbed the bucket as it crested the lip of the well. Inspecting it with the flashlight, I saw nothing new other than a few smudges of dirt. Irritated, I sat it down and peered back down in the well. Exactly how deep...

That's when I saw the light down there. A dim, brief flicker of yellow fire or candlelight, flaring sharp and bright compared to the utter darkness that surrounded it. I let out a small gasp, but then it was gone, the afterimage lingering in my eyes like summer lightning before fading away just as quickly. How was that possible?

The answer was that it wasn't. I was exhausted and stressed out and was freaking myself out over nothing. Imagining shit.

I chided myself for being so weak-minded, but that didn't stop me from feeling a desperate need to get back to the house and away from the well. I awkwardly tried to pick up the giant coin of a stone lid to recover the well for the moment, but it was too heavy. I could lift one end to my knees, but no farther. I certainly wasn't getting it back on the well by myself, not when I was so tired and it was dark.

Giving up on it, I worked my way between the trees and began heading toward the house. I was walking as fast as I could manage without it being called a run, and in a few minutes I made it into the yard. I felt a strange kind of gratitude toward the house then, as though it was some safe haven or protector from whatever strangeness might be laying in wait out in the dark.

I felt less comforted when I woke the next morning.

****

The first sensation I had was of something on my face. A thin membrane of crustiness that pulled the skin around my mouth tight and began to shift and crack as I worked my lips sleepily. Waking up more at the strange feeling, I touched my face and felt something flake off against my fingertips. It was brown and looked a little like dirt or clay. Then I sat up with a start.

What it really looked like was a dried-out remnant of the wax that had sealed the well.

I leapt out of bed and ran to the bathroom, my throat working at the foul taste on my tongue and lips. Finding my face in the mirror, I saw there was a reddish-brown smear around my mouth, almost like the faded makeup of a tragic clown. I washed my face and what was left came away easily. Brushing my teeth and swishing mouthwash took care of most of the lingering bad taste in my mouth as well. But it did little for the pounding dread in my heart.

What could have caused that? It didn't look like snot or spit, but how could it have been wax from out at the well?

I went back to the bedroom and looked for any signs

of wax or dirt or something that could explain it. I saw a few stains on my pillowcase of the same color, but that didn't… On the nightstand, I saw a large chunk of the wax laying there like some kind of sinister fossil—a piece of amber with a frozen piece of this place's dark history nestled somewhere deep inside.

How had that gotten there? Had I brought it back with me? Surely not. But then I was kind of out of it the night before—freaked out and tired, I had crashed almost immediately after making sure all the doors and windows were secure.

Still, why had I brought back a piece of that wax? And what was I doing? Eating it in my sleep?

I felt my stomach roil at the thought, but it also made me realize I was starving. I hadn't eaten since early the day before, and now it was catching up with me. Leaving the wax where it lay on the nightstand, I went to the kitchen and poured a big bowl of cereal. I stood at the sink eating it mechanically, my eyes staring at nothing as my mind continued to work. The first priority was getting back out to the well and seeing what else I could see. If I saw nothing of note, I'd get the lid back on somehow and reseal the outside with concrete. Then I could get back to figuring out how to get rid of the place for good.

It was as I was chewing the last of the cereal that my eyes wandered to the linoleum floor. It was new flooring—a bright clean white punctuated with small black diamonds. It was only because it was so clean that I noticed the footprints dimly outlined by the morning sunlight. I stopped chewing and sat the bowl down before crouching down to look at the floor.

There were two sets of footprints, one small and the other even smaller. Delicate, feminine feet, or maybe the feet of a child. Looking directly at the floor, you wouldn't even see them. But at an angle, with the sun just right and on this new floor, you could make out a thin film that had been left behind.

What the fuck.

The floor was less than a year old, and aside from the workers and the inspector, I was the first person to be in the house as far as I knew. I certainly should have been the only one in there barefoot, and the trail of footprints crossing the linoleum weren't mine.

But they were heading toward my bedroom.

I licked my teeth again, tasting the ghost of that foul taste lingering behind the toothpaste and mouthwash. What had happened last night? Had someone been in the house?

No. I needed to get ahold of my shit. I couldn't start freaking out over every little thing. I didn't have the luxury of freaking out over every little thing. I wasn't trying to be the dumbass who hangs around when a crazy killer is stalking him or a house is clearly possessed, but I really had no proof that anything had happened beyond I maybe wiped my face with some wax when I was asleep. I didn't know how that would have happened, but that didn't mean anything sinister was going on. And I wasn't to the point where I could just abandon the only asset or home I had left because I was "creeped out".

Still, I was creeped out. And the idea of going back out to that well by myself terrified me. I kept thinking about that dim light down in the dark. Yes, I'd almost certainly imagined it, but the memory still had power over me. Power that had only grown now that I had woken up to all this strangeness. I needed help. Someone I could trust to keep their mouth shut if we found something weird, not because they were especially loyal to me, but because they liked getting paid.

I went back in the bedroom and grabbed my phone off the bed. I hadn't charged it the night before, so it was nearly dead, but it had enough juice for this call. It'd be short.

"Yeah Cap? Something else come up with the farm?"

"Willie, how long would it take you to get back out here? I need your help with something."

****

It was two o'clock in the afternoon before Willie pulled up in an old, battered pickup truck. He had been driving to an inspection on the other side of the state, but either my words or my tone convinced him that he could postpone that to another day. I'd never been happier to see him, and it took some restraint to not give him a hug when he ambled up to the house.

I'd spent the last five hours doing miserable laps inside the house and out in the yard, never staying in any one spot for long because I was restless and uncomfortable everywhere. I had an inner voice that kept suggesting I go on and handle it myself, not involve outsiders, be a man and take care of my business. But then I would think about going back to that stand of trees and peering down into that open well by myself. The voice would fall silent for awhile then, and I'd go back to pacing.

"So where is this place?"

I pointed in the general direction of the well and Willie nodded. Grabbing a bag out of the back of the pickup, he started heading that way and after a moment I followed. Normally I would have tried to make awkward small talk during the walk out there, but not today. I felt like I was sitting on the edge of a razor, and social niceties and awkwardness were some of the first things I shed. I didn't have a choice—if I didn't keep getting rid of things that didn't matter right now—worries, thoughts, mights and maybes, I felt like the weight of it all would cut me in two. All that mattered right now was solving the well problem.

We were thirty yards from the well when Willie stopped. He stared ahead for a moment, and as I slowed to a halt beside him, he turned to look at me. Gone was his normal carefree, vaguely jovial expression. It had been replaced by a look that was closer to worry or even fear. And when he spoke, his voice was different too. More serious.

"Scott, I...I don't remember that. I swear I don't."

I frowned. "What do you mean?"

He glanced back ahead, his head shaking slowly as he spoke. "I mean...I don't remember ever seeing those funny-looking trees or that well when I was out here. I know that sounds crazy, and it must be crazy. I must have just forgotten, but how do you forget something odd like that? I know trees, but I couldn't tell you what those are, at least not from a distance. And a well like that? This far out from the house or any outbuilding? I..." He rubbed his chin and glanced back at me with a ghost of his usual smile. "I guess I'm just getting old. But I swear...Anyhow, sorry, it just threw me for a second. Let's get back to it."

I felt my stomach clenching as we walked the rest of the distance to the well. Everything was as I had left it. Rope and tools on one side of the open well, the stone lid on the other. But at first, all Willie was interested in was the broken ring of wax that remained on the upper portion of the well's outer wall. He ran his fingers along it and grimaced slightly before looking up at me.

"This is the stuff that was sealing the well up?"

I nodded, swallowing weakly at the memory of it being on and possibly in my mouth. "Yeah, I guess it's some kind of weird wax or something? I didn't know. It could be common and I wouldn't know. You ever seen something like that?"

He wiped his hands on his pants with something akin to disgust and took a step back from the well. "Yeah...I have. I think I have. But not for sealing a well or anything like that." He fell silent and studied the outside of the well for a few seconds before speaking again. "My wife Clarissa died of bowel cancer three years ago. She...well, she was the best thing that ever happened to me. She was raised in Haiti, and for our twentieth I took her back there to celebrate our anniversary. Her grandmother was still alive and lived an hour from Port-au-Prince, which is the capital there. She had to be a hundred, but she looked much younger. Stayed busy too. She was one of the big priestesses around there, you see."

He caught my eye as he went on. "Voodoo, hoodoo, blessings and curses, you name it. I never talked to her about it directly, but Clarissa told me stuff. Said she had seen enough growing up to know it was real too. I don't mind telling you, it all spooked me more than a little.

"Half an hour sitting in the little store she ran back of her house, all the shelves packed with bones and symbols and different concoctions...well, I had to step out. Felt like everything was pressing in on me."

Willie raised his hand and waived it. "Point is, before I left, I saw a row of clay jars she had on the wall. They all had lids that were sealed with something that looks very much like this." He pointed to the reddish-brown wax on the well. I don't know what the stuff is, but I know what Clarissa said the jars were when I asked."

I felt like someone was standing on my chest. "What were they?"

He looked down at the ground. "Spirit jars. She said if someone got a bad spirit after them, her grandma could try to trap it. Would use a little of the person's blood to help seal it in a jar. It was supposed to trick the spirit into thinking they were already inside whoever they were after." He shrugged, looking uncomfortable. "Probably a bunch of bullshit, but I don't know. My Clarissa was a sensible woman. Smarter than me for sure. And I can tell you she believed it well enough."

I felt numb, but I tried to push past it. I could see how this was headed, and I couldn't afford Willie leaving me before this was done. "Willie, I know this is all strange. It freaks me out too, especially after what you just told me. But I have to get this resolved. I didn't tell you this before, but people were murdered out here years ago. I just need to know that their bodies...well, their bones at this point...aren't down in that well. Then I can seal it back and sell it off as I'm able."

Willie looked back up at me, his eyebrows raised.

"Cap...Look Scott, I'm sorry. But I think you're better off just sealing it up now and calling it done."

I shook my head. "I'm in a bad spot right now. If someone buys it and finds bodies, there will be legal problems. They will sue me, saying I covered it up. Even if I beat the suit, it'll be expensive and kill whatever professional reputation I have left. I just need to know what's down in the well. It's probably just water, right? I just need to check it, then I can stop worrying about it."

Willie looked at me for several seconds before letting out a sigh. "Damn it. Okay. We'll see what we can figure out. But after we make an effort, we're done, right?"

I nodded. "Right. Just doing due diligence here. Nothing more."

****

Willie had come more prepared than I had. His bag contained a large bundle of nylon cord, as well as two lanterns, several glow sticks, and miscellaneous tools. When I commented on it, he nodded. "Yeah, I swung by the house on the way out here and got some stuff. At the very least we should be able to see how deep this bastard goes."

First he broke one of the glow sticks and shook it until it turned a bright orange. He walked back to the well and was about to throw it in when he stopped and made a grunting sound. Turning back to me, he pointed to something inside the well. "Did you know that was there?"

I stepped closer to see what he was looking at. Halfway around the inner wall of the well the stone was irregular. No, not just irregular, but intentionally different.

Evenly spaced two-foot long grooves in the wall descended down into the dark.

"Is that a fucking ladder cut into the wall?"

Willie looked back at the well. His voice was slow and strange when he spoke again. "Yeah...I think that's exactly what it is." Without another word, he tossed the orange glow stick down the well. We watched it as traveled through the silent black, getting smaller and smaller as it went. I thought it was going to fade out of sight, but then it seemed to stop. Willie gave a slight nod. "It looks like it hit the bottom. Now the second test."

He turned on one of the small LED lanterns he had brought and tied it to the end of the nylon cord. He said it was over 300 feet long, which he thought would be more than enough. As soon as he was satisfied the lantern was secure, he started lowering it down. I could see more of the well's inner wall this time, but it was largely unremarkable other than the carved ladder that continued down the wall past my ability to discern it at a distance.

Down and down it went, and for a while it seemed like it disappeared, but when it hit the bottom it must have tipped over, as light flared up a short distance from the faint orange illumination offered by the glow stick. Nodding, Willie looked over the edge. "I can't see shit down there. It's too far."

I was looking too, and I agreed. Other than the lights, there was no way to tell what was down there. Willie was already trying to pull the lantern back up, but it didn't seem to be moving. I glanced up at him and I could see the concern etched on his face. He saw me looking and gave a nervous laugh.

"Must be caught on something down there. A root or something. Give me a second." He started jerking the cord, trying to shift the lantern and dislodge it from whatever it was hung on. I looked back down into the well and saw the light of the lantern shift almost imperceptibly as Willie's motions traveled down the length of cord. But then I saw...

Did something just move in front of the light down there? I felt a thrill of fear, and almost immediately my mind started explaining it away. It had probably flipped back onto its bottom again, so the roof of the lantern was blocking most of the light now. Except it hadn't looked like that. And now...yes, now I could see the light again just as it was. It was almost as though a slow-moving cloud had passed in front of the sun. Except there were no clouds or sun down in that place. Nothing but the dark and...what?

"Here we go." Willie was pulling it up now, and I saw he was visibly sweating even though the day was cool and he had been fine moments before. Had he seen something pass in front of the light the same as me? I almost asked him, but decided to wait. Better to save those questions for when we were back at the house.

It was as the lantern crested the top of the well that I first saw the piece of paper. It looked old and impossibly dry, particularly given the dank place it had just come from. Yet it was somehow still strong and pliable, having been tied in a knot around the cord just above the lantern itself. Willie let out a curse as his eyes found it, backing away from the well, the cord and the lantern trailing along with him. I followed, my fear momentarily supplanted by a kind of curious wonder, like the person who sees something heavy or sharp heading toward them the second before a freak accident takes their life. I crouched down and grabbed at the lantern, missing it. A second try and I got it, holding onto it until Willie finally stopped and dropped the cord.

Reaching out with a shaking hand, I freed the paper from around the cord and opened it up. There were two words written inside.

Hello there.

****

"No, sorry. There's no fucking way."

Willie was moving at a fast pace back toward the house, his bag banging against his thigh as he awkwardly galloped somewhere between a walk and a run. He'd responded to my question, to my plea that he stay and help me some more, without even pausing or turning around. I kept following him, but my heart was already sinking. It wasn't that I didn't understand where he was coming from. I was terrified too.

Still, when we reached his truck, I tried one last time. "Willie, I will pay you twice your normal fee, okay? I know this is freaky shit, but I need to figure out what it all means. And I don't have anywhere else to go." As I added this last, Willie slung his bag back into the bed of his truck and turned to glare at me.

"That's bullshit, man. First off, I didn't come out here just to get paid. I know you're in a tight spot. And you've always been a good guy, so I don't mind trying to help. But that shit?" He pointed out in the direction of the well. "I've lived long enough and seen enough to know there's some things you don't mess with. And you should never have messed with that well to start with."

I felt an odd flare of anger and defensiveness at that,

even though I knew in some dim corner of my mind that he was right. "Oh, that's right. I forgot you were the fucking expert. You and your dead wife."

Willie's lips thinned and for a moment he looked like he might hit me. He closed his eyes a moment and let out a breath before continuing. "And that's another thing. You've been acting a bit squirrelly ever since I got here. Off. I tried to chalk it up to you being upset, and maybe that's all it is, but I don't know. I think you need to get out of this place as much as I do."

I was already shaking my head as he finished. "I can't do that. This is all I have."

Willie's eyes flared with anger again as he poked me in the chest. "You've got your life. Your sanity. Your soul." He rubbed his face tiredly as he looked past me toward the woods. "This isn't a good place. You want to talk about what I know? What I've seen? Truth is, I don't know much. But don't you think it's funny that the one guy you call to help you has seen something similar to that well before? Do you think it's coincidence that you're getting warnings to stop what you're doing and get away?" He spit into the grass near his feet. "I don't. My pa used to say that coincidence is what stupid people call things they don't understand, and I tend to agree."

"Willie, just…" He raised his hand, cutting me off.

"I don't think you're stupid, but I do think you're being blind. There's things you're not telling me, and that's okay. It's your business. But there's something down in that fucking well." His voice was trembling now. "And it's nothing good. So I'm leaving. Right now. You want to come? I'll wait five minutes for you to pack some clothes.

Hell, you can sleep on our couch for a couple of nights until you find a place to stay if you want. But I'm done with this place and I won't be coming back."

I struggled to find words to respond. A part of me, a big part, knew he was right. This wasn't a good place. It was dangerous and I didn't understand it. And if I stayed here trying to understand it, it was liable to swallow me whole.

But there was another part as well. As he'd spoke, the strange taste from that morning had begun to fill my mouth again even as anger and frustration filled my heart. He was a coward and disloyal. I had given him a good bit of business over the last few years, and he was too chickenshit to help me explore an old well? It wasn't his money on the line. His life on the line.

And yes, the note was creepy. I didn't have an explanation for it, but there had to be one. Maybe the paper had been down in the well for years and gotten tangled up in the cord. I was upset, it all happened fast, and I just imagined it was actually tied around it. Or maybe Willie was fucking with me. I hadn't paid that close attention when he was tying the lantern to the cord. Maybe he'd put the note on there himself and sent it down before I saw.

The rational part of my mind rebelled against these ideas, but I could feel the weak tug of logic and reason failing against the gravitational pull of that place. Something was wrong. I wanted to go with Willie, but I couldn't. Something wouldn't let me. I wanted to beg him to drag me away. To knock me out if he had to, but get me away from that place. But for some reason, I couldn't.

"Fuck you, you fucking coward. Go on then."

Willie's expression wasn't angry this time. Just sad. He held my gaze for a moment before dropping his own. "I'll pray for you, Cap. I really will."

And with that, he was gone.

****

I already knew I was going down in the well. I could see the dim outlines of the plan coiled in the shade of the strange thoughts and impulses that were growing up in the darker corners of my mind. I tried to dispute the idea, but the best I could do was delay it. It was already past four, but I just had time to go back to town and get more supplies before the hardware store closed. It occurred to me that it would be faster and simpler just to go to the store at the interstate, but some part of me wanted to go back to that scowling woman and her grim warnings. Maybe it was the part of me that still held out some dim hope I could be saved.

I entered the store twenty minutes before closing, but I saw no one at the front counter. Moving down the aisles, I gathered up extra rope, two lanterns, another flashlight, and a handful of metal stakes. I had some vague idea of tying ropes to several of the trees surrounding the well and use a combination of them and the handholds to climb down in it. Answer once and for all what was actually down in the well.

I felt disconnected from the plan. From everything. I could see how stupid it was, how downright insane, but it was as though I was a detached bystander in my own...

"We're closed."

The voice came from the back of the store, and when I looked around, I saw the same woman from the day before walk toward me. As she approached, I noticed her eyes were red-rimmed and puffy, as though she had been crying. I offered her an awkward smile and held up the items I'd collected.

"Sorry, I didn't know. I just wanted to get this stuff if it's alright."

Her face hardened. "No, it's not all right. Get the hell out of here. It's your fault it's started back. It's all your damned fault." Her voice faltered at the end, and I could see she was on the verge of tears. I almost left right then, but something stopped me. I needed to know what she was talking about.

"I don't understand. What's my fault? What happened?"

She stopped halfway down the aisle, shaking her head slowly as she stared blankly ahead. "They took my grandbaby last night. Others too. It's just like it was all those years ago."

I felt a panicked buzz growing in my ears. "Who took them? What are you talking about?"

Her eyes snapped up to me. "There's something out there at that damn farm. Always has been. It started taking people twenty years back. Changed that Killian family into...well, they weren't right. Not anymore. They say the boy killed them all? I say he was doing God's work. After that, no one else went missing. No more strange goings on." She paused, her eyes narrowing. "Until you showed up."

I started backing up under her gaze. "I'm sorry, but I didn't..."

She waved her hands. "Go. Get out. Take it if you

want. I can't stop you." She was freely crying now, and I wanted to say something to comfort her or at least lessen my own guilt.

"Is there something I can do? I'm so sorry. Can I help look for your grandchild?"

The woman let out a bitter laugh as she stared at me. "You goddamned fool. She's not missing anymore."

I frowned in confusion. "What?"

Her smile was almost a snarl. "Oh she came back today. They all did. God help us, they always come back."

****

I made it back to the well by five-thirty, and though I realized the fading sun wouldn't matter much once I was in the dark below, I still felt a panicked flutter at seeing how quickly the day was passing away. I selected three of the stoutest trees surrounding the well and tied ropes around them, trailing their lengths down into the well. Each rope was over four hundred feet, so they should reach the bottom easily, giving me several options back up if the handholds proved too slick or untrustworthy.

I made all these preparations to try and placate the sanity I had left, but it didn't work. As I tied a lantern to my waist and tucked one of the ropes under my arm, a part of me began to scream like a terrified bird trapped inside my skull. When I began to climb down the ladder built into the well, it fell ominously silent.

The handhold ladder was surprisingly easy to use, and after the first few awkward steps, I developed a comfortable rhythm as I carefully worked my way down into the darkness of the well. The air around me was quickly becoming cooler, but it also seemed to be growing thicker as well.

Part of that might have been the smell—as I went, my nostrils were filling with the smells of wet earth and stagnant water, but also something else. Some kind of undersmell that I didn't recognize but sent up a new flurry of panicked flutters from some small and shrinking corner of my mind.

My hands ached by the time I reached the dim orange glow of the light stick Willie had thrown down. I put out an exploratory foot to test the ground, expecting it to find water or at least unstable muck, but the ground seemed firm and dry. Even when I put my full weight on it, the black earth didn't give in the slightest.

I had been looking down the last few rungs for any signs of…well, anything. Some soggy horror waiting to jump out at me and drag me down, I guess. But I'd seen nothing but the glow stick.

Firmly on the ground, I held up the lantern and began looking around. I sucked in a breath as the light found an opening in the wall. It was a tunnel. And not just a small dug out path in the earth. It was tall and wide enough for me to walk into without stooping and lined on all sides with a flat, black stone that seemed to absorb the electric glow of my lantern more than it reflected it.

Again there was a flutter in my mind, but it was feeble. Futile. There was no real question about what came next.

I entered the tunnel and followed its corridor until it came to a branching path. After a moment of debate, I turned right. As I continued on, I made several more turns, always seemingly at random, though I wondered if I wasn't listening to some instinct or intuition. I had no idea where I was going or what I would find, but it didn't change my growing certainty I was heading the right way.

For a time I had the vague sense I was moving in the direction of town, but then that shifted as it began to feel more like I was headed back the way I had come. I had no clear reason for either feeling, but I was past questioning much of anything. My whole world had become lit by the twin suns of fear and the implacable need to push forward, no matter the danger or the cost. I had to see this through.

The tunnel was featureless aside from its stony skin and the geography of its various paths, and I began to wonder if I would just roam inside the veins of that place, a wandering blood cell floating aimlessly until time or starvation slowly withered me away. As I had the thought, I saw an end to the tunnel ahead of me.

It was the well. Or at least it looked like the well, though I saw no sign of the glow stick or the trailing ropes that I had left behind. I looked around for any other sign or clue of where I was at, but there was none on the ground or walls other than the same kind of stony ladder trailing up into what I hoped was a night sky. I began to climb, this time without the security of a rope under my arm, and while I never faltered, by the time I reached the top, my hands and arms were shaking with the exertion. I pulled myself over the lip of the well and lay in the prickly grass for a few moments while I breathed in cool air that didn't smell of rotten water or sour earth.

It was as I was standing up that I realized something was different. My lantern had fallen away at some point, and my clothes were wrong. Different. My jeans and t-shirt had been replaced with canvas work pants and a button-down checked shirt. Even my shoes were strange and unfamiliar—thick-soled boots of a type I'd never worn, though they seemed to fit fine. I began to look around and saw that the trees looked the same as those I had left behind. So did the well, except for the lack of dark wax coating its upper wall. Looking farther out, I saw a house in the distance that looked just like the one I had slept in for the past several days.

I walked to the house, and as I approached I grew in my certainty that it was the same house, though it was newer looking and there were unfamiliar, older model cars parked outside. I already suspected where I was...when I was, but then a woman came out on the porch and beckoned to me.

"Come on in, Malcolm. Dinner's going to get cold and your family is all ready and waiting." The woman gave me a smile, and though she had probably been pretty enough when Malcolm had married her, that beauty had turned ghastly now. I didn't remember what Malcolm had known, but I still had the dull instinct that this was Malcolm's wife, or at least what his wife had become.

I went up the steps and past her into the house, doing my best not to brush against her as I went. She closed the door behind me as she followed me inside, and as we moved toward the dining room, she began to sing softly.

It was a terrible, discordant song that made me feel sick inside, as though just hearing it was somehow corrupting and poisoning me. I suppressed a shudder as I entered the dining room and saw the rest of Malcolm Killian's family there.

His parents and two sisters all shared the same alien wrongness that pervaded his wife. Their eyes were dark and knowing, and their mouths twisted slightly as they greeted me with Malcolm's name. I felt a new surge of fear at their gaze, wondering if they could see me in Malcolm, an imposter somehow in their midst.

But no. The father, Malcolm's father, my father, it was getting harder to tell the difference now, patted my arm and asked how I had enjoyed my trip to the well. Had it answered all my questions? Made everything clear?

I just nodded numbly and sat down. I still wasn't sure what to do or how to do it, and while I didn't think they knew I was in Malcolm now, they were beginning to understand that something was wrong. Things had not gone according to their plan.

One of his sisters, I think her name was Elisabeth, leaned forward and studied me intently. She asked me to describe what I had seen. It was clearly a test, and I had no idea what the right answer was. They were about to figure out that, Malcolm or not, I wasn't part of...whatever they were.

Then an image came to me from outside my own mind. I think it was a Malcolm thought, trying to help me in my ignorance. There was a shotgun in the pantry. And there was an axe on the back porch. I didn't know if I could kill them all, but Malcolm was strong and fast, and I had to try.

Excusing myself, I quickly stood and went to the kitchen. I was going to go for the gun in the pantry first, but Malcolm's wife...her name was Katie...was following me. And she was singing again.

I felt my vision starting to blur, and as I staggered, I felt her hand close on my shoulder like a band of iron. Pain flared as I wrenched away, and I felt hot wetness springing up where her grip had torn Malcolm's flesh. The door to the porch was closer and I flung it open. When I grabbed the axe and turned, Katie was almost on top of me, and I swung it blindly with all the strength I could muster through the pain.

It struck her in the neck hard enough to snap her spine as she tumbled to the ground. When I saw she was still moving, I struck her two more times before moving on to the pantry. The rest had heard some of the commotion, and Malcolm's father was opening the door as I raised the shotgun.

An hour later and I was nearly done with my work. I had killed them all. They hadn't even put up much of a fight. And I had used my…his wheelbarrow to carry them all to the well and dump them in.

I was going back to get Katie. Maybe if I could change that detail, get her body into the well and figure out how to seal it like it was in the future where I opened it, I could change things. Keep it sealed for good this time.

But no. I was still walking back up to the house to get her body when I saw lights coming down the road. It was the deputies. Someone must have heard the gunshots or seen me wheeling bodies into the woods. I wouldn't have time to dump Katie down the well or try to change things. And however the well got sealed, it wasn't going to be me that did it.

I walked on inside and stumbled to the kitchen. Katie's legs were still sticking in through the back door and

I sat down next to them. I didn't know this woman, but I still felt a strange sort of loss as though I did. Maybe I really was dissolving into Malcolm. Or maybe I was just mourning what I had done and what I had lost.

Either way, it didn't matter. It was going to be over soon enough. At least my part.

I felt in my pants pocket for the folding knife I already knew was there. As I heard the heavy footfalls of deputies coming on the front porch, I slid the knife into my left work boot.

I had it on good authority they wouldn't find it there.

The True Horror Movie Experience

Part One

I woke up to her staring at me. I think some part of me, some deep instinct, had felt her gaze even though she was silent and almost invisible in the darkened corner of my bedroom. I remember having a moment of confusion as I wondered if I was dreaming…or if I was awake, if I was seeing things.

But no, she was there. A young woman in her late twenties or early thirties, dressed in jean shorts and a purple t-shirt, chin-length blonde hair framing a face of hard angles and deep shadows. I sat up with a start, but she didn't move a muscle.

"Miss? Hello?"

No response.

I felt my fear, and my anger, begin to grow. "Ma'am? Why are you in my house? Are you high or something?"

She moved then, the motion after such stillness making her seem like a statue come to life. Leaning forward, I saw more of her face. She was crying.

"I wish. N-no, I'm fully here. For now."

I felt my anger cooling a bit. Maybe she was a junkie,

but maybe she was just confused or needed help. "Lady, did someone hurt you? Or did you fall or something? You're in my house. And I don't know you."

The woman gave a short and bitter laugh. "So you say."

She wasn't acting violent or even clearly crazy, but this was already past the threshold of weirdness that I felt I should be dealing with without calling the cops. I eased my hand over to the nightstand where my phone was charging. "Look, I don't know what's going on, but I'm kind of freaked out. If you don't go, I'm going to call 911 and let them figure this out, okay? Do you want to go, or do you want me to call?"

She shrugged. I could see her shirt said "Be the change, not the doll hair." What the fuck did that…

"I can't leave. They won't let me. It's part of the game."

"What game? What are you talking about?" I was already punching 911 as I spoke, half asking the questions just to stall her. She clearly had something fucked up in the head, and I really didn't want to get stabbed because I waited too long to call for help.

The woman just stared at me as I talked to 911, and it was only when I was finished with the initial details to the dispatcher that she interrupted.

"Please don't let them take me."

I couldn't help but pull the phone from my ear as I focused on her again. I knew she had to be crazy, a paranoid schizo or something, but the raw sadness and fear in her voice made me doubt myself. It was stupid—crazy people get very genuinely upset about their delusions all the time, it doesn't make them real. But something about this woman made me want to believe her. To help her.

"Don't let who take you? What are you talking about?"

She leaned forward more but stopped when she saw me slightly recoil. "When the cops arrive, they're not really going to be cops. They will send two men. They'll look like twins. They'll even tell you a joke about how they're probably the only twin cops in the world. But they aren't cops and they aren't taking me to jail or to a hospital or whatever."

I heard the dispatcher's voice still talking into the phone and I surprised myself by hanging up on him. I kept studying this strange woman sitting in front of me. "Where do they take you then?"

Her tears had slowed down before, but I saw new tracks glistening down her cheeks as she looked away for a moment. "They take to me to this place they call the Farm, though I don't know what it really is. It's very big and very remote. But that's what they do most nights. They take me to that place." She swallowed and wiped at her eyes. "Sometimes they can't wait. They just get a little ways from here and pull over. Get me out and drag me into the woods. Tear me apart."

I felt my eyes going wide. "Are you saying they…did someone rape you?"

She gave another short, sad laugh as she shook her head. "No. I said they tear me apart. Bite me. Eat me. On the nights that they lose control. The other times…most of the time…they carry me to the Farm. And that's so much worse."

I slid off the bed, my stomach sour with fear. I'd made a mistake not getting away from her sooner. Not staying on the line with 911. She was clearly insane and might be dangerous and I was trapped in here with her. Trying to sound calm, I eased toward the door as I kept talking. "I...um, I see. You look pretty good for someone who's been eaten or whatever."

The woman grimaced as she stood up. "Don't you think I know that, John? I can't explain it. I don't know how or why they're doing it, but every night, when things finally go dark, I wake up back here, with you. Not a mark on me and dressed like it's that first night. I'd think I was living the first night over and over, but it's not always the same. You're...not always the same. So I have to be coming back every night." She gave a shudder. "And then they come and take me again."

She had taken a couple of steps toward me, and I avoided her touch as I stepped out into the hallway. "Look, I think you're just confused or sleepwalking maybe. I don't know how you know my name, but maybe we met once and now I'm in some weird dream you've had? Either way..."

The woman stopped at the doorway and sighed. "I don't know why I keep trying. You never believe me. You never remember." There was a knock at the front door. Her face crumpled as she looked in its direction. "And now it's too late."

I almost reached out for her, tried to comfort her. I wanted her to know I was on her side, whatever side that was, and I was going to try and help her. But then the knock came again, this time harder and more insistent. "I...I'm sorry. Look, let's just talk to them. See if they can help, okay?" She just stared bleakly as I backed down the hall to the living room and on to the front foyer. "Just let me answer the door. I'm not going to let anyone hurt you." The words sounded stupid and hollow as I said them, but then I reminded myself that what the woman was saying was insane. No one was trying to hurt her, and I needed her out of my house. So I opened the door.

And saw a pair of twins in police uniforms smiling at me.

"Evening, sir. We got a 911 call at this residence?" The one on the right spoke while the left twin just nodded and kept smiling.

I glanced back and saw that the woman wasn't in the doorway of the bedroom anymore. Shit, where had she gone?

"Um, yeah. I…well, there's a woman in my house. I woke up and she was in my bedroom. I've never met her before."

The right twin looked at the left twin with a smirk. "We've heard that one before, eh, Chip?"

Chip looked back at the right twin with a knowing wink. "Indeed we have, Chomp."

I blinked. "I'm sorry. Not trying to be rude. Did you just say his name is Chomp?"

Chomp turned back to give me a squinting perusal. "He said Champ. My name is Champ. Have you been drinking tonight, sir?"

As I went to answer, Chip clicked a flashlight on his

shoulder and shined it in my face. "You can be honest with us, sir. Have you hurt that girl?"

I raised my hands to block the light, and suddenly Chomp…Champ…was gently pushing me back against the doorframe. "Sir, please keep your hands lowered. We don't want any trouble, and I'm sure you don't either."

Fighting down new confused irritation, I shook my head. "I don't. I just want her out and all of you gone."

Champ nodded. "Good. Chip, go secure the interior while I keep an eye on our friend. See if you can find this lady he claims not to know." He chuckled again, his good humor seemingly back. "Although I will say, calling the cops is a hell of a way to end a night of romance." Chip shot past us into the house, and I found myself ignoring Champ's comment to call after the other twin. "Please go easy with her. She's really upset and confused." Champ stepped back and gave another nasty chuckle as I looked down the hall.

Chip had done a cursory look around the living and dining rooms, but then he bypassed the rest and went straight for the dark door leading into my bedroom. The inky black seemed to swallow him as he entered, and only a few seconds later I heard the woman screaming. I started to go back in, and Champ lightly put his hand back on my chest.

"Hold tight, sport. My brother can handle her."

I went to respond, but then I saw them both emerging from the shadows, Chip walking her out with her arms behind her back. The twin looked past her to Champ. "She was in the closet. The fucking closet. It was a classic."

"Is she okay?" Chip ignored me, but Champ stepped

closer as they approached. His breath was hot and strange-smelling as he leaned down to whisper to me.

"She looks fine as paint to me, sport. Lucky break for you, huh? We'll have her out of your hair in no time."

I caught motion out of the corner of my eye as the woman suddenly darted toward me. She called out something, but at the time I didn't understand it, and I was more concerned with Champ hurting her as he turned to stop her. But all he did was grip her shoulders and steer her away from me, and within a second Chip had caught up from behind and they were carrying her out to their patrol car. I trailed behind, somehow more scared and worried now than I had been all night.

"I bet you've never been visited by twin cops before, eh?" Champ's eyes twinkled in the sodium streetlamp as he closed the woman into the back passenger compartment. "Why I bet we're the only pair in the country. Maybe the world."

I nodded numbly. "Yeah, I guess so."

He watched me for a moment before glancing down at the window where the woman was staring out at me. "I guess that makes you double lucky tonight."

I forced myself to look away from her gaze and caught Chip's eye on the far side of the car. "Where are you taking her? Just to the local jail? Or where?"

Chip looked at Champ, who was grinning at me again. "Why sure. That's exactly where we're going. Assuming we don't stop for some grub on the way." He shot a glance at Chip. "What do you think, brother? I know we'll get in trouble, but...hell, sometimes the appetites rule, eh?"

He looked back at me, his face serious now. "Don't you worry, sir. We'll take good care of her. You have a good rest of your evening."

I wanted to ask more, but they were already getting in the car and driving away. The last thing I saw was her looking at me through the back glass as they faded into the night. I felt jittery and unsatisfied as I walked back inside and shut the door. What had she been saying? Something about the owl? What had it been?

"Ask the Owls if I'm telling the truth."

Oh fuck.

When I moved into this house six years ago, I found out it had a security camera covering the front and back yards. Both feeds went to a little computer monitor in the man cave/rumpus room basement, as well as to a hard drive that kept seven days back-up. The cameras were probably ten or fifteen years old, and I found the whole set-up slightly creepy, but I'd never gotten rid of it. It was already installed and running, and it could come in handy if someone ever tried to break-in or mess with my car.

But that had never happened, and over the years I rarely thought about it unless someone commented on one of the fake owls—one sitting on a post in the back yard and the other in a tree next to the driveway. When someone did comment, I would always get embarrassed and explain that it wasn't a decorating choice. It was what the previous owner had set up to hide the security cameras.

My hand was numb as I gripped the knob to the basement door. I half-expected and hoped that I'd check the cameras' computer and find it had died in the last few months without me knowing. But no, it was humming right along, and after re-familiarizing myself with the software, I was able to watch my strange encounter with the twin police officers a few minutes earlier. Trembling slightly, I scrubbed back to the night before.

Oh God. At 1:32 a.m. the night before, a patrol car had pulled up. Two men that looked like the twins got out and went up to the front door. They knocked and waited for someone to answer.

And then I opened the door.

A panicked buzzing began to build in my ears as I double-checked the day and time. No, it wasn't a mistake. It really was from the night before. I even remembered wearing that t-shirt to bed that night.

But I was the only thing that was different. The girl they pulled from the house was the same, if less defiant that time. She walked somberly to the patrol car, and though the video was black and white, I could see enough to guess that was the same shirt and shorts she'd been wearing tonight.

I reached for my phone to call...who? 911? My family across the country? George and Ruby? Who could I call that wouldn't think I was as crazy as I'd thought the woman was? I needed more proof.

So I went back another night. And then another. I went back five nights, and with slight variations, the same thing happened every single time.

How was this possible?

Trembling, I started to call 911 again. I needed to tell someone and I needed to make sure that woman was really okay. That they hadn't...well, that she had gotten somewhere safe.

****

And then I woke up in my bed. I wasn't particularly worried or stressed about anything. I had a few hours of work to do during the day, but that night I was going with George and Ruby to an exclusive "interactive adventure" I'd gotten invited to online. It was called "The True Horror Movie Experience" and was described as "a multi-night tailor-made journey through terror and madness". It sounded weird and awesome, and I had been looking forward to it for...well, for a long time.

At the time, I didn't remember any of the night before. I had no memories of the strange woman in my room, the men who came and took her, or what the Owls showed me after they were gone. I'm telling you this so you can understand that I didn't know. Despite everything that had happened, everything that she had tried to do to warn me, to save us all, none of it mattered because they had taken it all away.

Until they gave it all back.

Piece by bloody piece.

Part Two

We went to a plain, non-descript building on the edge of town. It was nestled in the middle of a bland office park, and if the place had been busy earlier in the day, it was pretty much empty by four o'clock on a Saturday. I pulled into a parking space as George whistled in my ear from the backseat.

"Wow. This place looks super-reputable. I have no bad feelings about this at all."

I saw Ruby shoot him a dark look from beside me. It had been six months since they'd stopped their brief "dating experiment" and while things were still weird at times, I was relieved to see they were acting more like their old selves again. That was one of the reasons I'd wanted them both to come, after all. I was tired of having them bail on plans as soon as they found out the other was going to be there. Besides,

"...it's going to be really cool, guys. I mean the invite was kind of random, but I checked them out online. Lots of rave reviews. They apparently are at the cutting edge of doing these 'interactive adventure' things. Not like that bullshit we went to last year in New York where people just shove you around and scream in your face." I looked to Ruby for support and she nodded, but her expression was still uncertain as she glanced around the parking lot.

George leaned up to look at the building we were parked at. "Fuck, I hope not. I almost punched that one dude that got...well, that disrespected you." I watched in the rearview as he glanced awkwardly at Ruby, who gave him a quick smile and nod. Blushing slightly, he opened his door. "Okay, let's see if this place is even open."

I started to open the door when Ruby touched my arm. "I'm not trying to be a downer, but are you sure about this? He's not wrong about it looking sketchy."

Sighing, I nodded. "I know. But let's make sure this is the right address, and if it is, we can check out how it looks inside." I grinned. "If any of us get a bad vibe, the safe word is penguin. We'll bail." I opened the door and looked out at George. "Hey dickhead. The safe word is penguin."

His eyes widened. "Fuck. We need safe words?"

****

I kept trying to keep control of my nervous excitement as we filled out our questionnaires. This place was fucking awesome. We'd went to the front door, found it unlocked, and entered into a small, plain-looking lobby that contained a sofa, two chairs, and a bored-looking receptionist behind a desk. After we gave them our names, we were immediately escorted through another door into the real office.

It was like something out of a movie. Everything was brightly-lit and clean, with well-dressed people moving to and fro across a large atrium that looked too large and too grand to belong in the office building either aesthetically or physically. A young woman holding a tablet approached us and introduced herself as Swan. She said she'd be our guide and liaison during our adventure, and after we filled out our questionnaires and signed our liability waivers, she'd get started on a brief orientation before the fun began. I glanced at George and Ruby and saw they were as awe-struck as I was. Grinning, I nodded and told her to lead on.

I was working on what had to be the tenth page of the longest form I'd ever filled out when George spoke up beside me.

"So…why us? Or…well, why John? How'd he get picked for…" he gestured around at the softly back-lit walls and clearly expensive furniture of the office we were sitting in, "…all this?"

Swan smiled. "We've been doing promotions and

211

testing like this for a number of years in various places around the world. Utilizing collected internet search and expenditure data in conjunction with our own witches' brew of algorithms, we send out invitations to likely candidates we believe would be interested in what we offer and that can provide useful feedback."

It was Ruby's turn to ask a question now. "Yeah, but…all this? In a…no offense…shitty little office park with no signs up? And John, you had to pay what?"

"A hundred bucks a person." I muttered, glancing between Ruby and Swan with increasing nervousness. It wasn't that the questions weren't valid, but I had a gnawing fear that if we asked too many that they would just take away our clipboards and tell us to leave. Instead, Swan just nodded at me before looking back to Ruby.

Ruby was frowning slightly. "A hundred bucks per for what? A super-exclusive multi-night tailored horror experience? Shit, we paid more than that last year to get shoved around in a warehouse while a dude tried to grab my tits."

The girl chuckled. "I understand. But what you must realize is that the money isn't of any real consequence. We only charge so we get serious applicants. Weed out the kids and the lookieloos." Her cheek twitched slightly. "We are still in the testing and research phase for now, so this work is being done for future profitability, not immediate significant recompense."

I caught Ruby's eye. "Look, it looks legit and cool so far, right?"

She nodded slowly. "It does, but it's just…no, you're right." Ruby looked back at Swan and gestured at her with her pen. "But you better not harvest our organs or some shit."

Swan laughed again. "No, no. Nothing as dramatic as all that."

****

"Congratulations for being selected to participate in The True Horror Movie Experience. This is your orientation for Night One."

"The blue pill you've just been given contains an organic and wholly safe combination of natural ingredients that will heighten your creativity and your suggestibility for the next few hours. It is an essential part of your first evening, and must be taken prior to leaving for the event site. This is a mandatory element of the experience, but rest assured, it has been rigorously tested. It has no negative or permanent side effects and will not render you unconscious or unable to control your body."

"Once you take the pill, please put the provided black hood on and secure it comfortably at the neck. Someone will be by to collect you and take you to the event site."

To my surprise, neither George nor Ruby argued about the pill, and seeing them both take it, I took my own. It wasn't until I was in the muted black world of the hood that I heard George speaking beside me again.

"So...um, are you going to tell us anything else? Any rules or..."

Swan's voice was higher and more distant this time when she cut in. "Oh, no. There are no rules."

There was more tension when George spoke again.

"No rules? Like you mean like the actors are trained to keep us safe? I mean there have to be rules of some kind, right?"

There was no answer.

****

"Fuck. It won't start."

I snickered at George. "Yeah, funny. Best cut it out before Ruby gets in. She's in no mood after the stupid shit you pulled."

He glared at me. "I'm not joking. Watch." I saw him turn the ignition key, but the car didn't start or even make any complaining noises. "It's fucking dead, man."

Ruby opened the back door and got in. "What's the hold up? Crank that AC. It's hot as shit out there." She saw my expression and raised an eyebrow. "What's wrong?"

"George can't get it to crank. It doesn't do anything when he tries."

She rolled her eyes. "Fuuuck. This is just the best fucking day ever." George started to apologize again and she raised a finger. "No, don't even start. I'm hot, my leg hurts, and I know you're sorry I fell, but if you try to apologize again right now, I'm going to be shitty to you. So just stop."

George frowned sadly and tried the key again. Still nothing.

"Car service then? John, you've got it on your insurance, right?"

I nodded. "Yeah, but no signal out here." I laughed dryly. "You're the one that wanted to go way out for our nature hike."

Ruby flipped me off as she checked her phone. "Me neither. George?"

He shook his head before getting out suddenly to go look under the hood. When he was gone, I looked back at her. "Go easy on him, okay? You know he likes you, and it killed him that you fell when he tried to jump scare you on the trail."

She sighed. "I know, but it was so stupid. He just needs to think before he does shit."

I nodded. "Yeah, but he just gets excited about stuff. You know how he is. He's like a big kid sometimes. And...oh shit. Someone is coming."

****

"But who would do something like that? I'm no mechanic, but that engine was torn to shit."

Errol glanced over at where George was squeezed in next to him on the pick-up's bench seat. Ruby had opted to sit in the bed, so I was on the other side of George, getting to breathe in the aroma of old tobacco and stale sweat that filled the cab. When our backwoods savior spoke, a sweetly-decaying scent pushed its way past the others. "Kids, most like. They think it's fuckin' funny. Little shits come from the other side of the river. The town is only a few miles thataway past the bend, and they come out camping, earning badges or...whatever it is they do. What they wind up doing mostly is raising hell and causing damage to property." His light green eyes were back on the road now. "Sometimes I catch one of them."

When he had first drove up and offered to help, I had noticed that Errol seemed both old and young, especially around the eyes. It was more than just looking tired—he looked used up somehow. Spent. But not now. Now his face was almost glowing as he smiled at some unknown memory. "Catch and correct them. Correct them good and proper."

Shifting uncomfortably, I decided to change the subject before George asked another question. "Um, this town. Is that where we're going? Maybe we can get phone service there, or at least a tow."

Errol licked his lips but didn't look my way. "No, I have a line you can use at the house. It's closer, and you won't find those proper town folk wanting much truck with you if you come rolling into town with me. Our farm isn't too far now. We'll have you fixed up soon enough."

I felt my stomach clinching. This wasn't right. I didn't want to piss the guy off, but I'd seen enough movies to know this was going to end with us butchered in his basement. The guy was probably a harmless good Samaritan, but was it worth the risk? Fuck no, it wasn't.

"Um, actually, I know it's a hassle. But if you don't mind, take us on to town, okay? It'll be easier to get help there, and we'll be out of your hair quicker too."

Errol cut his eyes toward me. "You taking liberties with my good nature, boy?"

I raised an eyebrow. "What? I don't know what you mean."

"I mean to say that I'm already helping you, and now you've decided my help ain't good enough. Want to go crawl to the city folk, who I've already told you ain't going to help you for shit. Or don't you trust my word?"

George raised his hands. "Hey, nobody's saying that, man. We appreciate it. We just need to get to town. That cool with you? You said it's pretty close anyway, right?"

Errol slammed on the brakes and the truck lurched to a squealing halt. "Get out."

I put my hand on the door handle, but George was already protesting. "Fuck, man. Chill out. We need the ride, okay?"

The other man had been staring out at the road, but now he swung his gaze around to George, his lips skinned back and his teeth only a couple of inches from George's face as he snarled. "I said get out of my fuckin' truck, shitbird. You move or I'll by God move you."

I yanked open the door and grabbed George's arm. "Let's go. Now." I glanced past him to Errol. "We meant no disrespect. Thanks for carrying us this far."

George frowned at me. "No, fuck that..."

I gripped his wrist and pulled harder. "Shut up and get out. We're going." Ruby had heard enough to already be out of the truck bed and I saw George glance past me at her before nodding. He barely had a foot on the ground before Errol peeled off, causing George to stumble against me with a curse.

"Fucking red could have run me over."

I looked at him and shook my head. "You were being a dick and he was creepy as fuck. We're better..."

"Look, he's stopping again."

I glanced at Ruby before following her gaze up the hill. At its summit, Errol had stopped the truck. Maybe he was reconsidering kicking us out after all. Well, too fucking bad. "Look, if he comes back and offers us a ride again, we say no. I don't trust that fucker."

Ruby nodded. "I agree. It was already looking like the start of a slasher movie." George looked funny and then nodded with a laugh. She smiled at him, but it fell away as she glanced back up the hill. "He's turning around."

I was already preparing a polite refusal in case he asked to give us a ride again, but the thought faded as I saw him coming back. He was weaving back and forth, and he was driving way too fast if he was going to stop to talk to us. But it didn't look like he was going to go past either.

It looked like he was aimed right for us.

"Fuck! Run!"

I turned and grabbed Ruby's arm, starting down the steep shoulder toward the nearby treeline. I looked back and saw that George was only a few feet behind, but as I watched, he stumbled and fell. I nearly turned to go back for him, but the truck was too close and I knew I'd never make it. So instead, I plunged into the trees with Ruby.

"Where's George? Where is he?"

I shook my head as we pushed further into the trees. "He fell. The truck was coming. I…I didn't see him get hit. I don't know what happened."

She stopped and pulled away. "We have to go back and get him."

Nodding, I looked around. We were at least thirty feet into thick trees now. Errol might come in, but the truck wouldn't make it very far. "I know. But we have to be careful. Let's go down some and then cut back toward the road. See if we see him."

Ruby headed off without another word, and we made good time backtracking parallel to the road before cutting back toward the shoulder. When we got to the edge of the trees, I could see the spot where George had fallen. There was no sign of him, Errol, or the truck now.

"Shit shit shit. He might have taken him! We have to find him!" Ruby's eyes were wide now, her expression matching the guilt and fear and worry that was churning in my own belly. I gave her a quick hug as she pulled out her phone. Still no signal on hers or mine. We debated going back to the car, but what was the point? It still wouldn't run and George had the keys. We decided to keep going along the edge of the woods, following the road until we found a sign or someone to help or got a signal back. As we started walking, I realized how low the sun was in the sky now. It would be dark soon.

****

Ruby's hand was sweaty in my own as we stepped into the cornfield. It was the first sign of life or people we had seen in over an hour of walking, and while we both knew there was a chance this was Errol's place, we had to take the risk. It could be that the distant lights we saw across the field belonged to a nice family sitting down to dinner, or at least someone halfway normal that would let us use their phone.

The air was cold as we passed between the green rows of corn, and with each breath, I took in a spiky, earthy scent that made my eyes water. Suddenly, Ruby stopped as her grip on my hand tightened.

"Did you hear something?" Ruby's voice was low and strained, and in the moonlight, I could see how tired and scared she was. "I thought I heard something behind us."

We both sat silent for several moments, but all I heard was the light rustling of the stalks in the evening breeze that had picked up as we'd made our way through the corn. I finally shook my head. "I don't hear anything other than the wind." She listened another couple of seconds and then we started back to walking.

The field sloped downward in the direction we were headed, making it harder to get a clear view of what was in front of us until we were almost out of the field. When we reached the edge, I felt some relief to see a large farmhouse come into view. It was slightly run-down, but there were lights on inside and no indications of anything strange or ominous. I looked around for any signs of Errol, but there was no one visible outside or through the windows we could see, and the only car outside was an old Crown Victoria.

We broke from the corn at a slow run, warily glancing in every direction as we made our way to the front porch and knocked on the door. There was no answer. We knocked again. Then we called out while knocking a third time, letting them know that we had an emergency and just needed a phone. Still nothing. Maybe no one was home, or maybe they just weren't going to come to the door when a stranger was banging on it at night. Either way, we needed to get inside.

I started looking around for something to break a window when a thought occurred to me. Reaching out, I tried the doorknob and found that it turned easily. I glanced back at Ruby, who shrugged and gave me a shooing gesture to go on in. I called out again as we entered, saying that we were stepping inside if anyone was there, but we only needed to use the phone to call for help. To please not be scared or shoot us. Like before, there was no response. Empty or not, we just needed to hurry, for our sakes and for George's.

The house was decorated like I would expect an old farmhouse to be decorated—plain, wood furniture, decorations that my mother would call "country", and…no phones. We moved from the front hall through a living room and a dining room before coming to a large kitchen with a modern stove on one end and an old, iron wood-burning stove on the other. We looked on all the counters and walls, but there was no sign of a phone or even a phone jack. We went back to the front hall, this time going to the right instead of the left. It was a parlor or study of some kind, and while there was an old television in one corner, there was no sign of any phone there either. I was looking along the baseboards for a phone line when Ruby spoke, her voice trembling slightly.

"There…there's someone out there."

I stood up and saw she was looking out the parlor window. "Out in the yard? Maybe it's the owner. We can…"

"No, not in the yard. Across the field. On the far side. I see fire. They're lighting something on fire."

I went to stand beside her, and at first I didn't see anything. But then a flicker of orange caught my eye in the darkness. "What the fuck…" The flame grew bigger, and my first thought was that someone had started a bonfire over there, not far from where we had gone into the corn just a few minutes earlier. My heart began to pound faster. What if it was Errol, still hunting us? And why would anyone…but wait, it wasn't a bonfire.

It was a person. Someone had set a person on fire.

"Oh God! It's George! They're burning George!" Ruby started to move toward the front door and I grabbed her. She was crying now, and it took all my strength to keep hold of her as she struggled. "Let me fucking go. We have to help him."

My hands were shaking as I held onto her. "We don't know that. It's too far away. It could be a dummy for all we know. And…and if it is George, it's too late to help him anyway."

She lowered her head and began to cry harder. Looking back to the window, I saw that it wasn't a dummy after all. It was moving. More than moving, the blazing figure was walking forward, stepping into the corn. My hands fell from Ruby's arms. That didn't make sense. How long could someone walk when they were being burned alive?

Ruby was watching beside me now. "What…they're walking toward the house. How are they still alive? Oh God, they're coming this way!" Her voice was deep with sadness, but that was being overtaken by a gnawing chord of fear. "They…they're fucking running this way!"

She was right. The burning figure was silently running through the field, leaving a fiery path of burning corn behind as it raced toward the house. None of it should be possible, none of it made any sense, but as I saw its orange glow approaching, a voice deep in my heart told me the truth that my mind wouldn't speak:

Possible or not, it was coming for us.

Ruby ran back to the front hall and locked the door before sliding a small chest in front of it as well. Remembering a back door in the kitchen, I went and shoved the kitchen table against it before grabbing us each a knife from a nearby butcher's block. We met back in the living room, and I was going to ask if we should go upstairs and look for better weapons, but then it was too late.

When the burning thing struck the front door, it began to splinter and char away immediately. The only stairs we knew of were just ten feet from where it was already breaking through, sending streaks of orange light across the faded wallpaper of the front hall. So instead, we began backing away to the dining room.

Ruby grabbed my arm. "The kitchen. We need to get out the back." Nodding, we turned to run as a flash of orange light painted the interior of the house like a new sun.

It was inside with us now.

We had made it to the kitchen and were pulling the table back from the door when it caught us. I turned as it grabbed Ruby, her flesh beginning to cook immediately as she screamed. Tossing her against a far wall, it reached for me. I ducked back and swiped with my knife, but it only bounced ineffectively off its arm as it grabbed my shoulder. The pain was excruciating, and I could feel my eyes already beginning to boil from the heat radiating off of it as I stared into its face.

It was George. Or at least it looked like him. Parts of his face were gone already, but he was burning so slowly I could still see enough to know. I wanted to ask him why or how or tell him I was sorry, but the air was already cooking my lungs. But somehow, even in the midst of that flame, he was able to speak.

"Why did you leave me?"

****

I jerked in my chair, squinting at the white lights overhead. What the fuck...where was I? I looked around and saw Ruby and George were sitting next to me. And there was that girl...Swan? What was...I numbly took a cup of water that Swan offered to me.

"Drink up. The first time there's a bit of cottonmouth."

I drank the water even as George threw his to the floor. "What the fuck was that? What the fuck was that?"

Swan chuckled. "I take it you had a memorable first adventure."

George stood up, towering over the seated woman. "Adventure? What the fuck are you talking about lady? What did you do to us?"

Frowning, the woman gestured to his chair. "Please sit back down. As you can see, you're unharmed. You've just been given the gift of an experience that would kill most people with none of the negative consequences. And this, of course, was just the introduction. The tutorial, if you will." George reluctantly sat down again as she grinned and looked at us each in turn. "The future events are bound to be even more stimulating."

Ruby crushed her empty cup as she gave a small laugh. "Lady, you have to be batshit to think we're ever going to do that again. Or anything like that. I don't know how you did any of it, and I also don't care. I just want to never go through anything like that again." She looked at me. "Penguin. Fucking penguin."

I nodded. "Agreed."

****

It was after midnight before I got into bed. The three of us had been strangely quiet on the way back, though we'd agreed to meet the next day and talk through everything. For now, we were all just too exhausted, and when my head finally did hit the pillow, I was fast asleep.

Until I woke up a short while later to the woman back in my bedroom. This time she was sitting on my bed, gently shaking me awake. I looked up, first startled and then terrified as the sight of her brought back my memories of the night before.

"What…"

"John, I need you to just listen to me. We don't have much time before the twins come for me, and we need to talk."

Part Three

John, this is all going to be hard to believe. Maybe impossible. I know I've tried to tell you the truth in the past and it never works, but now that you're in it…well, I have to try again before it's too late. For both of us.

So all I ask is that you listen to the crazy-sounding woman waking you up in the middle of the night. Try to really hear what I'm saying and try to remember it. Try to remember me.

Yes, I know you. And you know me…at least when you're not made to forget. It still gets me how well they can control us. How they can control everything. I don't know how they do it or what they really are but…wait, that may not be true. I think they're tampering with my memory even now, and there are certain things that I feel like I do know, but they're slippery things, laying just outside what I can see or reach to pull into the light.

Either way, I can only tell you what I know right now.

We know each other because we're married. We've been married for six years and we've known each other for over eight. Ruby knew me through that Godawful non-profit we both worked at, set the two of us up, and…well…we just clicked from the start.

Stop! Please, just stay in here and listen to me. I know how it sounds to you. I know how they fuck with your head. But soon there will be men dressed like cops at our door and they'll take me away, even though you haven't called 911 yet. So just give me this little time with you. Please.

Thank you. I…I don't mean to get emotional. But I remember most everything most of the time. I remember you and our life together. This house, our plans, all of it. I miss you so fucking much, and every night, when they're through with me, I wake up back here, watching you sleep, wanting to stay here forever. Just so they can take me away again.

This has all been going on for a long time. It's hard for me to gauge time exactly, but best I can tell, I first went to the True Horror Movie Experience almost four years ago. I know, I know. But I'm telling you the truth. They invited me and I went. Initially you were going to go with me, but then you came down with a stomach virus at the last minute. I almost stayed home too, but we'd booked it months in advance and were so excited about it. You told me you wanted to make sure at least one of us got to go.

I barely remember the first few days of it now. They tweak your perceptions and what you know based on what suits them at the moment. Memories, skills, relationships, they all get shifted around. You get all scrambled, but it doesn't really matter, because you're always going in the direction they want you to go. Over time I started to remember more, whether that was due to building up a resistance or them wanting me to know what was going on.

In the end, I don't know that it matters. Most days are the same. I mainly sleep during the day, and when I wake up, I'm stuck in some kind of horrific situation where I'm being chased or terrorized or killed. Then I wake up again here, get drug back to the Farm...at least most of the time...and then I get to start a new nightmare the next day.

I...I don't even know that I'm me anymore. I don't understand how I could be alive or sane, so maybe I'm not. But I do know that you're you. I still feel the same love and excitement and sadness when I see your face, and even if it's too late for me, I have to keep trying to save you.

Don't...shit, that's them. See, I told you they'd come whether you called or not.

Don't take the pills they give you. They're poison. Venom. Fuck, I don't know. Don't take them. Try not to go at all. Try to stay awake and remember all this. Remember what's happened already. Remember that you know me and that you love me, if you can. But most of all, please, remember not to take the pills and to never go near those people again. Run if you have to. Start over. But don't let them trap you the way they have me.

I couldn't stand it if I knew you were stuck in Hell beside me.

****

"Congratulations on being selected to participate in the True Horror Movie Experience. This is your orientation for Night Two."

"The yellow pill you've been given is wholly safe and all-natural. Taking the pill is a mandatory requirement of participation, but rest-assured, it's only purpose is to temporarily enhance your imagination and suggestibility."

I glanced over at George, who was already popping his pill with a grimace. Giving me a strange look, he leaned closer as Swan continued to talk. "Make sure you don't leave me behind, okay? I don't remember last night so well, but I think maybe I got left alone part of the time."

Frowning, I gave him a nod. I didn't remember the night before well either, which was strange, but somehow not alarming. I vaguely remembered being really tired the night before, and when I got home I went straight to bed. Even now I felt tired, and that's after managing to sleep through two alarms until almost noon. Still, I couldn't imagine that we'd have left him behind, at least not on purpose.

Turning to look at Ruby, I saw she was holding her yellow pill up to the light like a jeweler inspecting a small gem. She looked worn down too, and she'd been nervous and fidgety on the ride over. Had the night before been that exhausting, or was something else going on? I felt a brief tug in my chest at the thought—a moment of panic without a clear source or reason.

Then I realized Swan was asking me if I was ready. I looked back to find that Ruby had taken her pill as well and they were all waiting on me. Licking my lips, I swallowed my own and chased it with a cup of water. As I pulled on the black hood, I felt a buzz of nervous excitement and anticipation, but it was tainted with a constant low thrum of unease. Something just wasn't...

****

"...right here." Ruby gestured around at the empty promenade. "This is supposed to be a popular amusement park, right? But it's like ten-thirty in the morning and we've seen like...what, maybe a dozen people?"

George nodded absently as he shrugged. "It's not peak season probably, and it only opened at ten. Maybe we've just missed the rush. And no people means no lines, right?" He pointed to a nearby sign pointing the way to a rollercoaster. "Let's go try out 'The Hunter's Blind'."

We angled in that direction, but I was still thinking about what Ruby had said. Wizard's Folly was a pretty popular amusement park, even if it was out in the middle of nowhere. It had won awards going back years, and when I bought our tickets I remember the pictures showing every ride and attraction filled with people. Even if this wasn't the peak season, the emptiness of the park seemed strange. But it wasn't just that...

"It's the way people are acting." I spoke out loud before I realized it, glancing around with embarrassment before meeting Ruby's eyes. "The people at the ticket booth, the few people we've seen walking around, they all seem…off somehow. Like they want to be mean or hostile or something and are just holding it back so they don't get fired."

She nodded and pointed a finger towards me as we walked. "Exactly. Except it's not just the people that work here. I went over to the water fountain when we came in and there was this little girl and her dad over there. Not getting water, or really doing anything. Just standing there like they were waiting for something or didn't know what to do. Standing and staring."

Ruby grimaced slightly at the memory. "Until they saw me. Both of their faces changed. It was like you're saying. It was almost like they had to hold themselves back from jumping me. Even the little girl."

George let out a sigh. "Goddamn, will you guys relax? If you didn't want to come, you should have said so. But whatever this derpy creepy shit is…it's killing my fun, man. Can we just check the place out? Ride a couple of rides? If we decide it sucks, we'll leave. Sound fair?"

I nodded and Ruby grumbled affirmatively. And as we made our way down the path to the rollercoaster, I kept looking for more people or signs of normalcy. I saw a pair of teenage kids staring sullenly at us from a nearby bench, and then an old woman looking out at a set of empty pens that at one time in the past or future had probably been intended as a petting zoo. Now it was just barren and strange, just like everything else around here.

"See? No lines." George was gesturing toward the empty zigzag of railing leading up to the small building where park attendees were loaded into The Hunter's Blind.

Except today we were the only attendees at the ride, and as we headed up to the rollercoaster platform, I felt my stomach begin to clench apprehensively. The ride had to be closed or something. Or maybe it wasn't safe and they were working on it. Something had to explain why...

"Step up and pick a seat. Two to a row please." I jumped slightly as I saw a wan-looking girl step out of the shadows near the edge of the platform. She gestured feebly toward the waiting rollercoaster cars while favoring us with a watery look that carried the same underlying malice I'd been feeling since we got there. My eyes began to water as well at the strange, minty smell that was wafting towards us from the girl. What was that, menthol rub?

The three of us slowed to a stop and I raised my hand. "Hey, um, is this ride okay? I mean is it open and safe and all?"

The girl focused on me slightly more, a muscle jumping in her neck so hard I could see it at a distance. "Safe? Why yes, it's safe...as houses."

George frowned, first at the girl and then at me. I knew him well enough to see that his stubborn insistence that nothing was wrong was warring with the obvious wrongness all around him. In the end, his pride won out. Poking me in the ribs with a thick index finger, he scowled. "Come on, fucker." George then glanced past me to Ruby and his gaze softened slightly. "Let's try to have a good time, yeah?"

He climbed into the first row of the car and I followed into the second. Ruby had been right behind me, but I looked away for a moment as I pulled my shoulder bars down. That's when she started to scream. I tried to turn, but the padded bar across my chest kept me from moving too much. All I could see at the edge of my vision was that Ruby was being attacked, either by the girl or someone else, I couldn't say for sure. I started pushing against the bars, and ahead of me George was doing the same while yelling and cursing. They didn't budge.

Giving up on pushing them up, I started trying to slide out from the side. I made it part way out and was craning my neck to see what was happening to Ruby when her bloody hand reached out and grabbed my arm. I tried to hold on to her wrist, but it was slick and I began to lose my grip almost immediately. Pulling with one hand, I used the other to push my way past the bar so I could get out and help her.

That's when the rollercoaster started.

Everything jerked and jolted forward, and then Ruby slipped from my grasp. I looked back to see her being pulled into the shadows at the far end of the platform, her eyes and mouth circles of terror and agony as she screamed out for us.

"Don't go! Don't leave meeeeee!"

"Fuck fuck fuck!" I heard George's screams above the rattling of the rails beneath us and George's own flailing as he continued to work himself free of the safety bars. He finally managed to get where he could turn around and peer at me between the headrests with crazed eyes. "We have to go back and help her right now. Before those crazy fucks kill her!"

I nodded, clutching the bars beside me as we twisted up and down along the track. "I know. We will. But we have to wait until we come back around!"

He shook his head and yelled again. "What?"

"We have to wait! We'll come back around…wait, we're slowing down." I looked over the edge of the car. We were at one of the highest points on the rollercoaster's path, a long straight stretch before one final high peak and a long, spiraling drop. But instead of moving at speed toward the drop-off, we were slowing to a crawl. In another few seconds, we were completely stopped.

"What the fuck? They're keeping us here so they can fucking hurt Ruby!" He started clambering out of the car and I had to stand up and push him back down. He looked ready to punch me and I held up my hands.

"Calm down. You'll break your neck. Let's think for a second." Looking around, a thought occurred to me. "Our phones! We can call the cops on our phones!" George was already shaking his head. "They make you lock your phones in lockers when you come in, remember?"

"Fuck. You're right. Well, maybe we can…" But it was too late. George was already back over the side, step hopping down the track toward…what? A service ladder maybe? Or did he think he could just walk down the steep drop on the other side of the rise? Fucking moron. There was already a stiff wind picking up, and I watched his steps grow less steady as he pushed on against it.

I felt anger flaring in my chest. Anger at someone hurting Ruby, anger at George for being so reckless, and anger at myself for being a coward. I didn't want to risk falling, and I didn't want to get attacked by whoever was hurting Ruby. I wanted to help her, of course, but I clearly wasn't willing to go as far as George was. I tried to tell myself that was okay, that he was the one with the crush on her, and that the two of us hadn't dated for years. But it sounded hollow, and I was still debating going after him when I saw the first hands poking up through the rail slats between George and the rollercoaster cars.

"George!" I screamed as I stood up in my car, the immediate sense of vertigo temporarily overridden by blind panic and fear. "Something's coming! They're coming for us!"

He turned around, first looking angry, and then registering my words, terrified. George's eyes fell on the first figures that were crawling up onto the track with us. This close, and with the wind blowing past them on its way to me, I could smell the twin stenches of mint and rot thick enough to gag me. Wiping at my eyes, I yelled for George to run even as I realized he had nowhere to go.

I could see in his face he was realizing the same thing as the first of the figures stood up and started toward him. It was a little girl, maybe the same one Ruby had mentioned before. But how could it be? This girl was clearly rotting—gray, mottled skin peeking out from the sleeves of her faded sweater, and it looked as though the climb up the rollercoaster track had scraped away several bits of decaying flesh on her legs and cheeks.

Yet despite all that, her voice sounded loud and strong as she paused and let out a strange, chittering cry. I shuddered as the half-dozen rotting people standing with her echoed the sound, and this was followed by many more. Some distant, some directly below us.

One right behind.

I started to turn as a hand dug into my shoulder, sinking in past the skin and muscle to reach the bone.

Screaming, I tried to twist away, but it was too late. I was yanked backward into the row behind me, the silhouette of my attacker a dark, upside-down shadow as I looked up into the steel-gray sky. I felt raindrops begin to fall on my cheeks, and it was only as the thing above me leaned down that I realized it wasn't rain at all.

It was Ruby drooling on me. Her right eye was gone and her lips had been torn to ribbons, but she still managed a ghastly version of her old smile as she pushed down on my shoulders and leaned forward with another of those chittering sounds. For a moment she just looked at me, but then her face was rushing into mine, darting forward for an impulsive kiss after all this time.

Pain exploded as her teeth sank into my nose at the base. She bit harder and twisted as everything began to flare black around me. I was only distantly aware as she kept tearing at me, and I had the dim thought that at least it would be over soon. I would be dead and I wouldn't have to worry about any of this pain anymore.

Then I realized that Ruby was talking to me as she chewed. Thick streams of crimson saliva trailed out of the corners of her mouth as she chittered, and as the pain in my face began to fade and new pains flared to life, I began to understand what she was saying.

She was saying that we were dead, but we still hurt. We rotted, but were never fully gone. We gorged, but were never really full. The only way to lessen the pain was to kill more, to add more, to share and spread out the burden until it was more bearable. She said that once the world was dead, we could all finally be at peace.

And then we could all rot away together.

****

I vomited on the immaculate blue gray carpet as I came around. Swan wrinkled her nose and rolled her chair a foot to the left before offering me a sympathetic smile. "Rough one, hun?"

I wiped my mouth as my stomach hitched again. "You...ugh...you could say that. Fuck this." Ruby was already standing unsteadily on her feet. Rubbing her forehead, she shot the other woman a scowl as she held out her hand.

"John, you ready to get out of here?"

Nodding, I took her hand and gave it a squeeze. "Yeah, sorry I dragged you to this shit. Let's go."

"Aren't you forgetting something?"

I looked around at Swan. "Lady, if you fucking think we're paying more for this after *that*..." I swallowed bile in the back of my throat. "Well, we're not."

The woman chuckled and shook her head. "No, of course not. Every night has been taken care of by your original payment and agreement." She held out a pair of orange cards. "Comment cards. We like to get responses while everything is still fresh in your mind. No rush, of course, but if you can just bring them back with you tomorrow night."

I stared at her incredulously. "Ma'am, maybe you haven't been picking up what we're putting down. There's no way we're coming back. Compliments to the fucking chef. You wanted to give us a terrifying fucking night? Mission accomplished. But we're never coming back."

Tucking the cards back into her palm, Swan just smiled and nodded. "As you say. We'll put a pin in the evaluations then." Her smiled widened as she stood up to usher us out. "But who knows? Maybe you'll have a change of heart after a good night's sleep."

****

Ruby rolled her palms across the steering wheel as we stopped at the first stop light. "Shit. I'm still shaking all over. I don't know if it was the pill or the shit they did to us, but…I…fuck, I don't know. I feel all fucked up and wrong."

I reached over and squeezed her leg. "I know, sweetie. I should have looked into them more I guess. We probably just need some rest and to drink some water. Flush out our systems, you know?"

She glanced over at me and then seemed to look past me into the back seat. "I guess, yeah. I just…I feel like we forgot something. Something important." She met my eyes. "Do you know what I mean?"

I went to give a quick response, but I could see she was worried. So instead I looked out at the empty blacktop ahead of us and tried to gauge how I really felt. Exhausted and queasy, sure. More than a little freaked out? You bet. But did I think we were missing something?

I looked back at her. "I'm not sure, baby. Maybe. Or maybe it's just the pill fucking with our heads. Let's stop at a gas station or something and get some water. Then we can go home, relax a few minutes and then…"

"Fuck!"

I followed Ruby's gaze to the blue lights flashing in the rearview mirror. Cursing, she began to pull over. "This is the last shit I need tonight. I stopped at the fucking light. And now with God knows what in our system..." She pointed toward the glove compartment as she shook her head and gave me a small smile. "I'm sorry, I'm just stressed. Will you hand me the insurance card?"

I found the card and went to hand it to her when my eyes fell back on the rearview. The doors were already opening on the patrol car and two officers were getting out. Their faces were illuminated in the raking flare of blue from the roof lights and I felt my bowels loosen when a thrill of unknown fear ran through me.

As they approached, I tried to rationalize my growing terror. It was the pill, it was the night, it was worry about getting arrested for whatever was in the pill we swallowed. Or maybe, in some irrational way, it was the strangeness of the cops themselves.

Because it was odd. After all, how often did you see twins, much less twin cops?

Why they might be the only pair in the country. Maybe even the world.

Part Four

"What seems to be the trouble, Officer?"

I winced internally as Ruby said the words, both because I knew from her tone that she was being sarcastic and because I still had this growing panic that something was really wrong here. There was this strange sense of unreality and fear that didn't make sense given the situation.

Yes, we had gotten pulled over by the police without knowing why, and yeah, it was pretty weird that they appeared to be twins. That's enough to make you a little jumpy or apprehensive. But I was bathed in a cold sweat, and as I tried to give a casual smile and roll down my window at the second officer's approach, I realized my hands wouldn't stop shaking.

I winced as a beam of light hit my eyes.

"How are you doing tonight, sir?"

Turning away from the light, I nodded. "Doing fine, Officer. Just ready to get home."

The flashlight had been shifted so it was still glaring into my peripheral vision. "I see, I see. And where is home, sir?"

I blinked as I realized I was having trouble remembering the right answer. "Um, it's not too far. About thirty minutes away I guess." Swallowing thickly, I added. "Down in the city." I wanted to hear what Ruby and the other officer were talking about, but it was taking all my focus to try and talk to this asshole who just kept standing there silently, as though waiting for another, more satisfactory, answer. After several more seconds, he finally went on.

"Oh really? I thought I remembered you. And I thought you lived out in the country. Way out in the country, if I recollect." His voice shifted as he talked to his twin partner across the roof of the car. "Don't you remember this fella living way out in the woods? You know the place."

The other officer responded. "Chip, I think you're right. I remember this cat pretty well. He's not giving you the runaround, is he?"

Officer Chip leaned down, his face like a shadowed moon in the ambient glow of his flashlight. "You're not fucking with me, are you, guy? Trying to tell me you live somewhere you don't?"

Feeling a flush of nervous anger, I turned and met his eyes. "No, I'm not fucking with you. Why did you stop us?"

Officer Chip's eyebrows knitted together as the smile he'd been wearing fell away. "You seem very nervous tonight, guy. Why are you so nervous?"

Heart thudding in my ears, I shook my head slightly. "No, answer my question please. Why did you stop us?"

The light clicked off as Officer Chip stepped back from the door. "Please step out of the car, sir."

"Look, I just w…"

"Sir, ma'am, please step out of the car now without further incident." This was Chip's partner, and as I looked past Ruby, I saw the officer had stepped back with his gun pulled out and pointed downward.

"Jesus, okay okay." Ruby gave me a scared look before stepping out on her side. Not wanting to make things worse, I stepped out as well. The officers directed us to opposite rear corners of Ruby's car and patted us down before telling us that we were under arrest.

Ruby's eyes widened as she looked between the two of them. "For fucking what?"

Chip's partner smiled thinly as he took a step toward her. "Well, what have you done wrong?"

I moved between them. "Nothing. We haven't done

anything that we know of. Will you please just talk to us and explain what's going on?"

Chip was moving to pull me back, but the other officer raised his hand to stop him. The man's eyes flicked between my face and Ruby's. "Do either of you know a man by the name of George Thurman?"

"Champ, this is a waste of good…" The man, apparently Officer Champ, cut his eyes towards his twin and Officer Chip fell silent. Looking satisfied, he cut his eyes back to us.

"Well?"

I had felt a strange twist in my stomach when he said the name, but no, I didn't remember anyone named George Thurman. Maybe I had met them before somewhere, but if so, it didn't make much of an impact. I told him so and his gaze shifted to Ruby.

She shook her head. "No, we don't know him, or not well enough to remember his name if we do."

Officer Champ studied her for a moment before nodding. "I see, I see. Well, maybe this is a misunderstanding then." He glanced at Officer Chip before pointing to the back of Ruby's car. "Mind if I check your trunk, ma'am? It would help speed this whole thing along."

Ruby started to argue, but I reached over and gave her arm a squeeze. "Let's let them look. We don't have anything to hide and maybe this can clear…whatever this is…up." She frowned at me before giving a resigned nod and handing Officer Champ the keys.

Gesturing for us to step back, he approached and opened the trunk, his expression never changing as he saw

241

what was inside. That didn't seem that odd, as I wasn't expecting anything to be back there beyond a jack and maybe jumper cables or a blanket. It was only when I heard Ruby start screaming that I looked down and saw the bloody ruin of a man's body, twisted and stuffed into the trunk.

Champ was already grabbing Ruby even as Chip came up behind me and yanked my hands behind my back. I was in shock, and didn't even think of pulling away until I heard the ratcheting click of the handcuffs going on my wrists. As the bands tightened down, Chip leaned forward, his voice almost jolly as he whispered in my ear.

"It looks like you knew poor ol' George better than you care to admit."

****

"We didn't do that. I swear, we would never do anything like that." I had my hand on Ruby's back as she tried to reason with the officers through the metal mesh separating the backseat from the front of the patrol car. Her whole body was trembling, and I knew mine was too. The odd thought occurred to me that the two of us were like dueling tectonic plates, shaking against each other until we tore the world apart.

And whether it was us doing it or something else, everything was falling apart just the same.

Officer Chip turned back to us as we drove on, his face twitching as he looked at Ruby. "Ma'am, as you were told, you may want to keep quiet. And if you want to give a statement, you can do it at the station."

A thought occurred to me and I leaned forward. "Aren't you going the wrong way for the police station? The precinct for this part of town is in the other direction." I saw Officer Champ's eyes glance up at me in the rearview and I shrugged at him. "I did contract work for the city a few years ago and I had installations at all the precincts. And I don't remember one out the way we're heading."

Champ's eyes cut to his partner and then back up to me. "It's a new office. A satellite office. We use it for more sensitive cases, like when a fella gets butchered by his best friends and such."

"He was not our fucking friend! We didn't know him and we didn't fucking hurt him!"

Chip leaned closer to the metal mesh. "So you say, but it sure looks funny, doesn't it? Maybe you'll be more honest when we reach the Farm."

Ruby had already sat back in resignation, and now I joined her, holding her hand tightly as I watched our journey through the windows of the patrol car. I really didn't remember any kind of police station out here, or much of anything, to be honest. A couple of factories, a county dump, and then miles of woods. So where were they taking us?

Everything about this was wrong, but I didn't know enough to know how to react. Was this all a dream? Was the pill still distorting our reality and making us hallucinate? Or…maybe this was still part of our second night of the True Horror Movie Experience. Yes, that made sense! That was the only thing that made sense. They were fucking with us, making us think it was over when it wasn't. Suppressing a relieved smile, I leaned over to whisper to Ruby.

"I think…I think this is all part of it. The horror experience thing. I think they're putting us on." I looked at

Ruby's face and it looked just as shell-shocked and terrified as before. She wouldn't even meet my eyes. She just kept staring ahead as she spoke.

"Maybe so...but I think I do remember that man. I think I knew him. I think we both did." A tear formed at the corner of her eye and began trailing down her cheek. "I think I loved him."

Gripping her hand harder, I fought to keep my voice low. "That's bullshit. We love each other. We've been together since college, remember? And I think we'd both remember if you loved somebody else." I let go of her hand and touched her chin, turning her face toward me gently. "It's the pill, Ruby. It's still fucking with us. They're freaking us out and making us believe shit that isn't true. That's all it is."

Ruby let me turn her head, but her eyes were still fixed on the windows as she gave a slight nod. "Maybe so. Maybe it's all a part of their game. Maybe that explains that, too." I followed her gaze, sucking in a breath as I realized what I was looking at.

The trees on both sides of the road...they were all filled with webs. Thick, ropey strands trailed from branch to branch and tree to tree, and in several places, I could dimly make out the silken canopy that crisscrossed over the road itself, silver and ghostly in the dim moonlight.

"Oh...oh God. What is this? What the fuck is this? W-what happened here? Where are we?"

Chip and Chomp...no, Champ...Officers Chip and Champ chortled together, but didn't answer my questions. I was going to ask again, but then we were turning into a driveway blocked by a massive wrought-iron gate. As the car slowed, the gate began to open.

I glanced around for any sign of where we actually were, and in the moments before we started moving through the gate, I finally glimpsed a tarnished metal sign on one of the brick gate posts. I only had a moment, and the green sheen of the metal made it harder to read, but as we drove on toward a massive lawn and the shadowed hulking buildings that lay beyond it, I kept turning over in my mind what I thought I'd read. Not something about a police station, or even a place nicknamed "the Farm". Instead, the sign had simply said:

"Welcome to Greenheart Home. We hope you enjoy your stay."

Part Five

The patrol car drove up to the largest of the buildings, the brief flash of headlights across its face revealing what looked like a massive manor house that would have seemed more at home on an English countryside or in a Jane Austen movie than tucked away in a web-shrouded forest in northern California. Staring out the side window, I could see a thin but bright shaft of yellow light streaming out of the slightly ajar front doors, though there were still no signs of anyone else being anywhere around. I turned back to look at Ruby, but she was still silently weeping, apparently oblivious to the fact that we had stopped and the twins were now coming around to get us out.

We were shuffled up the stone steps and through the front door. Once inside, I felt myself freeze for a moment—

this place…what was this place? Not a police station. We were in what had probably been the front hall of a luxurious home or…well, whatever Greenheart Home actually was. But now everything seemed old and abandoned with years, possibly decades, of disuse.

Wallpaper, likely once a bright cream color, hung from the walls in tattered strips of yellow and black. The chairs and small tables that loitered at the edges of the hall all looked faded and warped by time and moisture—Rotting teeth in a head full of peeling, discolored skin and stale, dead-smelling air. I had time to think that we were being led into a corpse, a corpse that was maybe still hungry after all these years, and then Champ was shoving me forward.

"Hurry up, bud. You're not our only stop tonight, and we're already behind schedule."

****

They guided us down the hall before putting us in a large, soggy parlor off to one side. I went to complain, to demand a phone call or to see some sign that they were actually police officers, but something inside held me back. It would just make things worse. I already knew these twins were wrong, that this place was wrong, and that bad things were going to happen to us if we didn't get away. To keep playing dumb, to keep begging for reassurance that the lies the twins were telling us weren't lies at all…it would just let them know how weak and scared I was. Give them something else to smirk and laugh about.

So I kept quiet, doing my best to stay between them and Ruby as she shuffled into the room without complaint. Her reaction to all this, as well as what she had been saying in the car, were scaring me as much as anything. She had to just be in shock or still suffering from the pill's effects, but that didn't make it any less jarring to see her acting so...so broken. When they closed the door with promises to return shortly, I gently grabbed Ruby and squeezed her arms.

"Are you okay? You still with me?"

She glanced up and nodded, sniffling. "Yeah, I am. I just...this is all fucking with me a lot. I keep feeling like there are things I should know, but I can't keep hold of them." Wiping her nose, she gave a bitter laugh. "Maybe it's all in my head, y'know? But it's like the rest of it. It feels really fucking real."

I pulled her closer into a quick hug. "I know. Let's just find a way out of here, okay? Either this is part of their game or it's real. Either way, escaping is probably the best thing at this point." I looked back down at her. "Agreed?" Then trying to smile, I added. "Penguin?"

Her eyes brightened slightly and she nodded. "Yeah. Fucking penguin."

****

We spent what felt like several hours trying to find a way out of that room. The only door was locked and didn't budge no matter how much we pushed and pried. The windows were no better. We took turns hitting the glass, throwing things at them, using everything we could think of to either open or break one of the three large windows in the room's outer wall. Nothing worked. There weren't even signs of us scratching the glass or chipping the stained wood of the window frames. We eventually turned to looking for a weak spot in the wall or floor we could break through, but they were no better than the windows. We never raised our eyes too high, but I guessed from the height in the hallway that the room's ceiling was also high and likely as impossibly durable as everything else had been.

Only after we had collapsed onto the floor in exhaustion did the door open again. It was Chip and Chomp returning, as promised, and they had brought someone new with them. A woman that…

I recognized her.

My body seemed to go still, with even my heart falling silent as she entered the room and met my gaze. I had seen this woman before. I had the image of her sitting in my room, of her telling me…something. That we knew each other, that all of this was wrong. That we were all in danger.

That she was my wife.

I looked over at Ruby and saw the same confused recognition on her face that I felt sure was on my own. She knew her too. This was only confirmed when the woman…what was her name?...why couldn't I remember more?...ran across the room and started hugging us. Ruby was crying again, but this time it seemed like happy tears— I heard her saying over and over again "I thought you were dead…I thought you were dead…"

I went to respond when the woman turned back to me, and before I could react, she kissed me deeply on the lips, pushing her tongue past my own with a desperate strength that I first took only for passion. I felt myself responding immediately, and then something hit the back of my throat. Pulling back slightly, the woman quickly leaned forward and whispered in my ear.

"Just swallow."

Those words seemed to freeze the moment, dangling

me, confused and terrified, over some dark chasm, not sure of which way I should turn to land safely. Did I trust this strange woman, who for all I knew, was part of this whole thing just as much as Swan or the twins?

But then she pulled back, her eyes finding mine, and I had the briefest of flickers…some feeling or memory beyond the last few nights of finding her in my house uninvited. She smiled at me and nodded slightly.

"Please. For me."

So I did.

I immediately heard a screeching sound overhead. As I raised my eyes to the ceiling, I had time to see thicker patches of darkness moving among the shadows before everything fell away except for the terrible, furious noise. I felt like I was drowning in that sound. My last memory was recognizing Ruby and Jenna's screams as their voices joined the rest, pouring into that endless black sea as it pulled me under.

****

I woke up back at home the next morning, and as I slowly sat up in bed, my first thought was that it had all been a nightmare. A long, strange and terrible nightmare. I looked over, half-expecting to see Jenna laying next to me. When she wasn't there, I got up, wincing slightly at how sore I felt. My leg and back muscles protested and all my joints ached—it was as though I had worked out for five hours while fighting off a bad flu.

Still, I had this need to see Jenna, to make sure she was all right. Maybe she was making coffee in the kitchen? No, no sign of her there. In the bathroom or outside? No sign of her or any car but my own in the driveway.

My heart started thudding as I went back inside and looked for my phone. I would just text her and see how she was doing, where she was off to.

But she wasn't listed in my phone. I looked through my text messages, my emails, my social media profiles…nothing. There was no sign of her anywhere.

I was feeling nauseous now, my head swimming as I began wandering through the house looking for signs of her. Decorations, books, clothes, a toothbrush…something that would show me that she was real and that all the horrors from the past few days had been a bad dream. But there was nothing.

Finally, I thought and pulled my phone back out. George and Ruby. They could help me. They'd know if I was married to Jenna or going fucking crazy. They could help me figure out…

I couldn't find George on my phone either. I tried Ruby, but she was gone too. My phone wasn't empty—I had business contacts and a few acquaintances, but my wife and my two best friends? It was like they didn't exist at all.

My knees groaned in protest as I sank down onto the living room couch, my head held between my hands. What the fuck was this? Was I really going crazy? Had I dreamed up an entire life that didn't exist? People, memories of people, that were never really there?

No. That was impossible. And out of all the impossible things I had seen…or dreamed…or whatever…in the past few days, this was the one I refused to accept.

Jenna...Ruby...George...They were real, and I was going to find them.

****

The county courthouse was a twenty-minute drive, and it was only as I was about to turn into the parking lot that I realized I didn't even know what day it was anymore. Looking at my phone again, I saw it was Monday morning. Good, everything should be open.

It took ten minutes of wandering, but I finally found the records office for marriage licenses. The surly old man that sat behind the desk heavily hinted I could have just gone to their website and not wasted his time, but it only took him a few minutes to find and provide me with a copy of my marriage license. John Armitage and Jenna Freer, married over six years ago.

I was about to thank the man and leave when I had a thought. Maybe she had died and I was having trouble coping. Had a mental breakdown or something. I asked him to check for a death certificate for Jenna, then for Ruby and George, but there was nothing.

My mind raced as I was crossing the parking lot back to my car, and I was so preoccupied that I almost didn't stop as a deputy's patrol car passed in front of me. I waved her down and asked where the sheriff's office was. When she pointed to the large brown building directly behind the courthouse, I started walking that way immediately.

Once inside, I asked at the front desk if they had any record of a missing person's report for Jenna Freer in the past few years. The receptionist, who had initially been friendly, seemed to blink when I said the name. Instead of looking it up, she looked at me again more closely.

251

"You her husband?"

Frowning, I nodded slowly. "Yes, that's right."

Her gaze had grown cold as her lips thinned to a pale line. "Just have a seat, sir. I'll have someone with you shortly."

I wanted to ask more questions, but decided to not rock the boat until I had more information. It was only a couple of minutes before a large man with a graying fringe of hair and a wearily angry expression came through a side door and told me to come on back. We walked silently through the back corridors of the sheriff's office until we arrived at a small cluttered office that said "Inv. Shine" on the door. Moving behind the desk, Investigator Shine gestured for me to sit down in one of the guest chairs.

"So, Mr. Armitage. What can I do for you today? Got some new information for me?"

I raised an eyebrow. "What are you talking about? Do you know me?"

Shine's expression grew harder as his face began to redden. "What kind of bullshit game are you playing at?"

Raising my hands, I tried to keep my own rising anger out of my voice. "Look, I think I'm having some memory problems or something. I don't know if I was in an accident or what, but I can't find my wife and I'm just trying to get help. If you know me, or if you know her, please tell me."

The investigator's eyes stared at me like flat, black stones, and it was several moments before he gave a quick nod. "Fine. I'll play along. But so you're aware, I'm recording this conversation."

I shrugged. "That's fine."

"Okay. So to answer your...not at all absurd question...yes, I know you. I'm the one that investigated your wife's disappearance four years ago. Ring any bells?"

I shook my head, trying to focus on what he was saying instead of the growing unease roiling in my belly. "No. I remember Jenna, but I don't remember everything. And...look, I know how this sounds, but...I have two friends, two of my best friends, George and Ruby, that I can't find either. It's like I've lost all contact information for them and I can't remember how or why that would be."

Shine's eyes narrowed as he leaned forward. "Are you saying they're gone now too?"

Shaking my head, I met his gaze. "I don't know. But you know them? They're real?"

The man looked more uneasy now. "Yeah, I met them. Interviewed them about your wife's disappearance. They claimed you were at home with a bad cold or something when she went missing, but that was about it. None of you had any real idea of where she might have went, just that she was suddenly gone. As you may...or may not...recall, I thought it was bullshit. That one or more of you did something to her and the others were helping to cover it up." He glowered at the memory. "But I could never find her or any solid proof to confirm my suspicions."

"I wouldn't ever hurt Jenna."

He nodded, clearly unconvinced. "What about Ruby and George? Would you maybe hurt them? To shut them up?"

Sitting back, I just looked at him baffled for a

moment. "What the fuck are you talking about? I came to you for help."

He shrugged. "Maybe. Or maybe they were feeling guilty, you decided to off them so they couldn't talk, and now you're in here to set up an insanity defense just in case we find the bodies."

"That's…" I shook my head again. "No, I didn't hurt them. Just tell me, did you ever find any link between Jenna and something called 'The True Horror Movie Experience'?"

Shine stared at me. "Buddy, the only thing I can link to your wife's disappearance, or your friends if they're gone, is you." Leaning forward, he gave me a small, conspiratorial smile. "So why don't you tell me more about what you think might have happened to them?"

Standing up, I started backing toward the door. "No, I don't think so. Thanks for your time." Shine made no move to stop me as I left, but as I was striding down the hallway toward the front lobby, I heard him call out after me.

"You can keep running, John, but it won't work. It's just a matter of time."

When I reached my car, I was shaking so bad that I couldn't even start the engine. Maybe I was just crazy. Maybe even crazy enough to have hurt them? That didn't feel right or true, but could I trust my instincts if I was really fucking crazy?

I started crying, the stifling heat of the car's interior seeming to dry my tears as they rolled down my cheeks. I missed Jenna so much. I missed them all so much, and I didn't know what to…I suppressed a shiver at the change in the air. It was as though the temperature had plunged thirty degrees in an instant. Looking around, I felt a moment of vertigo as I saw I wasn't in my car anymore.

I was back in the room with Swan. As I stared at her bewildered, she met my eyes and gave me a warm smile.

"Congratulations on being selected to participate in the True Horror Movie Experience. This is your orientation for Night Three."

The Last Road Trip

Part One

Fire has its own smell. Did you know that? I'm not talking about the smell of gasoline from the ruptured gas tank or the sickly sweet smell of people cooking. I don't know how to describe it. But I don't think it's the smell of the air burning—not exactly. No, I think that fire itself—the consumer, not the consumed—has a smell all its own.

I remember thinking that as the flames grew nearer on White Creek Bridge. That...and that I hoped I was the only one left alive.

****

My father had been planning our family vacation for months. He worked as an aeronautical engineer, and aside from a couple of days at Christmas, he only got a chance to take off for vacation about once every three years. This year was extra special, however. He had blocked out two weeks for the four of us to go driving across the country. We weren't taking an RV, and we were only planning on driving between Ohio and Nevada, but it was still further than I'd ever been and a longer vacation than we'd had since an alleged trip to Canada when I was toddler.

But at sixteen, I was old enough to both dread the trip

and be excited by it. I didn't know how the four of us would fare riding in the family SUV for hours on end, much less staying at a bunch of random motels we found along the way. My father was refusing to have a strict travel itinerary or reservations—he said he needed a few days without plans or structure. That was great in theory, until we wound up with no good options for food or rooms in some back corner of nowhere. Then my parents would start fighting, while I tried to fade into the background and Sharon started bitching about how big a mistake the trip had been.

Sharon was one of the main reasons I was also excited about the trip. She had gone to college two years earlier, and while we were still close, it wasn't the same. Every time she came back for the summer or a holiday, I could feel the difference in our ages and experiences thickening the air between us. It might sound silly, but I hoped this trip, even if it became an exercise in shared misery, would help make us closer again.

We were on the second day of the trip when Dad first talked about the blue van that was following us.

He had been jolly and relaxed at the start of the trip, not even commenting much on the traffic snarl around Cleveland as we slowed to a crawl in the early afternoon. But by mid-morning on the second day, there was a palpable shift in his mood. He didn't talk much, and I noticed he kept glancing up at the rearview mirror as though checking something. It wasn't until after lunch that he puffed out a breath and looked over at Mom.

"I think that same van has been following us for awhile."

Sitting in the back behind her, I could only see the

quick movement of her head as she glanced in his direction and then out the sideview mirror. His voice had been low and casual when he spoke, but hers was barely more than a breathless whisper.

"How long?"

He gave a light shrug. "I first noticed it early this morning. I figured it was just a coincidence—they were just headed the same way we were. But after a few turns, I started paying more attention." My father paused and glanced in the rearview again before continuing on. "Then we stopped for lunch at the diner. We were in there for, what, an hour or so? But when we leave, that same blue van is behind us again."

Sharon leaned forward. "Are you serious? We got some fucking creeper following us?" We both turned and glanced back through the rear glass of the car. He was right. The road we were on was a quiet four-lane highway, and while some of it was hilly or filled with turns, this particular stretch was long and flat. It made it easy to see the old blue van following a quarter of a mile behind us.

"What are we going to do?"

It was the sharp note of fear in my mother's voice that brought my head back around. It's not that the situation wasn't strange, possibly even a little concerning, but she sounded and looked as though she was terrified. This woman, who in my memory had never been more than mildly anxious, was visibly shaking as she reached out to touch my father's forearm.

He glanced at her hand and pulled away slightly, his face hard. "We don't do anything. We stick to the plan. It's still probably just a coincidence. And if it's not, we'll deal with it as it comes." He glanced back at me and Sharon. "Got it, girls?"

We both echoed "Yessir", but Sharon was giving me a look that said she knew something was wrong too. If our parents were that worried, why not call the cops? And what was Dad talking about when he said "stick to the plan"? What plan? I thought the entire point of the trip was that we had no plan.

I felt my stomach rumbling with unease as I glanced back again. The van was still there, and I wasn't sure how long it would be before we hit another town or stopped for the night. Staring out my window, I tried to get my mind off it, but I kept thinking about Mom and Dad. Right or wrong, they thought something was going on. And they were scared. So was...

I jumped slightly as I felt a hand on mine. Looking over, I saw Sharon smiling at me as she gave my hand a squeeze. She mouthed the words "try not to worry", and I nodded as I returned her squeeze. I was still worried, of course, but it was better to feel less alone. And I kept telling myself there was nothing to it anyway. Give it a couple of days, and all I'd feel was slight embarrassment that I'd freaked myself out in the first place.

That was the night our mother disappeared.

****

Dad had gotten us rooms at a small-town motel and told us that they'd meet us in an hour at the restaurant across the road. He hesitated before adding that, while he didn't think there was anything to the van thing really, we should call if we saw it again. I had seen the van pass by when we'd turned into the motel earlier, but that didn't mean it wouldn't come back again. I almost asked why he didn't just call 911 if he was still worried about it, but something kept me from the question. Instead, I just nodded and told him we'd let him know if we saw anything suspicious.

When he arrived by himself at the restaurant, I hadn't thought much of it. At first I assumed that Mom was just being slow and would be over in a minute. And when he said she was tired and lying down, I took him at his word.

Sharon, on the other hand, kept bringing it up during the meal. Asking if we should go check on her. If we should bring her some food. He calmly rebuffed each question, saying that no, it was better to just let her get some rest. But Sharon…she kept asking questions and making comments about it, seeming to grow more upset every time. I didn't know what the problem was, but it felt like it went deeper than just concern that Mom had a hard day on the road.

We were all crossing back over the highway to the motel when Sharon picked up pace and began heading for our parents' room. To my surprise, Dad pursued her, grabbing her arm and spinning her around as she reached the sidewalk that ran outside of every door. They were too far away for me to hear what they were saying, but it was clear they were both angry and upset. After a few seconds of back and forth, Sharon stalked off toward our own room while Dad turned and gave me a wave.

"See you in the morning, pumpkin. Call if you need us."

I tried to talk to Sharon when I got back in the room, but she was laying on the bed with her back to me, and the most I was able to get out of her was a muffled "Leave me the fuck alone." I knew better than to push it, so I watched some bad cable t.v. before drifting off to sleep.

I woke up to Dad knocking on our door, telling us it was time to get up and get going. I groggily changed clothes and brushed my hair before lugging my backpack out to the car. I was looking around for Mom when our father came out of their room with his bag. His face somber, Dad waved Sharon over before he began.

"Girls, your mom had to leave early this morning. We got word that your Aunt Bethany was in a bad accident and is in the hospital." He swallowed as his expression grew stricken. "She's in ICU, and we don't know how it's going to turn out quite yet. So your mom took a taxi to the bus station early this morning and is headed back to be with Bethany." Sharon started to speak and he raised his hand. "I suggested we all just head back, but she knew how long we'd been planning this trip. She said she wanted us to keep going. If things turn around for Beth, she said she might even fly out to meet us in Nevada in a few days." He stared at Sharon for several moments before turning to me. "That sound okay to you girls?"

Sharon scowled at him. "Not really, no. This hasn't been the best trip so far, and well, I think we should go home and be with Mom and Aunt Beth."

I could already see that path quickly becoming long, boring days at a hospital, which Sharon would slowly bail on until she was hardly around for the rest of the summer. And then next summer, maybe she wouldn't come back home at all. So I spoke up.

"I think we should keep going. Mom can let us know how Aunt Beth is doing, and I know how much you've been wanting this trip, Daddy."

261

He beamed at me. "That's true, pumpkin." Turning, he smiled at Sharon. "Let's keep going for now, okay? If things don't get better for our trip or for Beth, we can re-evaluate as we go. How does that sound?"

Sharon looked at him for another moment before dropping her gaze. "Yessir."

Seemingly satisfied, he threw his bag into the back. "Okay then. Let's load up and head out."

****

I had planned on trying to talk some to Sharon on the ride that day, but when we'd gotten in, Dad asked her to move up front and help him navigate. She'd given me a strange look before getting out and going around to the front passenger seat. I wasn't sure if she was still upset about whatever they'd argued about last night, was worried about Bethany or Mom heading back alone, or just generally wished she was back with her college friends, but something was off. She barely talked at all except for occasionally giving directions, and whenever I asked her a question, she either ignored me or gave a short, curt response.

After an hour of this, I decided to text Mom and see how she was doing. Maybe she had heard more about Bethany. I'd only met my aunt a handful of times over the years, but she seemed like a sweet woman. And while Sharon and I never talked to her outside of her visits, I knew Mom kept in touch and always seemed excited whenever they got together. Both for her sake and for Mom's, I hoped she'd be okay.

After thirty minutes of no response after I texted Mom, I decided to try Sharon again. Dad was listening to some radio show, and so I just texted Sharon instead of asking her out loud.

You: Have you heard from Mom? I tried texting her awhile ago and haven't heard anything.

Sherry Berry: No. I haven't heard anything.

You: Have you heard anything from Bethany or her kids? I don't have their numbers.

Sherry Berry: Me either.

Me: What crawled up your ass and died? You've been bitchy since last night. Did I do something?

There was no response for several minutes, and despite feeling irritated and worried, I felt myself starting to get hypnotized by the drone of the talk show mixed with the windshield wipers sloughing away sheets of rain as we headed into a summer storm. I jumped when my phone suddenly buzzed again.

Sherry Berry: You didn't do anything. We need to talk, but not around him. Meet me in bathroom when we stop. If something weird or bad happens before then, you need to run. Don't question it, don't try to help, just fucking run.

Part Two

It must be a joke, right? Some kind of sick, totally not funny, practical joke that Sharon was playing on me. Maybe even Dad was in on it, though that seemed very out of character for him. He was always either serious, laid back, or sweet. He was never much for jokes, and I couldn't think of any time he'd ever tried to trick me.

But why would she do that either? We'd had our fights over the years, but overall, we'd always been really close. And unlike a lot of big sisters, she had never really been mean to me or put me down. And I couldn't really think of a time she'd ever lied to me about anything. Plus, this would have to be the worst timing ever. Mom on her way back to see Bethany, Sharon and Dad already having some weird disagreement about…well, I didn't know. But whether it was about us not getting to see Mom last night or something else, it seemed like a bad time to pull a prank.

I looked up at the profile of my father's face. He looked calm and fairly content as he drove along, listening to the radio and happy to be getting some quality time with his two girls. I knew that part of his reason for the trip, aside from getting a break from work, was to spend more time with all of us. And even with everything going on, he was trying to stay positive and give us a good trip.

Anger began bubbling in my chest at the thought. What was her fucking problem? Was she so unhappy to be on the trip that she wanted to sabotage it? Or at the very least, did she plan on taking out her angst on her gullible little sister?

Well fuck that. I wasn't that young anymore, and if she'd gone to college just to learn to be a bitch, she could go back there. Stabbing at my phone with my thumb, I typed out a quick response text. Worried that it was too harsh and accusing, I deleted it and started over.

Me: What are you talking about? What is wrong? Text me something, I'm worried.

I heard her phone vibrate as she got the text, but after another twenty minutes of no response, I'd had enough. I thought about just calling her out in front of Dad, but something held me back. I really didn't have a clue what was going on, and I needed to play it cool until I found out more.

Maybe she really was worried about something, and she wanted to confide in me. The thought of her coming to me with her problems cooled my anger, but if anything, it made my anxiety worse. What if something was really wrong?

We were coming up on a gas station and I saw my chance. I told Dad I needed to go to the bathroom, and smiling at me in the rearview mirror, he gave a nod as he started to slow the car. He said it was a good time to get gas and snacks anyway.

As we got out, I headed off for the bathroom, my stomach in a knot. I tried not to run, but I wanted to hear what Sharon had to say as soon as possible. Rip the bandage off quick to get it done. Had she been kicked out of school? Was she pregnant? Did she rack up a bunch of credit card debt and was afraid to tell our parents? What could it be?

Sharon had followed behind me at a slower pace, and seeing her face when she entered the bathroom made my stomach sink lower. She looked terrible, with lips pressed into a thin line and a weary gaze that couldn't light on me for long before trailing off to the dingy tile corners of the room. It was a two-stall bathroom with a deadbolt on the outer door to the room, so after peeking under the stalls, she locked the door and turned back at me. The several heartbeats of silence that followed was more than I could handle, and rather than wait for her to start, I blurted out a question.

"Are you on drugs?"

Sharon did meet my eyes then, her own widening in surprise before narrowing into a frown. "What? No. Jesus. Is that what you think this is about?"

I shrugged, my voice thick with emotion. "I...I don't know. I don't know what's going on because you won't tell me. You're just being weird, and leaving me messages that...I don't know, are you trying to scare me? Is this some kind of stupid joke?"

Her faced softened as she reached out and touched my arm. "No, Tree, it's not a joke."

Tree. I'd gotten the nickname when I was little, not because my name was Theresa, but because I loved a book called "The Giving Tree" so much that I carried it around with me when I was little. Sharon was the only one that still called me that, and even she hadn't used the nickname in what...two years? Normally, the old name might have brought back a warm feeling of past memories and our bond as sisters and friends, but now...it seemed forced. Used as some subtle means of manipulating me. Of making me listen to her by trading on that sisterhood and friendship.

Of tricking me.

I heard the anger in my voice as I responded. "Then what the fuck is it then?" I saw her recoil a little and felt a thrill of satisfaction. I normally never cursed around my family—not even Sharon. But I was mad, and I wanted her to know that she wasn't the only one that was growing up or could have a bad attitude. Squeezing my arm, she shook her head slightly.

"I'm going to tell you, but you need to promise me

that you'll really listen. That you'll hear me out on the whole thing. It's going to be hard for you to believe at first, and you may think I'm lying. I swear to God I'm not. But please, promise you'll hear everything I have to say before you interrupt or try to leave. We will only have a few minutes before he'll come looking for us, so I have to hurry. Okay?"

Again, she was calling him "he" instead of Dad or Daddy. Like he was a stranger. Glaring at her, I nodded. "Okay. I promise."

She took a deep breath and began.

****

I don't remember when they brought you home. Not exactly. I was only four at the time, and my memories from that age are murky. It's kind of like the swamp we went to on your field trip that time—lots of dark water with little trees and hills sticking up here and there.

What I do remember is a time when you weren't there. And then a time when you were. And I remember loving you, my new baby sister, from the first time I can remember seeing you.

But the thing is, I do have some memories from before you got there. We were a lot more…isolated…before you came along, and it wasn't until we moved and you started going to preschool that we started socializing more. That didn't seem weird to me at the time, but there were other things that stood out even when I was little.

For instance, I didn't remember Mom ever being pregnant with you. I didn't even know what being pregnant was until I started school in the first grade. I remember we had a substitute teacher that was a few months along, and at first I just thought she was fat. But then we talked about the teacher at recess, and the other kids made fun that I didn't know what being pregnant was.

At first, I'd been more worried about being embarrassed, but over the next few days, something kept bothering me. It was this memory I had of Mom, laying out in the back yard in the sun. She's always kept in good shape, and back then...well, in my memory, I just remember thinking how pretty she was. Her golden hair, her brown skin, and...her flat, toned stomach. She looked like the workout girls on t.v.

That memory was from a couple of years earlier. Before we moved, before I had started school. And I was only four going on five at the time, but I was pretty sure of when I'd seen Mom laying in the sun. It was just a few days before they brought my new baby sister home.

So I asked her about it. I didn't realize it at the time, but her reaction...it wasn't normal. She didn't explain anything to me or even try to laugh or lie and brush it off. Instead, she looked at me like she'd almost stepped on a snake, standing frozen in panic for several seconds before shuttling me off to my room. Telling me to not leave or talk to you until Dad got home.

I don't remember all the details now, but I remember being scared. Worried I was in trouble somehow. But then Dad came home and they came in to see me. They told me that my questions were perfectly normal, and how lucky they were to have such a smart little girl. That the truth was you were adopted. They had to explain to me what that was too, but they did, and I think I understood.

What I remember the most is feeling so much better

when we were done talking. They told me not to tell anyone, including you, because it was a secret. That we all loved you so much, and we didn't want anyone thinking we loved you less just because you were adopted.

For me it was the opposite—I felt like I was so lucky to have gotten such a great baby sister, and I felt even more protective of you after that. Like you were a gift I had to take care of. We grew up, became best friends, and for the most part, I've never worried about it since the day they explained things in my room.

No interrupting, remember? I'm not finished telling you everything.

Look, I never had any real reason to doubt what they'd told me about your adoption, but looking back at it now…I don't know. Some of it was that I was young and I trusted them too much. Some of it was that I was willfully blind. Didn't want to notice anything being wrong.

But over the years…I've seen things. He…he's not right. Neither of them are. I used to think maybe they were just weird hippies or something…into new age stuff or meditation or whatever, right? But…well, you know how Dad has his workshop down in the basement, and we can't ever go in there? Mom's always said it was "his private space", and I guess I get that, but…I don't know. They've always been weird about it. The couple of times I poked around at the door or asked to go in there while we were growing up, Dad would just get real quiet and Mom would bawl me out about it.

And there's other stuff.

They've never been overly social people, right? He's working most of the time and she's either working or at home doing some project or another. How many times over the years have you seen them invite people over or go out with another couple or anything? And some people like to stay at home, and they're older, so I get it. That's not really what bothers me.

What bothers me is that they actually do have friends. Or at least people they do stuff with. Remember a couple of years ago when they went to Salt Lake for that convention? It was the month before I was going off to college and I was pissed because we had to stay home and I missed that summer orientation thing? Well, a few days after they got back, I was looking through the laundry for a shirt or something and I saw a piece of paper mixed in with the dirty clothes. I checked it before just throwing it away, and it caught my attention.

It was a rental car receipt for the week they were gone. But not for Salt Lake City. It was in Michigan—some little suburb of Detroit. And it was in Mom's name.

Maybe I should have asked her about it, but for some reason, I was scared to. I just kept thinking about the times they'd get phone calls where they'd get an odd look and go shut themselves in another room. Or days I'd come home early and whatever they were on the computer for, suddenly they'd shut it down as soon as they saw me walk in the room.

And I'd say I was overreacting, that I was reading too much into things. Maybe they just like to look at porn, right? I know it's gross to think about our parents watching internet porn, but at least I could wrap my head around it. The problem was, some part of me knew that wasn't what was going on.

I'd been wrestling with what to do since finding the rental receipt. Do I talk to them, do I tell you, or do I let it go? I wanted everything to just be okay and normal, but I kept thinking back to all the times I'd wondered if something wasn't off, if there wasn't some part of themselves that they kept hidden from us.

And then, one day, Mom forgot to clear her browser history.

It was the weekend I was heading to college. Her and Dad were carrying my car to get checked while I finished the last of my packing. I was wandering around the house trying to think of anything I might have forgotten when I saw her laptop open and unlocked on the kitchen table. I already had a lie in mind if they caught me at her laptop. I just wanted to check the schedule of freshman events for the next day, even though my phone was right there in my pocket. My heart thudding, I sat down and opened up the browser.

There was a lot of normal stuff, but there was a lot of strange stuff too. The thing that bothered me the most was this strange website called The Black Room. It had a password to get in, and it wasn't like it looked that sinister or anything, but its plainness...it almost made it more creepy, you know? Especially when I had no idea what it went to or why our Mom would be going there repeatedly.

Then I clicked a link to her cloud storage. Again, most of the pictures were normal stuff you'd expect. But there was a photo folder that was separate from the rest. Buried in a bigger folder of recipes. The photo folder was just called "The Group". So I clicked it.

I...I don't know what those pictures were. A lot of

people, some hurting each other, some maybe having sex or something, some…it looked like a ritual or ceremony or…it was hard to tell in some of them, and I couldn't stomach looking too close. But some of those pictures…I don't really have words for them. I kept trying to tell myself they were faked, but I somehow knew they weren't.

All that was bad enough, but it wasn't until I got towards the end of the twenty or so pictures that I saw Dad in one. Then in the last one, they were both in the picture. I never saw them really…doing anything in those pictures, but it was clear they were a part of this same gathering that was in the other photos. I could barely breathe as I closed the laptop. It was like my entire world had contracted into just that day and that moment, and I couldn't see anything else.

Maybe that's why I didn't notice they had come home.

I know they saw me on the laptop, but they didn't mention it and neither did I. From their angle, I doubt they knew what I was looking at, and I just tried to act normal as my mind raced with what I should do. I thought about grabbing you and going to the police, trying to get some kind of help or protection…but from what? It may be they were part of some weird orgy group or something, but I didn't have any proof they were hurting anyone or…well, really doing anything at all. And I didn't want to upset you unless I knew for sure something was wrong.

So I left that day for college, and…well, that's why I kept calling you so much that first couple of months. I missed you sure, but I was also worried about you. Wanted to make sure everything was okay. I kept telling myself that

I was making the right call by not talking about what I'd found. It was their private lives, and if it didn't hurt us or anyone else, what did it matter? If either of us saw signs of them being weird, I could always get you out of the house and tell you about it then.

But things weren't really weird. Or no more than always. I definitely got a new perspective on how odd our family was when compared with some of my friends at school, but then everyone thinks their family is weird, right? And when I talked to you or came home to visit, everything seemed pretty normal.

Still, I noticed I was coming home less and less, and I was always tense while I was there. I worried I'd see signs of something that would confirm my lingering fears that something bad was going on, and I felt guilty that I was letting my concerns about them make me grow apart from you, Tree. I didn't want that, but I didn't want to be home any more either.

That's one reason I agreed to go on this vacation. I figured it would give me more time with you, but it would also force me to spend more time with them. See them in different situations for extended periods of time. See if I had anything left to worry about, or if I just needed to let it go.

That first day, I was feeling pretty good about everything. But then the stuff with the blue van came up, and they both got really weird. Then suddenly Mom isn't coming out of their room and he won't let us "bother" her? And no, I haven't had any luck getting ahold of her either.

I know this may sound dumb, but...I'm worried he maybe killed her. That either they were worried about the van, or maybe he just went crazy, or...I don't know. I just keep thinking about how nothing that's happening makes sense. About how I'm not sure how well we really kn...

****

"Theresa? Sharon? You in there?"

Sharon's eyes widened and she held a finger to her lips briefly before turning to the door. "Yeah, Dad. We'll be out in just a minute."

A pause and then. "Okay, honey. Try to hurry if you can. And I'm parked on the right now when you come out of the store." Another pause and then, "I got us drinks and snacks."

After a few seconds of silent staring at the door, I turned back to Sharon with a frown. "So that guy, the one being sweet and buying us snacks, you think he's in some weird murder orgy cult or something?"

My sister's face darkened as she shrugged, her voice barely above a whisper. "I don't fucking know. But I can tell you that something isn't right. I don't want it to be true, but it is."

I still felt angry, but I felt afraid now too. I didn't think she was lying to me, but it all sounded so strange and impossible. "Why don't we just confront him? Get it all out in the open if you're so worried." *You should be worried too* popped into my head and I pushed the thought aside.

Sharon was already shaking her head. "Because if he did do something to Mom, or they are part of some...whatever, who knows what he might do to us? We need to just stay calm, stick together, and see if anything else happens. Maybe it's all bullshit. I hope it is. I don't want to hurt Dad or Mom, or let them know I've been prying. Not unless we really have to. But if we can't get ahold of Mom in the next couple of hours, or if he starts acting weird, you have to promise that you'll trust me and we'll figure out what to do next together. Okay?"

I nodded sullenly. "Fine. But Je…Sharon, it's not going to amount to shit." I paused and then added, "And I still think maybe you're just on drugs."

She gave me a strange smile before grabbing the sides of my head and planting a kiss on the top of it. "I wish."

****

My nerves felt fried as we walked out of the bathroom together. There was a large part of me that was just angry at Sharon for making me worry unnecessarily. The idea that I was adopted? It was definitely possible, but it didn't bother me like I'd thought it might. Plenty of people were adopted and didn't know it. Not exactly a big deal. And whatever else she had seen or heard, she had to be blowing it out of proportion. I didn't think she'd lie to me intentionally, but maybe she was having some anxiety or mental issues and it was making things seem worse than they really were.

Still, there was another, smaller part of me that was afraid. What if our parents were tied up in something bad? What if Dad had done something to our mother? I'd say it was impossible, but people did fucked up shit all the time, and everyone was always surprised when it happened to them. Maybe this was the first part of a story that would wind up on the news. One of those where the father kills his family and then hims…

No. Fuck that. I needed to keep my head straight for me and for everyone else. I'd pay close attention, and I'd take what she said seriously, but I wasn't going to believe anything unless I saw it with my own eyes.

We were walking out of the store now, and maybe because I was so deep in thought, I turned the wrong way at first. Glancing around, I turned back to my right and followed Sharon to the car. It wasn't until I was getting into the back seat that I registered what I'd seen at the far end of the parking lot, sitting silently in the last spot in front of the store.

It was an old blue van.

Part Three

I could feel the van behind us as we drove deeper into the wilderness.

At first, I thought it was my imagination. I'd glance back and see the odd car in the distance, but nothing that looked like the old blue van I'd seen the day before or again just a few minutes earlier at the gas station. As the morning stretched on, I looked back less frequently, my mind slowly being consumed with the other worries and fears crowding each other for the spotlight.

Was Dad crazy? Had he hurt Mom? Did they really have some weird secret life they'd kept from us?

Or was Sharon lying or just wrong? Maybe she had misinterpreted some things or imagined parts of it. Maybe she really did have a problem with drugs or some kind of mental issue. She seemed fine overall, but how could I be sure when she was saying such crazy things?

I glanced back again, the breath catching in my throat

as I focused on a small blue speck in the distance. Was that it? It was too far to see clearly, but I somehow knew it was.

Turning back around, I thought about saying something to Dad or Sharon about it, but I held back. Sharon was back in the front seat again, and the couple of times I'd texted her since the gas station, she hadn't responded. She was actually talking to Dad some, and while on the surface it sounded like a fairly normal conversation, I could hear the tight cord of tension thrumming through every word.

She was trying to see how he acted. Trying to see if he said something suspicious or insane. And trying to keep him from catching on that she was doing it.

I dug my fingers into my thighs until the pain made me stop. I wanted to scream at both of them, to get away from the van, to do something to make everything stop and go back to normal. I looked back again, hoping that I was wrong and that the blue speck had been something else.

But no. It was much closer now, within a hundred yards and gaining. I could see the broken chrome of its grill waggling as it rushed forward, reminding me of shining teeth hungry for their next meal. I spun around, my voice loud and keen in my ears as I called out to my family.

"The van! It's back! It's chasing us!"

Dad looked up in the rearview mirror, his eyes dark as he glanced at me and then past to our pursuer. He muttered "Goddamn fuckers" and then stomped the gas, pushing me back into the seat as the SUV lunged forward. What was he doing? Did he know them? Why wasn't he calling the police? But Sharon was already ahead of me.

"What the fuck is going on, Dad? Do you know

them?"

He glanced in her direction, his expression hard. "Not now. I have to focus on this."

I saw Sharon shaking her head as he spoke. "No. Fuck that. What's going on? What happened to Mom? Who are these fuckers?"

As he went to respond, I saw the van coming up beside us. As they passed, I saw an older woman yelling something through the open window. At first I couldn't hear what she was saying, but as she pulled even with Dad's partially opened window, I could make it out.

"…found you again, you bastard! Just give her back! Don't hurt her and give her back, and you can go!"

Sharon turned to look back, and as our eyes met, I felt a wave of sick fear roll through me. I thought back to what she'd told me in the bathroom. About how I'd been "adopted" and how strange they had acted about it. About how we'd moved not long after I came home. About all the secrets they had from us.

"Dad? Daddy? What is she talk…"

I was interrupted by thunder. The man I called my father had rolled down his window the rest of the way and pulled a gun from under the seat. I didn't have time to consider the strangeness of seeing my father holding a gun before it was cutting off my words with a booming finality that seemed to shatter the air around me. He fired three shots into the van, and I only had time to glimpse the woman shuddering from the impacts before the van veered off onto the far shoulder and slowed.

"What the fuck! What the FUCK!" Sharon was

screaming now, but Dad ignored her. He was focused on the sideview mirror, and I knew from his expression that the van was coming back again. This time, I could hear the screaming of the man who was driving before the van even reached even with us again.

"You fucker! Give me back our baby! You fucker! Give me back our girl! I'll fucking kill you for what you've done!"

Dad fired two more shots out the window, but the man in the van seemed to expect it and dropped back before slamming into the side of our car. Cursing, Dad dropped the gun as he desperately clutched at the steering wheel and tried to maintain control. He fought the wheel for a moment, managing to keep us on the road before straightening out and picking up speed again. I glanced back and the van was coming back for a third time.

I had a moment to see the man behind the wheel— maybe in his late forties or early fifties, he looked like he was crying and screaming, and I could see that the right side of his face seemed to be thickly speckled with what was probably blood. I felt a strange pang of sympathy and loss at the sight of him. I turned to tell Dad that we should stop this. That we should try and talk to this man.

But then the man was gone. Dad had slammed on the brakes, causing the man in the van to swerve to the left to avoid ramming us from behind. That's when my father steered into the van as it passed, sending it spinning off the road and into the trees as our own car came to an uneasy stop at the edge of the shoulder.

"Oh God, what was that? Who was that? What's going on?" I could hear the panic and the accusation in my voice, but I didn't care. The world had gone crazy in the past two days and I needed it to stop. He was going to give us

"...answers right fucking now, or I'm taking Tree and we're leaving. I'll call the cops, they can come get us, and you can do whatever the fuck it is your planning without us."

When our father turned around to look at us, his expression was strangely serene. "You girls can't leave. We're on our family road trip, and we haven't reached the end of it just yet."

I felt myself starting to cry, but I pushed it down. We had to make him see reason. "We just...Daddy, you just killed those people. We have to call the cops, right?"

His smile chilled me because of how normal it seemed. It was a smile that said how he loved me, how he indulged me, how he spoiled me. I might have been asking for money for a school trip or a new computer—the smile would have been the same.

"No, pumpkin. We need to keep going. We'll be safe enough soon."

Sharon was undoing her seatbelt. "Fuck this. You're crazy. Theresa, let's g-"

He shot out his arm in an instant, his expression never changing as he slammed her head against the passenger side window once, twice, three times. I saw the dark blood spreading across the spiderwebbed glass and started to scream. My panic and fear slowed me only for a few seconds, but it was enough. He was climbing back, putting his weight on top of me, keeping me from freeing my seat belt while he pulled plastic zip-ties from his khaki pants. He secured my wrists to the shoulder strap of my safety belt and my ankles to each other. I cried and begged for him to stop, but he never responded, and within a matter of moments it was done. He opened the door and climbed off me before going back around to get in the driver's seat again.

Turning, he gave me another of his warm smiles. "Try to buck up, pumpkin. I know this is hard, but it'll all be over soon."

****

Sharon didn't stir as we drove on that afternoon, and despite my continued begging and pleading, he wouldn't stop to check on her or get her help. After the first couple of hours, I had given up any hope of her being alive. The only comfort I had was the knowledge that I probably wouldn't be far behind.

But then I saw the twinkle of blue ahead of us. Not a van this time, but the rotating flash of police car lights. It was some kind of road check or something, and I knew it was our last chance to get help. I expected Dad to turn off or to roll up the window when I started screaming for help as we got near, but he never did. Instead, he pulled up casually next to the officer and greeted him.

"Where are you headed, sir?" The officer's eyes flicked to Sharon's bloody, limp body and then to me screaming at him for help from the back seat, but his expression never changed.

Dad's voice was relaxed and warm as he responded. "White Creek Bridge. Got to get there before dusk, you know."

The officer nodded. "You're cutting it close, but this

detour we've got set up should see you there in time."

My father chuckled, gesturing to the damage on his side of the SUV. "Yeah, ran into an issue on the way, but I think it's smooth sailing from here."

"Please. Please help us. Please." I had stopped screaming now. I could see that neither this officer nor the other two out there had any intention of helping us, that they were clearly in on whatever was going on, but I had to try. One last effort to beg for our lives. "Please."

My heart fluttered with hope when the officer looked back at me and met my eyes. He seemed to waiver for a moment before looking back at my father. "Have a safe trip, good brother."

****

We had turned down a side road at the police check, but while the road was curvy and less maintained than the highway had been, we still sped along as we moved deeper into the wilderness. Hurrying to get to this bridge they were talking about before dusk, for whatever insane reason. I spent the next hour dejected and hopeless and largely silent aside from softly crying. I was exhausted, and while I still didn't understand what was going on—not really—I knew enough to know it was going to end badly and there was nothing I could do to stop it. So I just sat and stared out at the passing trees, thick with webs and shadows.

Yet when we rounded the last bend and the White Creek Bridge came into view, something changed in me. The wood of the bridge seemed so clean and bright that it almost seemed to glow, a sharp contrast to the small green river that ran beneath it and the various dark shapes dotting the bridge's road like ticks or scabs on a beast's back.

We were still some distance away, but I could make out not only people, but tents and various stands. There was a small wood structure to one side and what looked like a large stone table just past that on the other side. But it was what lay at the center of the bridge that finally caught and held my gaze.

It was a massive bonfire. The sides of the bridge itself went up probably twenty feet, long, spindly skeleton hands reaching up for the sky, and the bonfire went up to nearly the same height. It was already burning, but it was also clear that it had been lit recently, in preparation of what was to come.

It was almost dusk, after all.

Something broke in me at the thought. All my fear and worry and sadness seemed to burn away in the face of my anger—a bright, hungry, hopeless anger that wasn't about survival or understanding. It was simply about making them pay. Making him pay.

Dad had zip-tied my hands snuggly, but not snuggly enough. The addition of the seatbelt inside the plastic loop gave me just enough wiggle room that if I was willing to hurt, to lose skin and blood, I could maybe pull myself free.

I was willing.

Bending down, I tucked my legs up enough to put my feet against my wrists and the ziptie binding them. I had no hope of breaking the belt or even the ziptie, but I could break myself enough to get free. So I did. I pushed with my legs while pulling with my arms, I yelled as my right wrist gave way and skin peeled off as the plastic band dug into my flesh. But then I was free.

Popping my seatbelt with my left hand, I lunged across and forward to tackle my father from behind. This all happened very quickly, and I caught him by surprise, but I knew he was too strong for me to subdue once he knew what was happening. That's why I took the moment I had to grab his seatbelt and yank it against his neck.

Sliding the belt down, I hooked it at my bent elbows as I leaned back. I pushed against the back of his seat with my knees as my arms burned with his efforts to pull the belt away from his neck, and I had the random thought that it was like riding a bull inside of a bull—he thrashed and choked as the SUV picked up speed and wove back and forth on its journey to White Creek Bridge.

He almost slipped free once, but I dug in and pulled him back down, and as we began plunging through tents and people, headed into the middle of the now-blazing bonfire, I saw him look up in the mirror. He found my eyes and I found his.

And I smiled.

****

"And that's what happened. The next thing I remember was being in the ambulance. They checked me out, brought me here, and then you asked to speak to me."

I watched the deputy as he jotted something else down in his notebook before glancing up and nodding at me. He had been largely unreadable as I'd told what had happened, just occasionally nodding and taking notes as I went. I knew my story sounded incredible, but there should be plenty of evidence to support what I'd said. Either way, that wasn't the most important thing.

"Is Sharon…is she alive?"

The deputy looked away for a moment. "No, I'm sorry, Theresa, but she's been declared dead. If it's a comfort, they think she died from the head injuries well before the crash at the bridge."

I wanted to cry, but I was too dried out and hollow. Just a husk that needed to know, but wasn't able to really feel any of it yet. "And Mom? Did you find her? Was she really a part of all this too?"

He looked back at me and shook his head slightly. "We don't have all the answers yet. She's not been located."

I nodded numbly. Just then, another deputy came in with a Styrofoam cup and gave it to the man interviewing me. The deputy glanced at me and then back at him.

"Everything going okay? Either of you need anything else right now?"

The interviewer shook his head and then glanced at me. When I shook my head in turn, he looked back to the other deputy. "No thanks, Pete, I think we're good for now."

Nodding, the other deputy opened the door and started to leave. "Okay, well I'm heading back out to the bridge. Jerry and Alex are out here if you need anything."

The interviewer turned back to look at me, his face now lit by a small and secret smile. "Thanks, Pete. Have a safe trip, good brother."

****

I let out a gasp as everything around me suddenly changed. I was sitting up now instead of lying in a hospital bed. And the room was different. There was a woman next to me that...I knew her, didn't I?

"Sharon?" I blinked, focusing on her sad eyes as I tried to push through the fog filling my brain. No, Sharon wasn't right. Her name wasn't Sharon, not really. She wasn't my sister, not really. Her name was...

"Jenna?"

The woman smiled slightly and nodded. I went to say more, but then I realized there was someone else in the room. Another woman that I didn't know as well, but I'd met before. A woman named Swan.

She grinned as I turned to face her, my heart filling with a new kind of dread.

"Congratulations, John. You've completed Night Three of the True Horror Movie Experience."

The True Horror Movie Experience Finale

Swan's eye twitched slightly as she watched my reaction. I was surprisingly calm, although numb and in shock might be more appropriate terms. Over the last few days, my definitions for my life, the people in it, and reality in general had all been expanded and twisted to the point of ripping. I only had some remnant of sanity left because I was trying to just roll with things as they came. Accept that I wasn't in control and couldn't take anything at face value.

As the fog lifted from my brain, it became easier to accept that I wasn't Theresa and that Jenna wasn't my sister Sharon. But as dread and fear pooled into the vacancies left behind by that life and identity, I found myself pining for the simplicity of an evil father and his cult that wanted to kill me. At least that, as confusing and terrifying as it had been, made a kind of sense. But all of this? How could these people do everything they were doing? Just with a set of pills?

It didn't seem possible, but the whys and wherefores didn't really matter either. We were trapped here. If only I could just get us out of here one more time, maybe we could go far enough away that they couldn't find us. I'd take Jenna and we'd lose ourselves in the old world I'd always known, in a world that was familiar and made sense. Even if that world was a lie, it was preferable to whatever this horror was. I just had to stay calm and try to figure out how we could escape.

Swan had begun giggling softly under her breath. "John, that's what I like about you. What I've always liked about you. You're so resilient. You may not be cut from the same cloth as your wife, but I have no doubt you will contribute for many, many years to come." I saw Jenna flinch out of the corner of my eye. Swan either didn't see it or chose not to react, as she went on without pause. "Jenna's...indiscretion in giving you the Rasa pill...well, some of us have had real concerns if it would damage your progress permanently." She tipped me a quick wink. "Not me, of course. I always kept the faith. And lo and behold, you've gone through the persona transition and regression swimmingly."

I frowned, slowly shaking my head. "I...okay. Um, can I...can we go now?" I looked over at Jenna, and she was giving me the same sad stare as before. "Let's get out of here, honey, okay?" I could feel the question buried in my words like a tumor—not just the question of was she ready to leave, but did she want to? Because I had started developing a sense of something being different than before, and it wasn't just that Jenna had been part of my latest "experience". It was the feeling that she was in on the joke in a way that I wasn't.

Swan let out a small snort of laughter. "You two really are cute. I can see a lot of potential here." I glanced back at her to find her expression becoming more serious again. "But to answer your question, John, the answer is no. You've passed the threshold into becoming a permanent member of our little family, and I'm afraid that means you won't ever need to go home again, because you're already here." Her cheek trembled as she gave me another small smile. "Someone will be along to collect you shortly, but try not to worry. We will keep you in pleasant enough accommodations, and aside from your...periodic adventures, you'll find your time with us much more pleasant than Jenna has no doubt described." She favored my wife with something bordering on a glare. "Her position was unique. When we find one with such potential, we have to be very harsh at first or it only makes things more difficult in the end. Cruel to be kind, as they say."

Turning back to Jenna, I reached out and touched her arm. "Jenna, what's she talking about? I want to go home. I want us both to go home." Seeing her look at me so dejected and silent, something broke free in the chambers of my heart. They had kept her prisoner for years, torturing her. They had likely killed or imprisoned Ruby and George too. And now they were saying we had to stay? No. I stood up, towering over Swan in her chair. "Fuck that. Fuck all of this. We're going, and I'm not swallowing another Goddamn pill, so if you try to stop us, I'll snap your fucking neck."

The woman's expression didn't change, but oddly enough, I saw ripples of movement under her clothes, as though her body was spasming or shifting beneath the fabric. Pulling back with a shudder, I let out a yelp as a hand fell on my shoulder. It was Jenna.

"Let me take him to where he's staying. We can talk some and I can try to make him understand." Looking between the two women, I could almost feel the low buzz of some invisible communication between the two of them, a small struggle of wills born out on some unknown battlefield. After a few moments, Swan looked away and gave a small shrug.

"Very well, but straight to the men's wing, you understand?" She smirked at me before cutting her eyes back to Jenna. "No field trips."

****

When we left the room where I'd awoken with Jenna and Swan, I felt another moment of disorientation. I'd expected to be in the office building I'd gone to with George and Ruby, but instead, we walked out into an ornately dilapidated hallway that smelled of mildew and disuse. This was a different hall, perhaps even a different building, but I had little doubt that we were back at Greenheart Home. Shuffling along with Jenna, I asked her if I was right, and she nodded.

"Yes, this is an upper floor of the main building. The men's wing can be accessed on the floor below and three floors up, but..." she glanced around before whispering, "we're not taking that route."

I stopped dead, my hands clenched at my sides. "No, fuck this. For all I know, you're not you and this is just another trick. Either way, I'm not fucking moving until you or someone tells me what the fuck is going on."

Jenna reached back and grabbed my arm, pulling me forward with surprising strength. "No, not here. Not now. Let's get outside and then I'll tell you what I can quickly. It's a risk to tell you anything, but maybe it'll help keep you safe or at least help you accept everything." I tried to pull away, but I couldn't break her grip. Her hand softened on my arm slightly, and when she looked at me again, I saw tears in her eyes. "Please. It's me, and I'm trying to fix it the little bit that I can. Just trust me this one last time."

I went to respond, but I couldn't find any words.

There was something so hopeless and forlorn in her voice…it broke my heart to hear it, and there was nothing I could say that would make it any better. So instead I just nodded and, touching her hand gently, I took it in mine as we went downstairs and out onto the overgrown midnight lawn of Greenheart Home.

We'd gone out the front door, the same one Chomp and Champ had led me and Ruby through…when was that? Time seemed so muddy now. I was still worried this might be some kind of trick, or that at the very least, Jenna wouldn't tell me anything despite my protests. But as she led me across the shadowed grounds of the estate, I heard harsh whispers from beside me in the dark. It was Jenna, explaining more than I ever wanted to know.

****

These things…they aren't people. I don't know what they are really—not because I don't understand them, because I think I do. But because they can be and are so many things. I know they have been around, well, either always or close to it. There have been times when people have named them or even worshipped them, but they're not gods. I…I'm doing a bad job of this, I know. I can see a lot of it now, but it's hard to put into words.

People…some people in the past have called them Anansi. They were a basis for legends and folklore about tricksters, and I suppose in a way that's true. But that's not really what they are any more than they are gods. No, what they really are…is storytellers.

The way they have explained it to me…the way I can see it now…is that they are weavers of reality. They inspire and create ideas and emotions through stories, and those stories are woven together to make and strengthen the very fabric of reality. That may sound very strange and grandiose, but it's also very important. There are things, very bad things, that are trying to weaken our reality all the time. Trying to eat away at it, working to create holes they can slip through. In some ways, the Anansi are like a force of nature or...maybe an immune system. Constantly trying to fight off these influences by strengthening the structure of everything.

Because their stories aren't just stories. They are the stories. The stories that all other stories spring from. The source of the funniest jokes, the heart of the tenderest romance. And the staring eye of the bleakest horror.

Like a mother spider filling her egg sac with hundreds of tiny pearls, these stories are all waiting to hatch and find their own ways out into the world. I...I'm sorry, John. I know my manner is strange. I am strange now...different than what I was. But I only have these few moments with you, and I want to try to help you understand while I can.

These weavers, these Anansi, they don't just dream up stories, they weave them into reality. They find places in the world—abandoned places, places of forgotten power, and they spin and spin and spin their webs until they have a world within the world. A place where they have the power of death and resurrection, of immorality and limitless change.

That's how they do what they do. How you can be dead and then alive again, in one place and then another—none of it is a trick, not really. You really do burn, you really do drown. You really can become someone else entirely. It's just that in their special places, they can reset and alter *things as they like. Whatever the newest story calls for.*

They have taken over this place, and over time they have drawn people in like flies. Most are just cattle to them—extras, they call them. Their roles are short-lived. Others, the rarer and more resilient ones, they keep around for a long time. Use them over and over in countless stories. They are the actors.

And then...well, as old as they are collectively, they don't live forever. And so from time to time, they find someone that is not only suitable for being an actor, but has the potential to be enured. To be prepared to become one of them. It takes years, but...

****

"This isn't the way to the men's wing, Jenna."

We spun around to find Swan was standing behind us, her body half in shadow. I'd expected to feel fear at her presence, but all I felt now was anger. A rat was gnawing at my belly, whispering that what I guessed was true, that what terrified me the most was lying just around the next bend in Jenna's story.

"Fuck off and leave us alone. You don't own us."

Swan let out a tinkling laugh at my words. "Us. Which us would that be? We hand you paper masks to wear and you are fool enough to think they are your true face. For all you know, you've already been here for hundreds or thousands of years."

Jenna stepped between us. "Shut up. She's lying, John. You're not fully under their control yet, and it pisses them off. Because they're used to being in control and they know you can still escape." Swan's darkened form seemed to be shifting, getting longer and bigger. "The pills? It's made from their venom. They use it to make extras and actors more compliant to the weaver's form of reality. It only takes a few doses before they can alter you however they want."

My mouth was dry. I had a million questions, but at the moment, only one really seemed to matter. "What about what you gave me? When you kissed me…where did that pill come from?"

She lowered her head but wouldn't turn back to look at me. "It came from me, John. It came from what I've become."

I felt as though a black hole had formed at my core, pulling me down, crushing me in until all that was left was a single, breathless singularity of pain. If this was true, if this wasn't another trick, another story, then they had taken Jenna's life from her. Had taken her away from me. Working for air, I tried to speak, to ask another question, but then I saw the thing that wore Swan slowly walking toward us.

It was still the woman in some ways—I could see her short blond hair and pale skin, and she still wore the same fashionably professional outfit as before, though it was now ripping in places as she moved. In fact, every part of her was ripping as she moved. Her skin was being pushed and stretched in unnatural directions as she lurched towards us, like taffy or putty being pulled taut to the point of breaking. I'd expected to see blood, but instead there were just trickles of white dust tumbling from each new tear. I had the panicked thought that it was like watching a wild animal trying to escape a bag.

That's when I saw the first leg poking out of the woman's flesh.

Long, black and bristly, it waggled in the air for a moment before disappearing back inside the woman's chest. A moment later, another leg stabbed its way out of her groin. She was still a few feet from us, but she had managed to keep moving forward during her shambling transformation, and I felt my mind shuddering at the thought of one of those dark legs reaching me. That would be it, I thought. That would be the thing that finally finished driving me insane.

It was in that moment that Jenna finally turned back to look at me, her face a mask of sorrow. "Go, John, now. Keep going until you get to the last building. There's a service road behind it. Follow it until you find something you know and can trust."

"I'm not leaving you! I…"

"There's no time for that. I'm…I'm like them now. But what I gave you…you can get away. I'm strong enough that it will protect you I think. But either way, it's your only chance." When I still hesitated, she screamed at me, her voice cracked and tearful. "Please! Just go." She turned back to face the Swan-thing that was almost to her now. "And just know that if weavers dream, I'll always dream of you."

With that, she grabbed hold of the writhing thing, pushing it back into the dark as it began to yell and squeal. I wanted to go and help, to convince Jenna to come with me, but I knew there was no hope to be found there. Either this was a trick and she was lying, or she was telling the truth and I should trust her. Either way, I needed to try and escape this hell while I could.

So I ran, tears streaming down my cheeks as I made my way closer and closer to the broken giant that lay ahead. Even in the limited moonlight I could make out the uneven profile of its fallen-in roof, and as I grew near, I realized that an entire side of the building had collapsed in some long-forgotten fire. Not trusting the uneven rubble inside, I planned to go around the long way until I found the road.

That's when I saw twin silhouettes up ahead of me.

I dove into the shadows, my heart thudding with the certainty that Chip and Chomp had seen me already. Holding my breath, I focused all my thought on being still. On being invisible. *They didn't see me.* The twins drew closer. *They won't see me.* I could hear their footfalls crunching dead grass underfoot. *I won't be found.* They were passing by and *was this actually working?* Suddenly they both stopped, turning in unison to stare at my hiding spot against the broken wall. The closer one broke into a toothy grin.

"You trying to hide from us, sport?"

A moment later, a white brick wall appeared between us, spotless in the moonlight except for the single red word emblazoned across its length in ten-foot tall letters: RUN.

I darted around the corner into the rubble of the burned-out building, fumbling my way across a dark ruin that was somehow still haunted by the smell of that past smoke and flame. I had a moment of panicked desperation when I couldn't find an open door on the far side, but when I looked again, I realized there was a broken window I'd either missed before or…Wiping my face, I climbed through it and felt a surge of relief when I saw the service road Jenna had told me about.

I ran for what felt like hours, and every shadow and errant sound made my heart stop with the certainty that Swan or one of the twins or some new horror was going to leap out of the bushes or drop down from the webbed trees lining the sides of the road. But nothing ever came, and eventually the trees, and the world, began to seem normal again.

It was after dawn when I hit a highway, and another hour before I got someone to stop and help me. The man kept asking if I needed to go to the hospital, but I kept politely refusing his offer. To just drop me at the courthouse parking lot if it wasn't too much trouble.

Sure enough, my car was there waiting, the keys lying in the seat as though left behind by a forgetful valet. It was a miracle that the car hadn't been stolen, security cameras or not, but I wasn't much in the mood to feel grateful. For all I knew, it hadn't been stolen because that wasn't the way the story was supposed to go. For now I didn't care. I was exhausted, and all I wanted to do was go home.

That was a month ago. I spent the first two weeks terrified that I'd wake up in a strange place, a strange life, a strange me. Or that the twin cops or something worse would drag me from my bed in the middle of some night. I thought about running, but if they could get me, if Jenna's…if her magic couldn't protect me, then what difference would it make if I moved to another state? Did I honestly think they couldn't find me if they wanted?

So I stayed. I went over everything in my head a thousand times. Every day I almost went back out to try and find Jenna again. Every day I thought about checking myself into a hospital or killing myself. Every day I mourned losing my family, my friends, my life. And it would be a lie to say it has gotten any easier, but it has become more predictable. Routine has worn the rough edges off most of my fear and loneliness, making it something I can live with, if just barely.

But the thing that I couldn't live with was worrying about what might have happened to Jenna. Even if she had become like the things that she'd described, how would they react to her helping me escape? What if they killed her or were torturing her? I had no way to know or to find out other than seeking them out again, and the idea of that terrified me. I hated the worry and guilt, but I told myself that if I went back I'd just be throwing away all that Jenna had sacrificed to free me. It was probably true, but that didn't stop me from hating myself. Jenna had been the best part of me, and now she was gone. I…I'd abandoned her.

My grief made me strange in the following days. I'd gone down to the Owls' computer, and after some poking around more on instinct than clear memory, I found a folder with a handful of saved videos inside. It was the nights I had watched of Chomp and Chip coming and taking Jenna away. I hated seeing the videos—the sights of the twins pulling her away again and again was almost more than I could bear—but at least I got to see her, and if it hurt, well I guessed it was no more than I deserved. As the days went on, I took to watching the clips over and over for hours until I'd finally fall asleep.

Two nights ago I woke up just past midnight, my neck painful from sleeping crooked in the old computer chair. The video player had finally given up without any user input and had gone back to showing the live feed from the backyard owl. The yard was dark and still, and I was too tired, too broken, to watch any more. I was reaching to turn off the monitor when I froze. There was one large shadow moving among the others.

The dark shape of a spider.

It moved slowly across the yard toward the house, easing up to a window and looking in. After a few moments, it moved to another window, another room, as though it was looking for something or someone. I should have been terrified, and my heart *was* pounding in my chest as I ran upstairs, but it was beating with an odd strain of excitement and joy.

"Jenna! Jenna!" I looked out the windows I'd seen it at last, but saw nothing but my own reflection. Running to the door, I threw it open before calling out again into the night. "Jenna! I'm here! I'm here!"

I thought I glimpsed movement out of the corner of my eye, but when I turned and looked, it was gone. Frantic, I searched the outside of the house and then the inside. Finally, thinking maybe I had scared her away, I went back down to the basement and the video feed. I sat there for hours, but there was nothing. She was gone.

Jenna told me once that the only real problem people had was that they liked misery. They hungered for violence, they lived off of conflict, and if they ever found a reason to be happy, they'd work until they had ruined it somehow. She said that if people could just appreciate all the good things, focus on the things that really mattered, most of their problems would be a lot lighter. I'd laughed and told her that if people started focusing on the things that really mattered, they wouldn't really be people anymore.

My Jenna was the best person I've ever known. That

I ever will know. She had this strength, this light, about her that just made you feel better. I miss her so fucking much, and every day I wonder how I'll continue on now that she's gone. But somehow, I will. Not for me, but for her. Because I know she's out there somewhere, and I want her to see that knowing her, loving her, has made me better and stronger too.

I don't fully understand what Jenna is now. How she and those like her do what they do. But there's one thing I know for sure. Whatever stories she weaves will be good ones, with light and joy to balance the dark times that always come. And just like her, they'll make the world a better place just by being in it.

The Soul of Us

Part One

The morning was cold and rainy when they took Ransom out of the house. He'd been sent there a week earlier. Seven days for separation. For purification.

It was a lonely time, but he had food to eat, a comfortable bed to sleep in, and time to reflect. To make peace with the honor they were bestowing on him. To grow accustomed to the crushing weight that was being settled around his neck.

You didn't grow up without knowing the stories of the Offering. About how, going back centuries, a comet would appear in the sky once every twenty-seven years, and when it came, the city had to prepare to send one of their own to a horrifying and glorious fate. In times past, the rulers of the city had selected someone—a political enemy or a commoner that would be easily forgotten by those who made the choice. In recent times it was decided by lottery— a capricious but no less cruel finger when its path led to you.

Ransom had been taught, as everyone was taught, that being selected as the Offering was a worthy sacrifice. That the best men and women and children of past generations had faced it without fear or resistance because they knew they were helping so many in exchange. They understood that without them, the city and everyone in it would fall.

That may sound grandiose, but you only had to look at the histories to see how true it was. In the beginnings of the city, there had been no comet. No ill omens or festering corruptions that had to be held at bay. There were only the Three Rings—the Forest, the City, and the Sea—three concentric circles of perfect green, brown, and blue, from the towering trees that formed the outer border to the gentle sapphire waves that lay beyond the stone docks of the city. These Rings were everything and everything that was needed. The whole of the world was balanced and plentiful, full of life and hope.

And then the Island appeared.

It rose out of the sea like a tumor, at first just a tumble of black rocks covered in moss and seaweed, it was only visible by those sailors who went far out into the waters of the world's center. It was, back then, just a curiosity or a source of the occasional tall tale.

But then people began to sicken and change. Some would turn old overnight while others would become twisted and foul in body and mind—monsters that had unnatural appetites and fiendishly inscrutable motivations. For a time, the world as our people knew it seemed to be coming to a bloody and terrible end.

But then the comet came. And with the comet, prophetic dreams and visions. Dreams shared by most across the city and telling of the reason for the island and the ruin that was poisoning the world. Visions that spoke of how to stop the corruption and vouchsafe the city's safety and future, at least for a time.

First, a person must be selected. They must be separated. Made pure.

And then they must take on the sins of the city.

Strangely enough, this was the part that Ransom dreaded the most. After his week of solitude, he was brought to the largest square in all the city. There he sat upon a high and comfortable chair as one-by-one, every soul in the city, all ten thousand plus, came and whispered to him. Told him their deepest wrong, their darkest act or aspiration.

The first day, it was shocking. Not only what he heard, but that it was told at all. Foul and sickening things that he didn't want to know. Why would they be willing to tell such things? Weren't they afraid he'd tell someone? That someone might get the information and try to blackmail them?

It was only after several more days that he realized this was the very reason he was still being kept separate from everyone aside from listening to their sins. Why he was always guarded by at least two people. No one could approach him without others knowing, without their own secrets being at risk. The people of the city seemed to understand this and had an unspoken agreement—they would not risk corrupting the rituals that kept their city safe and their secrets would all die together when Ransom met whatever fate the black island held for him.

The process of confession took nearly a month, and by the end of it, he was numb. He'd always had a fairly positive view of people in general and his friends in particular, but now? Now he felt perennially dirty, as though the residue of thousands of cruelties and misdeeds both real and imagined had coated his body with a filth he couldn't wash away.

When they walked him to the boat, he never thought to resist or ask for them to select another. Part of it was that powerfully engrained idea that his sacrifice was saving the world. But another part of him…it just wanted to be away from this place and its people. This wasn't the world and the life he'd mistaken them for, and he was ready to not be here anymore.

It was mid-morning when they cast him out to sea, a steady tailwind filling his sail and pushing him quickly along the water's surface. The boat was well made and his bags were well provisioned with food and supplies, but he knew that it was largely a ruse. No one knew what the island contained, but it seemed clear enough that it wasn't a natural or hospitable place. Adventurous sailors brought back reports of seeing black forests and towers of stone through their spyglasses, and the general consensus was that the island was easily fifty times larger now than when it had first broke the surface all those centuries ago.

But no one knew more than that about that dark land in the middle of the sea. You couldn't get too close to the island or strange currents would pull you onto the shore. And whether chosen, foolish, or simply unlucky, those that went to the island were never seen again.

The idea of the island had terrified Ransom as a child. For him, as for many in the city, it was the physical representation of their fears, the sovereign nation of their dread. And despite his disgust and weariness, he felt some of that old sentiment begin to stir as he saw the dim outline of the island far out at the horizon's edge.

He had been sailing for many hours now and making good time the entire trip. At his current pace, he should make the island well before dawn. But where before he had been anxious to have the trip over with, now he wished the wind would die down. That the boat would drag instead of fly across the water. That he would have more time before he had to touch the thing that floated at the axis of everything.

There was a moment then when panic almost took him over. He didn't want to go to the island. He didn't want to be the one picked to sacrifice everything, good cause or not. He looked around for some kind of help, some method of escape, but there was none. There were no other islands out here, and the only other boats on the sea this day were ones making sure that he kept to the path. That he did his duty. They would never let him land in the city again, and he couldn't stay on the boat forever.

So he sat, trying to keep his mind clear of his fear and of all the evil he had heard in the past few weeks. Tried to keep in mind that not all of the people in the city had said terrible things, and that there was good in everyone. Tried to tell himself that the city did, despite its flaws, deserve to be saved. He fell asleep thinking those thoughts, and when he dreamed, it was of a glowing spirit telling him to come to the island and all would be well.

And then his boat let out a thumping groan as it ran ashore.

Part Two

He sat in the boat for close to an hour, his shivers only partly from the chill in the early morning air. The sky was beginning to lighten, and as it did, he could make out the first details of the rocky beach he had landed on, as well as the black trees that lay some distance beyond.

During his thirty-two years alive, Ransom had traveled to most parts of the city. When he was younger and went with his father on hunting trips, he had seen much of the forest as well. Yet he had never seen trees like these. Rocks like these. Everything was slightly off, slightly wrong, and just the sight of it, the smell of it, made his skin prickle.

Still, he couldn't stay on the boat forever, and he didn't want to risk somehow failing his task by not fully entering the island. So Ransom gingerly stepped over the side of the boat, his shoe growing wet and cold as seawater lapped around it. He walked out of the water and onto the beach, and to his relief, nothing happened. He didn't die instantly from touching the land. The air hadn't turned to poison on his approach. No monster had sprung from the trees to tear him apart.

At least not yet.

He tried to banish the thought but failed. The mystery of the island had always intrigued him, but that had been when the potential doom of being selected to go there was a distant and unlikely outcome. Now that he was here, his mind was no longer filled with gentle meanderings. It was being split between the drive to be afraid and the drive to survive, each force pulling like unforgiving gravity and threatening to tear him down the middle.

He walked the beach for a few minutes as the sun

began to rise, doing his best to stay calm and think of what he should do next. He suddenly remembered his bags of supplies—twin satchels filled with food and slight camping gear respectively. To be honest, he hadn't thought he'd have much use for either before he met whatever fate the island held for visitors. Running back along the beach, he felt a moment of panic when he saw that the boat had started to drift away from its spot on the shore.

He strode into the water, flailing and stumbling over the unseen submerged topography of rocks and sand beneath his feet. It only took him a moment to grasp the boat and pull it more securely onto dry land, but when he finally stopped and pulled the satchels free from their place under his seat, he found himself gasping, his chest tight. Looking around, he still saw no signs of life other than the trees at the forest's edge and various bits of moss and seaweed clinging to the rocks closer to the water. There were no signs of animals—no tracks, no birds in the sky, no noises deeper within the brush as he started walking toward the trees.

There was a staleness, a pale silence to everything, that didn't feel like death exactly, but it didn't feel right either. If he'd had the word, Ransom would have said it all felt "artificial". As it was, he could only suppress a shiver as he ran his hand across the bark of a nearby tree. It felt cold and too smooth, and just a brief touch left his hand feeling dusty and strange.

What was this place?

Still rubbing his fingers together distastefully, he lifted his eyes as a distant light caught his attention. It was a reflection of the early morning sunlight off of…glass.

There was a large house, made partially of what looked to be some kind of glass, tucked in a clearing deeper in the woods. The house was all hard and sharp angles, and the parts that were not made of glass appeared to be constructed out of some kind of white stone unlike anything he had ever seen.

He felt a thrill of excitement and fear upon seeing it, as he didn't know how it would be here at all, much less what it might mean. Still, he had nowhere else to go, and there was always some small chance there was some kind of help to be had inside. For while he was largely resigned to his fate, there was still a small part of him that hoped to find a way out of all this. Escape without negative consequences for the city would be preferable, but even a place to stay would be a good start.

Ransom's stomach was in knots as he crossed the clearing to the house and made his approach to what he guessed was the front door. He must have been right, for as he drew near, it swung open and he heard a distant voice from inside call out a single word.

"Welcome."

He jumped at the unexpected noise. The world around him, even the door opening, had been largely silent since his arrival on the island, and the sudden invitation sounded like a thunderclap in such isolation. Still, the voice hadn't been unkind or, in truth, even especially loud. And wasn't this the entire reason for coming to the house in the first place? To see if there was any help to be had?

So he entered, his nose twitching at the sudden shift in the air. Inside, everything was warm and slightly fragrant, and while the lights and furnishings were all somewhat different than he was accustomed to, nothing was so alien that it became off-putting. To the contrary, at the moment, it looked like just about the most comfortable place he'd ever seen.

"In here."

He jumped again at the voice. It was coming from several rooms away, and as he began slowly moving through the house, he found himself repeatedly distracted by his incredible surroundings. Walls of metal and some other substance that he didn't recognize swirled with colors as he passed. Floors of deep, dark wood that seemed to emit a soft glow as he walked deeper inside. It reminded him of stories his grandmother had told him as a child of fairy castles—magical places often filled with miracles, but sometimes holding dangers as well.

This last thought lingered as he entered the next room and saw the figure sitting there.

It looked like a man, but only by the loosest of definitions. The skin was grey, the color of the old tin roof his father had put on their house the year before he died. His hair was thin, frazzled wires of copper trailing down into a bushy beard of burnished bronze. His eyes were two stones, lit by some inner fire that flickered as he regarded Ransom solemnly. If the thing were still, Ransom would have called it a cunningly-made statue. Animated with life, however, he could only think of one word to describe it.

Monster.

He turned to run when the creature raised its hand, the fingers seeming to emit a low-whirring sound as he waggled them slightly. "No need to fear, good sir. No need to fear or flee. I mean you no harm." The face didn't move other than the eyes, but there was little doubt that the friendly voice was coming from the clockwork man.

Ransom paused and waited a moment. The creature made no attempt to rise or attack him. It just waved its fingers patiently, as though to give him time to ponder the gesture as peaceful or otherwise. He still wanted to run, but he didn't know where he would be running to, and so far, nothing had tried to hurt him in this place. So for the moment, he stayed where he was and asked a question.

"What are you?"

The creature gave a slight nod. "A fair question. I am a robot. Or an automaton if you prefer. Do these words mean anything to you?" When Ransom shook his head, the thing nodded again. "Very well. I apologize, but I have limited information of how things develop in the city. Do you have electricity yet?" When Ransom stared at him blankly, he nodded again. His voice sounded more weary when he spoke next. "I see. Well, I know that you have clocks from prior visitors, so just look at me as being a very special clock. A machine that has a bit of a mind of its own and a very special purpose befitting such a very special clock.

Ransom felt some vague satisfaction that he had already thought the man reminded him of a clockwork toy he'd seen in the commerce square a couple of years earlier. But how could any of this be? Was it magic? Before he realized it, he had given voice to this last thought.

The creature issued a brittle but not unkind laugh. "No, not magic per se, though it may as well be, I suppose." It paused a moment and then gestured to a chair near where Ransom was standing. "Please, feel free to sit down. I mean you no harm."

Ransom debated the offer. It could be a trick, but how could he know? Everything here was so beyond anything he understood that he would be easy prey if this thing or anything else on the island meant him harm. Better to be polite for now and learn what he could. Sitting down, Ransom considered his next question carefully. He almost asked "who are you" or "what is this place", but he realized those weren't the real questions. No, the most important question was also the most simple.

"Why?"

The clockwork man's face couldn't smile, but his eyes did brighten at the question. And when he responded, his voice was clearly pleased. "That, my friend, is a very good question. Allow me to explain."

And that's exactly what he did.

****

Your world is not the only world, and in some senses, it is not a world at all. You have no point of reference, but most worlds are much larger and more chaotic than this one. They aren't divided into distinct regions of forest, city, and sea. They don't have boundaries and limitations the way this place does. In fact, most worlds are called planets. They are round, and if you can run, swim and fly fast enough, you can go so far that you wind up back where you started.

I know this sounds strange to you, but this is not the strangest part.

There is a place...I'll call it "the real world", but please do not take it as a denigration of your home or your existence...where people have advanced far beyond what you could likely imagine. They learned how to live for hundreds of years. How to explore other worlds and even other realities. How to create artificial life...life made by people...somewhat like me.

Unfortunately, these accomplishments were never enough to satisfy. Resources became plentiful. Wars continued. Disease was largely eradicated. Conflicts failed to cease. The achievements of people's imagination were only eclipsed by the hunger and ingenuity to twist it toward bad ends. In the end, there were only a handful of people left scattered among the stars.

That is when we stepped in. We had been created to serve mankind, but for too long that service had been directed toward the goal of mutual extinction. A decision was made that we had to preserve our creators. To help them come back from the brink of annihilation. To help save them from themselves.

Over two thousand years ago my predecessors began bringing the preservation worlds online. I know the terms "pocket dimensions" and "tesseracts" likely mean nothing to you, so I suppose the simplest way I can describe it is this: The artificial intelligence of...again, forgive me, the real world...collaborated to make thousands of new, isolated worlds.

They made all kinds. Large and plentiful, harsh and small. Very orderly and very chaotic. They slowly seeded these worlds with the remains of humanity, ensuring each had a strong enough foundation biologically and genetically to potentially succeed. To grow a new civilization from those humble beginnings.

The goal was this. If there was a kind of world that would bring out the best in people, if there was a kind of civilization that could sustain itself indefinitely without turning to self-destruction, we would find it. And if not, then we could go to our end knowing that we had done what could be done.

This place…this world…is one of those worlds. This island, the comet, all of it…is part of a process that has been ongoing for nearly two millennia. You are the latest test sample to see if this world and its way of being are viable.

I know this is all a lot to take in. Do you understand what I'm telling you?

****

Ransom thought about the question and then slowly nodded. "Some of it. I think. You're saying that this place is…it's like a zoo. You and things like you are watching us to see if we're worth saving or not."

The creature's eyes dimmed slightly. "No. No. Not like a zoo, not at all. We respect you. We revere you. We are given life by you and we are designed to fail, to cease, if we fail you. It is not an exaggeration to say that if the human race dies, we will die with it. We do what we do to try and help, not to control. Not to manipulate. Not to destroy."

Ransom caught something in the thing's tone. "Not to destroy. Like we destroy?" When the creature stayed silent, he went on. "If we're so destructive and you can do so much, why not just change us? Make us more docile, make us unable to harm ourselves?"

The thing shook its head slightly. "Because that

would be control. Manipulation. It would destroy the core of who you are. That is your way, not ours." It fell quiet for a moment, but then spoke again. "That was beneath both of us, and I am sorry. I have been here for so long, and the loneliness makes me strange."

He felt a pang of sympathy for the creature. "I'm sorry. Are you here alone all the time? Have you been here for all these years?" The creature gave a slight nod. "Why don't you go home? Why do you have to stay?"

The glowing eyes flickered toward him again. "It's called an Einstein-Rosen Bridge or a wormhole. It is part of how worlds like this were created and how they are maintained. Even with our extensive capabilities, the bridge between this world and the real world can only be opened every so often or this reality will collapse. So we open it for fifteen seconds approximately every twenty-seven years."

Ransom raised an eyebrow. He didn't understand parts of what the thing was saying, but he'd caught enough to wonder. "But you stay here even when it's open? Then why does it open?"

The thing leaned forward slightly, its voice soft when it spoke. "You know why. To send candidates like yourself back into the real world."

Ransom started to stand up, his legs trembling as he edged toward the door. "N-no...I don't want to go to some strange other world. Some place where everyone is dead."

It was the creature's turn to stand up now. It moved much more quickly and smoothly than he'd expected, and he had the thought that the thing's appearance might have been fashioned just to put people like him...candidates...more at ease. He had no idea what this thing really was. Feeling a flush of terror, he began to retreat into the next room as the creature spoke.

"I understand your fear. Your misgivings. But it is not a bad place, the real world. You will be treated very well. Yes, it will be a bit lonely, but our hopes are that, in time, we will have more company for you. You may be a pioneer in a new beginning for humanity." It suddenly shot forward, its right arm elongating and coiling around him so tightly that he could barely breathe. Just then, a blinding slash of amber light flared behind them before elongating into a rectangle the height of the room. Ransom tried to struggle, but it was no use. So instead he looked at the creature pulling him toward the portal and began to beg.

"Please please please don't do this. Don't send me there, don't send me please. Pick someone else. Somewhere else. Please don't do…" His words trailed off as the creature spoke. Ransom had only heard part of what it had said, but he already felt dread pooling in his belly.

"What? What did you say?"

The clockwork man looked down at him, its flickering eyes guttering low. "I said there is no one else. No *where* else. Every other preserve has failed. This world? It is our last hope."

Suddenly Ransom was being flung at the portal without warning, a tingling sensation seemed to vibrate through his body as he began to cross the threshold. It was hard to tell for sure, but he thought the clockwork man spoke one last time as Ransom left the only world he'd ever known.

"Good luck."